"I think my baby was switched with yours."

Janette spoke with firm, almost frightening conviction. "Adam, I think Amy is the baby I gave birth to."

Adam's handsome face, which moments ago had reflected warmth and love, was tight with shock and disbelief.

"I know that losing a child can do strange things to a woman's mind," he said, aghast. "But this! You made me think you were interested in me, when all you wanted was to get close to Amy out of some sick maternal need."

"No," she cried. "Don't think that...."

Adam turned away from her and stormed toward the door.

She ran after him. "Adam, listen to me."

Never, he thought. He would never listen to her. And he wouldn't look at her. And, if he had his way, by God, he would forget she was the one woman who had very nearly filled the aching emptiness inside him.

ABOUT THE AUTHOR

Born in Britain, Megan Brownley now lives in California with her film editor husband, George. She has always loved writing. In 1986, she gave up her teaching job and began writing full-time. She has published several novels and magazine articles and tells us that *Cry of the Seagull,* her second Superromance novel, "is the result of a day I spent at the beach watching globs of oil from a tanker mishap floating into tidal pools. A seagull flew overhead and I couldn't help but feel its piercing cry echoed my own."

Books by Megan Brownley

HARLEQUIN SUPERROMANCE
466—SILENT WALKS THE MOON

Don't miss any of our special offers. Write to us at the following address for information on our newest releases.

Harlequin Reader Service
P.O. Box 1397, Buffalo, NY 14240
Canadian address: P.O. Box 603,
Fort Erie, Ont. L2A 5X3

Cry of the Seagull

MEGAN BROWNLEY

Harlequin Books

TORONTO • NEW YORK • LONDON
AMSTERDAM • PARIS • SYDNEY • HAMBURG
STOCKHOLM • ATHENS • TOKYO • MILAN
MADRID • WARSAW • BUDAPEST • AUCKLAND

Published May 1992

ISBN 0-373-70501-8

CRY OF THE SEAGULL

The author wishes to express appreciation to
Kelly A. Hatfield, attorney-at-law,
for her help and interest in this story.

For Robyn with love

CHAPTER ONE

DR. KEVIN YOUNG stroked the soft gray wing of the seagull lying motionless on the examining table of the Fur and Feathers Pet Hospital; its right leg twisted into an L beneath the bulky still body. "I think this little fellow is going to have to manage with one leg," he said softly. The seagull's dark beady eyes were closed and only the gentle rise and fall of its white downy chest revealed any sign of life.

Janette Taylor felt both pain and anger. Pain for the little seagull whom she'd rescued earlier that May morning from the rusty bedsprings that had been discarded on the beach behind her house. Anger toward whoever was responsible for the little creature's mishap.

She glanced at her watch. She was scheduled to give a backstage tour of the Crystal Beach Living Masters Pageant where she worked. She already was a half hour late. She grimaced at the thought of the havoc thirty fifth graders could be creating at the pageant grounds while they waited. What a way to start a Monday morning!

"How long will it take?" she asked.

"Not long," Kevin replied. "You better leave him here. You can take him home this afternoon. He'll need to be nursed back to health for a good forty-eight hours. His wound will be healed by then and you'll be able to let him go."

Wonderful, Janette thought. This was her busiest time of year and now she would have to play nursemaid to a seagull. "Will it be all right if I pick him up this afternoon?"

The vet nodded, adjusted his eyeglasses and turned to the sink to wash his hands. "Would you like to know how much it is going to cost you this time?" he asked, glancing at her over his shoulder. This was the third seagull in as many months that he'd treated for Janette. Unfortunately, he hadn't been able to save the other two, but he'd done wonders for a sandpiper she'd brought him with a fishhook caught in its wing, and a tern who'd gotten its beak stuck in the ring of a pop-top can.

Janette groaned. She had a running account at the pet hospital and she didn't even own a pet. "Is it going to ruin my day?" she asked with mock severity. Kevin was an old school chum and she suspected he charged her a reduced rate. Something he soundly denied.

Kevin turned off the long-handled faucets and reached for a towel. A grin spread across his boyish face. "Probably. But I think we can save this little fellow. Birds adjust quite readily to the loss of a leg."

Janette sighed in relief, her mouth softening. Maybe the day wasn't going to turn out so bad after all. "You do that and you'll not hear a word of complaint from me no matter what you charge."

Janette slipped the strap of her bag onto her shoulder. "Say hello to Cynthia and the kids for me, will you? And—" she took one last look at the motionless seagull "—take care of my little friend." With a wave of her hand, she turned and hastened along the corridor of the pet hospital to the exit sign.

She drove the short distance from the hospital to the beautiful wooded grounds of the Fremont Bowl which was home to the Crystal Beach Living Masters Pageant where she'd worked for the past five years. The Living Masters recreated famous paintings using live models. Although the pageant lasted for only six weeks during the summer, her job as a director was a full-time one. Cutbacks in the funds used for public education had all but eliminated the teaching of fine arts in the schools. It had been Janette's idea to make up for this by providing tours each spring for school children explaining how the art tableaux are produced. During the last two years, the tours had become so popular that it was now necessary to book them months in advance.

Janette's office was one of several wedged behind the stage of the amphitheater. Her assistant, Pat Haley, glanced up from her desk as Janette breezed through the open door on the way to her own office, anxious to join the teacher, Mrs. White, at the picnic grounds as promised. Pat's face brightened at sight of Janette and an audible sigh of relief escaped her.

"Thank goodness you're here," she said dropping the receiver of the phone into its cradle. The assistant grabbed a pencil and pad and followed Janette into her office, her high heels clicking steadily behind Janette's more practical Reeboks.

Janette's office was a small cramped room with high windows that let the sunshine spill across her paper-laden desk.

"I was just dialing your number," Pat explained. "Do you know you're nearly an hour late and those kids!" She threw up her arms. "Another ten minutes and we won't have a pageant this year because there won't be anything left! I've chased two boys off the roof, one out of the water fountain and one was actually trying to shimmy up the flagpole."

Janette couldn't help but grin. Pat could handle any crisis as long as it didn't involve children. Anyone under twelve completely overwhelmed her, which was one of the reasons Janette conducted the school tours herself.

"I'm sorry I'm late," Janette said, slipping her purse into the bottom drawer of her desk, and grabbing a large canvas bag that contained enough brochures and discount tickets to the actual pageant for the entire class. "The leg's got to be amputated."

Pat's perfectly manicured hand flew to her chest, and the gray eyes behind her jeweled frames grew round with alarm. "Whose leg?"

"The seagull's. Stella and I rescued the little guy this morning." Stella was her best friend; they shared a Victorian house overlooking the ocean. "Anything that needs my attention?"

Looking confused, Pat nodded and sank onto an old leather chair. "Afraid so. Joe Whittaker was in a car accident last night. Nothing serious," she added hastily. "Just a few broken ribs."

"Thank God for that," Janette said. "Did you call his replacement?"

"That's the problem," Pat explained. "Joe's replacement is going to Europe for the summer."

Janette frowned. The Living Masters models were carefully chosen according to size and bone structure. The costumes and props were then designed around the model to capture every nuance of the painting they were meant to depict. Joe Whittaker was one of those rare compact men who stood only five foot ten, but was so well proportioned he looked taller. Finding a man whose proportions matched Joe Whittaker's would be no easy task.

"Send Joe some flowers," Janette said. A child's voice outside her window sent her scurrying for the door, calling over her shoulder. "See if there's anyone on file who's Joe's size."

She hurried outside and glanced around. There was no sign of the children. Taking a deep breath of the clear ocean air, she started along the winding path that led from her office to the picnic grounds where she'd arranged to meet Mrs. White. She could hear the high-pitched voices of the students long before she emerged from the thick grove of stately pines where the path took a sharp turn and started to incline.

A woman's voice shrill with frustration, called out somewhere in the distance. "If you children don't come out of those bushes, I'll send the whole lot of you back to the school bus!"

Janette glanced guiltily at her watch, and decided she'd have to be extra patient with the children to make up for the wait. As late as she was, however, she couldn't resist slowing down and peering through the bushes that were alive with rustling sounds and muffled whispers.

She walked to the edge of the path where the growth was thickest and studied a bush that was positively vibrating. Standing on tiptoe, she peered curiously through an opening in the heavy foliage. She caught a glimpse of a gray-haired woman on the opposite side of the thick natural barrier and assumed it was Mrs. White. Her attention was drawn to a flash of yellow at ground level and she reached down to push aside a leafy clump. She was greeted by two brown eyes, round and shining with mischief. A closer look revealed that the eyes belonged to a boy with curly hair as dark as night, and an uncertain grin that disappeared at the sound of his name.

"Matthew, is that you in there?" the teacher called, her voice followed by a loud piercing whistle.

Matthew ducked out of sight, leaving Janette smiling like a child herself. Oh, to be that young again, she thought, starting down the path. She looked up, startled, into a face that was all eyeglasses and freckles, its owner hanging upside down from the branches of a sprawling sycamore tree that shaded the path. After gently admonishing the boy to get out of the tree, and waiting until he had safely done so, she continued along the path.

Without warning, someone shot out in front of her, stopped in surprise at seeing Janette and looked about ready to dive for cover again in the bushes. The wayward offender was a girl, tall and wiry and dressed in blue jeans and a green striped shirt that matched her eyes. Her blond hair, long enough to reach her waist, was brushed back from her face and held in place with a shiny green barrette.

Janette stopped the girl's retreat with a friendly smile. "You must be in Mrs. White's class."

The girl glanced over her shoulder at the empty path, then turned back to face Janette. She opened her mouth to answer, but stopped at the sound of her name.

"Amy, when I get my hands on you, I'm going to march you right over to the telephone and call your father," Mrs. White shrilled again, her voice loud enough to disrupt the crows from their perches at the top of the trees. An uproar sounded from up high as the birds took flight, cawing raucously as they circled overhead.

Janette could hardly take her eyes off the girl named Amy. The eyes, Janette thought in awe, why they're as green as all get-out. Janette was taken back by the thought. "As green as all get-out" had been the way Janette's grandmother had described Janette's eyes those long years ago, when Janette was but a school-girl herself, and had eyes the color of emeralds. Her eyes had grown lighter over the years and now at the age of twenty-seven, they appeared more turquoise than green. Few people ever mentioned the green in her eyes anymore, for it could only be spotted if someone peered closely at her, and it had been a long time since she'd allowed anyone close enough to do that.

Janette never knew what "all get-out" meant, exactly. Her grandmother had grown up on a farm and used the most rudimentary language to convey a world of meaning. But the expression had seemed apt back then when she was young, and it seemed appropriate now in describing the eyes of this girl with the appealing face and the lithe young body that was posed like a deer ready to take flight.

Mrs. White rounded the curve, bedraggled and winded. She wore red pants and a gaily printed blouse and a silver whistle dangled from a black cord around her neck. Right now the whistle was bopping up and down in the center of her heaving bosom. "Two more years," she puffed. "Two more years before I retire and then I won't have to take any more field trips."

Amy paled at the sight of her teacher and glanced at Janette beseechingly. Janette felt herself drawn to the girl and had the strongest urge to throw her arms around her and protect her. Even stronger was the urge to brush back the wispy lock of hair that had escaped the barrette. *Hair as blond as all get-out.* Janette blinked with a start. What was the matter with her? Her grandmother had died when Janette was fifteen and she had missed her something fierce over the years. Still, it had been a long time since Janette had actually thought about her. Now, suddenly, in the span of a few moments her grandmother's soft gentle voice with the decidedly midwestern drawl had come back to haunt her twice.

Janette held the canvas bag toward Amy. "Will you carry this for me?" she asked, keeping her voice low.

The girl glanced at the bag a moment before lifting puzzled eyes to meet Janette's. Janette nodded encouragement, and Amy took the bag, sliding it up her arm, and letting a soft grateful smile touch her mouth as if she sensed she'd just made a friend. Feeling a warm glow wash over her, Janette smiled back.

Mrs. White reached them, scolding and complaining and looked as if she was about to pounce on Amy like a cat ready to jump on a mouse. Janette quickly extended her right arm, surprised at the strong urge to protect a child she didn't even know. She wasn't even certain that Amy needed protecting. A closer observation of Mrs. White's face revealed enough friendly lines around her mouth to prove that the teacher was probably not as threatening as she appeared. "You must be Mrs. White. I'm Janette Taylor. Amy is helping me carry my things to the picnic grounds."

The diversion worked, for Mrs. White immediately forgot Amy as she shook Janette's hand and regarded her with a disapproving frown. "When I spoke to you

on the phone you said the tours started promptly at ten."

Janette nodded. "I apologize for the delay. But I had a family emergency."

"Oh, dear," Mrs. White exclaimed, her scolding voice edged with concern. "I do hope everything's all right."

"Yes, thank you," Janette said vaguely, not wanting to explain that the family emergency involved an injured seagull. It wasn't a lie. She considered seagulls part of her family. Each morning the birds gathered outside her kitchen window where she threw them pieces of fish that she kept especially for the purpose. Janette didn't have a conventional family. Her parents and both sets of grandparents were dead. She'd almost had a family of her own once. But that had been a long time ago, ten years ago to be exact. Now she depended on friends and seagulls to fill the void. Of course, none of this could be explained to a stranger.

A clamor came from the bushes, and a young voice called out, "Over here!" This was followed by the sound of running footsteps.

"Oh, dear," Mrs. White cried. She grabbed her whistle and put it to her lips as she tottered toward the bushes. The long piercing shrill almost burst Janette's eardrums.

Janette exchanged glances with Amy, puzzled by the feeling that she knew this child. Amy's green eyes were shining with humor and something else—a glow of recognition as if she, too, had the same feeling. But Janette knew that wasn't possible; she would have remembered meeting such an appealing child.

Feeling sorry for the harried teacher, Janette reluctantly drew her eyes away from Amy's and called after

Mrs. White. "If you have the children form a line, we can get started."

"Yes, yes," Mrs. White cried eagerly. She blew her whistle again and clapped her hands. "Line up, children. We're going to start the tour now. Line up!"

Boys and girls appeared from every direction, scrambling out of bushes and jumping out of trees, chattering and moving constantly like baby chicks scrambling for grain. After taking a nose count, Mrs. White introduced Janette and stepped aside, obviously relieved to turn the class over to someone else.

Janette cleared her voice and welcomed the children to the pageant grounds. She then gave a brief description of the pageant. "Every year we choose about two dozen paintings to recreate on stage," Janette explained. "We use living models, music and special lighting to give the impression that the tableau on stage is an actual painting." As she spoke, Janette found herself searching out Amy, who had moved toward the back of the group to join two other girls, but whose eyes seemed unwilling or unable to let Janette out of her sight.

For the first time, Janette realized how tall Amy was in comparison to the rest of the class, standing at least a few inches taller than the other girls and as much as a head taller than the boys. *As tall as all get-out.* Her grandmother's voice echoed again. Janette shook her head and concentrated on the task at hand. She gave a brief history of the pageant and then said, "If you follow me, I'll show you how we create these living pictures."

Janette led the class up the path leading to a building fronted by an open-air stage. She turned and cautioned everyone to be quiet, and then led the students single file through a side door and down a long corridor to the brightly lit makeup room. Large mirrors, framed with glaring white lights, rose from countertops, which were crammed with makeup jars, boxes of tissue, cotton swabs and sponges.

Lester, the stage manager, was perched on one of the stools in front of a mirror, half his face painted like a clown. Sally, one of the makeup artists, leaned over and applied a sprinkling of freckles across his clown-white cheek with the tip of a tiny brush.

"Say hello to Sally and Lester," Janette said.

The class said a greeting in unison, and Sally waved her brush and smiled. Lester turned and put on a clown's expression that brought laughter from the students and even coaxed a smile from Mrs. White.

"If you come to the pageant this summer, you'll see a painting called *Bring in the Clowns*," Janette explained, drawing the students' attention to a photo of the painting that was taped to the mirror. She glanced over the heads of the boys and girls and allowed her eyes to linger on Amy who stood in the back, listening to every word with rapt attention. Again, Janette felt a glowing warmth bubble up inside. She had the strangest feeling that every part of her was reaching out to this child. More puzzling still was the warm and wonderful feeling that Amy was reaching back. "See how Lester's face looks like the clown's in this painting?"

A girl with long braids raised her hand. "How come only half of his face is painted?"

"That's a good question," Janette said. "If you look closely at the painting, you'll notice that only half of the clown's face is showing. To make our tableau appear two-dimensional like a real painting, half of our model's face will be set into a hole that is cut out of the backdrop."

As she spoke her eyes gravitated toward Amy. Her mouth went dry as an unexpected tug inside awakened feelings she'd promised herself never again to feel.

Turning abruptly, Janette quickly led the way through a narrow hallway, which opened to a large room filled with costumes. Wondering why she felt the sudden need to flee, she waited until everyone had crowded into the area before holding up a boy's suit that appeared to be made from blue velvet, promising herself not to look at the girl.

"This costume will be worn in a famous portrait painted by an artist named Gainsborough," she explained, raising her voice so that those in the back of the room could hear her. "The painting is called *Blue Boy* Even though it looks like this might be made out of velvet it's actually made out of unbleached muslin and painted to look like the costume in the painting."

After showing the children the costume department, Janette ushered them into the sculpture department, where Timothy Marsh was working on a piece of Styrofoam with a saber saw. Tim stopped working as soon as the children started filing in, straightened and grinned at Janette.

Janette introduced him to the class. "Tim makes all the animals we need for our paintings."

A boy whom Janette recognized as the mischievous Matthew, asked why real animals weren't used. Janette explained that real animals would move around on stage. "Once the curtains open, the models mustn't move a muscle for ninety seconds, otherwise the re-creation won't look like an actual painting."

Janette led the class from the sculpture department to the headpiece department where everything from helmets to wigs and masks were created from latex, and then up a short staircase to the open-air stage, where two male artists were painting a backdrop for a barnyard scene.

As soon as they were gathered on stage, Janette pointed to the hole in the backdrop for the "farmer's" arm. "These are the backdrops I mentioned earlier. They are made out of wood frames," she explained. "We use nearly two miles of lumber for each show. Then over six hundred yards of unbleached muslin is needed to stretch over the frames. Our two artists here will need nearly seventy-five gallons of paint to make the backgrounds look identical to the real paintings."

She then explained that during the show, the sets are lined up one behind the other to allow the scenery to be changed in seconds. "As soon as the curtain comes down, the stage crew has only two minutes to prepare the next tableau before the curtain rises again."

After Janette finished answering the children's questions, she led the class down the narrow stairway leading to the outdoor seating.

The tour ended at the picnic grounds where the children grabbed their lunches, then scattered across the grass to find a place beneath the sprawling shade trees to eat. Amy handed Janette the canvas bag and ran to join her friends. Then it hit Janette! The reason she'd had so much trouble keeping her eyes away from the girl was that Amy looked exactly like the portrait Janette's artist father had painted of her when she was ten. Of course!

She was amazed that it had taken her so long to recognize the likeness. She hadn't looked at the portrait for years. It was too painful to look at, for it brought back unresolved hurts and resentments she felt toward her father. But if her memory served her correctly, the resemblance between herself as a child and this tall, lovely girl was remarkable.

Feeling slightly dazed, Janette handed Mrs. White enough brochures and discount tickets for the entire class. An idea began to form in her mind. "Would it be possible to ask Amy's parents to get in touch with me?" she asked.

Mrs. White looked surprised. "Amy? You mean Amy Blake? All she's got is a father. Her mother died a few years ago. Why do you want to talk to her father?"

"I'm thinking about the possibility of using her as a model," Janette replied slowly. Although she had agreed to stage one of her father's paintings this year, it had never before occurred to her to stage the portrait he'd painted of her. Not until today, this minute. The idea, seeming to come out of the blue, left her shaken.

"I'll see what I can do," Mrs. White said vaguely, her attention caught by two arguing boys. She stuck her whistle in her mouth and marched over to where the boys stood shouting at each other. Janette doubted that Mrs. White would remember to talk to Amy's father, but it was probably for the best that she didn't. Janette didn't relish the thought of digging out the portrait of herself, anyway. It would evoke too many memories.

She glanced one last time at Amy who was sitting on the grass beneath a tree with two other girls. Speckled sunlight touched Amy's hair, turning the long silky strands into glittering gold, and making the green barrette shine like a strand of emeralds. As if she sensed Janette's gaze, the girl glanced up, her green eyes wide and filled with life and laughter and so much more as their eyes met and held.

Janette thought about her infant daughter who had died at birth. If Stephanie had lived, would she have looked like Amy? Would that explain the longing, the aching need that Amy evoked in her? A painful squeeze in Janette's chest brought a lump to her throat and an unexpected sting of tears to her eyes. With a silent sob, she spun on her heel and practically ran up the hill to her office.

THE FOLLOWING FRIDAY, Janette sat at her desk thinking about the appealing blond girl with the laughing green eyes. It had been odd, to say the least, to have felt so close to a stranger—especially one so young—and the fact that Amy bore a striking resemblance to her as a child hardly explained the strong pull Janette had sensed—still sensed—between them.

The buzzer on her desk sounded and Janette leaned over and pressed the black button on the intercom. "Yes, Pat."

"I may have found someone to take Joe's place. His name is Art Milton. He'll try to come in around noon. He says he can stay for only a few minutes."

Janette wrote the name on a scrap of paper and glanced at her calendar. A reporter from the local press was due at ten. She'd asked the music director to come in at eleven to discuss the music for the Egyptian tableau, and there was the Velcro problem to deal with. Wardrobe had ordered five hundred yards three months ago and it still hadn't arrived. Heaven only knew what people did before the invention of Velcro!

"Has he modeled for us before?"

"No, but his brother has, so he knows the routine."

"All right, it should only take a few minutes to get his measurements. By the way, will you call and see when we're going to get that Velcro? Wardrobe's having a fit."

Janette released the button and glanced at the notations on her calendar where she'd jotted down Joe's measurements. The *Wild Wild West* scene required the model to be perched upon a bucking horse that had been masterfully reproduced in Styrofoam and chicken wire by Tim's expert hand. Since the original artist hadn't left much sky showing above the cowboy's head, there wasn't much room for error. Another consideration was the size of the model's thigh since one leg had to be thrust through a carefully concealed hole in the backdrop.

Grateful that the model problem was so easily resolved, Janette concentrated on the other problems clamoring for her attention.

It wasn't until after her meeting with the reporter that she had time to glance at the notes she'd scribbled out regarding the Dresden piece. During the previous night's rehearsal she'd thought the model had the complexion of the Pillsbury doughboy instead of the look of fine porcelain. Trying to decide if this was the fault of lighting or makeup, Janette's thoughts were interrupted by a strong firm knock on the door.

"Come in," she called, checking her watch and discovering to her surprise it was already noon.

She glanced up as a tall man entered her office, his rich baritone voice floating across the room as smooth as velvet. "Miss Taylor?"

Dark, shining eyes stared at her from a rugged square face. Brown hair dipped from a side part, falling across his forehead as it swept down and upward in a generous wave. A voice suddenly echoed in her head and for the fourth time that week she distinctly heard her grandmother put in her two cents worth: *As handsome as all get-out!*

CHAPTER TWO

"AM I GLAD to see you!" Janette managed. Appalled
to find herself staring. She glanced down at the piece
of paper on which she had written the model's name.
Art Milton. Remembering what Pat had said about
Art's limited time, and not wanting to keep him a moment longer than necessary, she grabbed her tape
measure and jumped to her feet. "Stand over here and
I'll measure you."

Once she had managed to pull her eyes away from
his face, she became acutely aware of the rest of him,
and she took in the long form of the stranger with sudden dismay. "My, but you're tall."

The man looked confused for a moment, lifted his
shoulders in a shrug and walked over to the spot she
had indicated. "I'm afraid it runs in the family," he
said.

"Mine, too." Janette dropped to the floor at his feet
and wrapped the tape measure around his upper thigh.
And what a thigh it was!

Amy Blake's father looked down in astonishment at
the woman who crawled around him on hands and
knees, muttering to herself. He caught a glimpse of soft
velvet eyes, a pleasing mouth and a nose that was
turned slightly upward. But it wasn't astonishment that
prevented him from pulling away from the gentle touch
of her fingers that worked from the front of his thigh

to the back, as she wrapped the tape measure around his leg; he didn't know for sure what it was. All he knew was that he was willing to stand perfectly still and let this stranger do whatever she wanted to do without argument.

One thing he did know, however, was that the woman was tall and shapely. Curved hips flared from a slim waist and tapered into long jean-clad legs. Her yellow knit top hugged the soft curving mounds of her breasts; the open V collar offered an enticing view of the soft warm shadows at the hollow of her neck.

"Open your legs," she said, and without comment he did as she asked, feeling a lurch inside as he watched her draw the tape measure beneath his crotch, her delicate fingers brushing a part of him that hadn't been touched by a woman since his wife died three years earlier.

"Oh, my," she cried in disbelief. "Twenty-eight inches." She glanced up and for a brief moment, he thought they'd met before. It was the eyes—something in the eyes. They were wide with dismay for some reason, their turquoise depths boring into his as if he'd done something wrong. She had blond hair, soft and feathery, that hugged her heart-shaped face. Almost as soon as the thought took shape, he amended it; her hair was blond, but it shone red in the stream of sunlight that fell through the window and seemed to seek her out no matter where she moved. Blond-red hair, that was better, he thought and decided that blue-green was a more apt description of her eyes.

He decided he was mistaken; they couldn't have met previously. Not even the grief and despair that had marked his life over the last few years could have made him forget meeting someone so beguiling.

What in the world is she doing? he wondered, not wanting the delicate pressure of her fingers on his thigh to stop. Measuring for a suit?

Janette felt his eyes on her as she worked. She glanced up the length of his long legs wondering what Pat could have been thinking of when she'd asked him to audition for the part. He was far too tall. More than that, he was far too muscular and too restless, as well. Although he stood perfectly still for her, she could feel restless energy surge through the powerful muscles of his thigh, and she doubted seriously that he could hold the precarious perch on a bucking horse for the entire ninety seconds that would be required of him.

Her gaze drifted upward, taking note of his taut stomach. At last her eyes reached his dark handsome face, tanned by the sun to a rich bronze that she would give the world to be able to duplicate in the surfing scene they were staging that year.

If the color of his skin wasn't enough to confirm him as an outdoors man, the fine lines spreading out from the corners of his eyes certainly did. Her instincts had been right. He definitely wasn't model material. Suddenly realizing she was staring, she found herself blushing.

She was used to measuring men, seeing men in various states of undress as the models were whisked in and out of costumes for the summer-long show. There was no room backstage for dressing rooms or false modesty, nor was there the time or inclination to knock. But there was something about this particular man, the way his presence filled up the room, that made her all too aware of how his chest strained against the fabric of his short-sleeved dress shirt, and the perfect fit of his brown silk pants that hung from his hips in a smooth straight line. He was fully dressed and yet she was all too aware of taut muscles, hard thighs and warm flesh.

My goodness, she thought, he'd positively upstage the rest of the models, even the bucking horse. If only he didn't look at her so... So what? Intimately? She could at least concentrate on what she was doing.

Feeling flustered, she measured his thigh for the second time, her pulses racing like a galloping horse as she drew the tape measure between his legs, aware of the proximity of his manhood, and feeling her cheeks burn. There was no mistake. The man wouldn't fit on the Styrofoam horse, no matter how much Tim might manage to reinforce it.

She dropped one end of the tape measure and stood. "I'm sorry," she said breathlessly, suddenly lost in the depths of his blue eyes. "You're just too tall."

It wasn't the first time Adam had been told he was too tall, but she made it sound as if it were his fault that he stood six foot four. All through his youth, he'd been too tall to play in organized sports with other boys his age, having far exceeded the height limitations. But never had he heard the complaint from a woman.

"Would you like to lodge a grievance with my ancestors?" he asked wryly.

Not sure whether or not he was teasing, she was saved from responding by the buzzer on her desk. "Excuse me," she said, pressing the button of the intercom, grateful for the diversion. "Yes, Pat."

"Art just called to say he can't make it in today. He'll be in first thing Monday morning."

Janette's mouth dropped open as she swung around to gaze at the tall stranger. Meeting her alarmed gaze with an amused grin, he extended his hands outward and shrugged. She gulped, finding her cheeks burning again, and stifled a moan. "Thanks, Pat."

She flipped off the switch and lifted her lashes in apology. "I'm so sorry. I thought you were someone else."

"I know," Adam said, rewarding her with a smile that intimated more empathy, this time, than amusement, and somehow managed to ease her embarrassment. He tugged on his tasteful silk tie, then held out his hand. "My name is Adam Blake. I'm Amy's father. Your secretary was busy so I took the liberty of knocking on the door with your name on it. I believe you asked to see me."

For a moment all Janette could think about was the feel of her hand lost in the warm safe haven of his. It wasn't until he let her hand go and drew his arm away that she was able to recover enough to remember that Amy was the child who'd haunted her thoughts all week.

"I'm so pleased to meet you," Janette said, trying to gain control of her senses.

As handsome as all get-out.

The thought, very much her own this time, nearly upset what control she'd regained. She braced herself against her desk for support. "You have a delightful daughter." Not only did he have a delightful daughter, Janette added to herself, but he seemed to have the same magnetic appeal as the child. Disconcerted by the thought, she wondered in dismay if she would now be haunted by the father, as well.

Another smile lit up his face, followed by a look of fatherly pride. "I think so, too."

"I would like her to model in the pageant," Janette explained, anxious to prove that she wasn't completely inept. "I'm not happy with one of our tableaux. I'm thinking about scrapping it and replacing it with another—a portrait." She wasn't sure if she should tell him the rest; that the reason she wanted to stage the portrait was because Amy looked identical to herself as a child. She hesitated. "Are you familiar with the pageant?"

"Yes," Adam replied. "My wife..." He paused and began again. "I've attended a few in the past."

She remembered Mrs. White telling her that his wife had died. But even if she hadn't known in advance, she would have guessed it from the look in his eyes when he mentioned his wife, the softness, the sad resignation that told her he was past the grieving stage, but not the hurting stage.

"The pageant lasts about six weeks," Janette explained, and then carefully outlined what would be expected of Amy. Modeling took a lot of time and energy, and required endless hours in makeup and costuming and waiting around for curtain call. Although most people imagined it was a glamourous job, modeling in the pageant was extremely hard work.

Adam listened attentively, sensing the woman's love for her job. She talked of capturing the essence and spirit of the artist's work, and explained how a panel of professionals was consulted to make sure that the artist's intent in creating the work was in no way compromised by its stage interpretation. He liked that. In fact, he liked everything about Miss Taylor and it was easy to see why Amy had talked so highly about the pretty woman who had supposedly saved her from Mrs. White.

"Do you have any questions?" Janette asked, suddenly aware of how closely Adam watched her as she spoke.

"Did you know about the green?" he asked suddenly.

She stared at him in confusion. "I beg your pardon."

"The green . . . in your eyes."

Her heart throbbed, her legs threatened to buckle beneath her weight. And your eyes sparkle like champagne in candlelight, she wanted to say, but didn't dare. "I . . . I know," she stammered. She glanced away, willing herself not to blush. "About Amy . . ."

"I think it's a great idea," Adam said, obviously unaware of how his observation about her eye color had affected her. "Of course it depends on how Amy feels about it."

She met his gaze and sensed he was still assessing the green flecks of her eyes. It had been a long time since a man looked at her the way Adam Blake was looking at her. "Of course," she said, managing to keep her voice under control.

He hesitated slightly before continuing. "Amy is a sports nut, I'm afraid. The pageant would cut into some of her games and knowing Amy . . ."

Janette nodded. "I know how hard it is for a child to remain still."

"Softball, soccer, you name it," he continued. Since the death of Amy's mother, he had raised her himself, with some help from his mother-in-law, Virginia Spencer, who lived nearby. It had seemed more natural to him to take her to a football game than to a ballet class or an art museum. "I think it would be good for Amy to learn a bit about the arts, Miss Taylor,'' he added with a grin.

Janette felt her heart take flight. "Janette," she said softly. "Call me Janette."

"Janette," he said easily. He checked his watch. "I'm afraid I must be going. I have a one o'clock appointment." He glanced at the tape measure in her hand.

"Will you be needing Amy's measurements if she decides to be a model?" he asked, trying to hide a smile.

Remembering the feel of his thigh beneath her fingers, heat spread upward from her cheeks. "Yes. But first I need you to fill out a form giving your permission," she said softly, hoping the erratic beats of her heart hadn't drowned out her voice. "It's for insurance purposes." She dropped the tape measure on the desk and reached into the top drawer for a form, which she handed to him. "If you like you can fill it out now and then if Amy agrees to model, I can complete the paperwork."

"Sounds like a plan." He pulled a gold pen out of his shirt pocket and flicked the top with his thumb, before leaning over her desk to write.

Janette sank into her chair, grateful for the moment of reprieve from his probing gaze. Nevertheless, she felt no qualms in allowing herself the luxury of studying every inch of him as his strong square hands made bold strokes on the paper. From there, she found herself hungrily taking in the set of his firm chin, the way his mouth softened at the edges as if filling out the form on his daughter brought him pleasure, the faint furrow of concentration between his brows.

He sighed his name with a flourish and straightened. Clicking the tip of the pen before slipping it back into his shirt pocket, he handed the form back to her. "Would that be all?" he asked, his eyes lingering on her mouth.

She wondered in alarm if he knew she'd been staring. "For now," Janette said, pressing her back into her chair, grateful for the desk that spanned between them. "Can you let me know Amy's decision no later than Monday? We've already begun rehearsals and we're going to need some time to work on the costuming and backdrop for the portrait."

Adam thought for a moment. "She gets out of school around three. I'll have her grandmother bring her here, say, at four, if that's all right with you. That way if she has any questions she can ask you herself."

At the mention of Amy's grandmother, Janette felt a wave of disappointment that Adam wouldn't be bringing Amy himself. "That'll be fine," Janette said, rising.

Adam grinned. "I'm really looking forward to this year's pageant," he said. He wondered irrelevantly if the moonlight would bring out the blond or the red in her hair. Probably both, he thought, for he was having a hard time trying to separate the colors himself.

She returned his grin. "So am I," she said, wondering if she had only imagined the underlying message behind his words that suggested his interest in the pageant had nothing whatsoever to do with art.

He backed away from her desk, as if not wanting to take his eyes off her until the last possible moment. At the door he nodded and turned.

In an instant he was gone, but it took a long time for Janette to get her heart to resume its normal pace and her legs to stop shaking. When at last she had gained control she reached for Amy's application. Fingering the form carefully, and remembering the strong hands that had touched the paper a couple of minutes earlier, she scanned the sheet.

Adam's bold handwriting practically filled every line with Amy's vital statistics, including the child's weight and height. Janette was impressed that Adam knew these things about his daughter; most fathers didn't have the information so readily available.

At the moment, however, Janette was not particularly interested in Amy's weight or height. It was the father that claimed her interest. She glanced farther down the page in search of information about him. Anything that would satisfy her curiosity. Under "father's place of employment" he had written Ashton Tex Corporation, which she knew was an oil company outside of town.

He didn't look like one of the many geologists she knew the company employed. Those people were always digging and drilling in the area. Judging by the quality of his clothes, she guessed he was in management, high up on the corporate ladder, no doubt.

That was all she could discern from the information at hand. Her eyes drifted upward again, lingering on the handwriting. Surely the strong bold lines of his pen told something about him. The large loops of his *y*'s, the strong bold dots over his *i*'s, the capital *S* in the word September—Amy's month of birth.

Suddenly, Janette felt as if her very foundation had crumbled beneath her. Overcome by astonishment, she fell back in her chair, her breath caught in her throat. She blinked her eyes in disbelief and stared again at the line that jumped at her as if it had taken on a life of its own. September 1, 19...

She could hardly believe it. Amy had been born on the exact month, day and year as Janette's baby.

CHAPTER THREE

THAT NIGHT, Janette helped Stella prepare dinner in the cozy kitchen of the quaint Victorian home they'd shared since Stella's divorce three years earlier. Janette could talk of nothing else but Adam and the astonishing coincidence of Amy's birth date.

"Don't you think it's remarkable?" Janette asked. She was sitting at the butcher-block table, stripping dry papery husks off ears of fresh corn. "I mean, what are the chances of meeting someone who was born on the same date as Stephanie?" She said her baby's name softly, afraid that saying it louder would awaken the pain inside that she had tried so desperately to keep buried.

Stella was one of the few people who knew about this painful chapter in Janette's life, or at least she knew about most of it. Janette had a baby at the age of seventeen, who'd died at childbirth. Stella, a year older than Janette, had been away at college at the time, and Janette had given birth alone, the father of the child having taken off as soon as he learned that Janette was pregnant.

Janette's own father, the renowned portrait painter, Cameron Taylor, unable to forgive her the shame she'd brought the family name, had stubbornly refused to come to the hospital, forcing Janette to face the ordeal alone. What Stella didn't know because Janette doubted that she or anyone else would understand, was that even after all this time—eleven years come September—she still grieved deeply for her child.

It was hard to explain why she'd never come to terms with losing her baby. Months of counseling hadn't helped, nor had the passing of time. It was as if some vital part of her had been snatched away the day she lost her baby, and the only thing she'd come to accept was that she would probably have to endure the gaping hole inside her for the rest of her life.

Stella carried a pot of water to the stove and wiped her hand on her apron. Her hair was a vivid color, more orange than red, and she wore lipstick to match. Long yellow hoops dangled from her ears and an oversized gold chain fell from her neck to adorn the long colorful tunic she wore over black knitted tights. Stella's somewhat eccentric appearance belied her sharp mathematical mind that had made her a success in the financial world. It amused Janette no end to walk into the White, Evers and Murphy stock brokerage company where Stella worked and see all the grim-faced men dressed in impeccable suits looking to Stella for financial advice.

"You lost your baby over ten years ago," Stella said, her normally deep throaty voice soft and gentle. "I guess it's not so surprising that with as many school children as you see in a year's time, one of them would have the same birth date. It's called the rule of twenty-eight. You stand on a street corner and ask twenty-eight people their birth dates and one of them will have the same birthday as yours." She turned on the front burner of the stove. "Guaranteed, every time."

Janette gathered up the discarded husks and dumped them into the trash. Trust Stella with her logical mind to come up with a plausible explanation. "And what are the chances of that person looking exactly like me as a child?" she asked.

"As far as I can tell, this girl had green eyes and long blond hair. That probably describes 8.2 percent of the student population."

Janette grinned. Eight point two. Anyone else might have said ten percent. "I still think it's a remarkable coincidence," Janette argued and thinking of Adam Blake added, "A very nice coincidence. Did I tell you how tall he was?"

"Yes, and you also told me his thigh measurements, the color of his eyes, his hair, the way he walks and..."

Janette laughed as she crossed to the stove and dropped the corn into the pan of water. "I guess I've bored you to death, haven't I?"

"Listen, I may be living the life of a cloistered nun, but I'm not dead yet. If you want to talk about a good-looking man with size twenty-eight thighs, don't let me stop you."

After they had finished dinner and had stacked the dishes in the dishwasher, Janette scraped off pieces of corn from the cob she'd saved, and placed the yellow kernels in a saucer. She carried the saucer outside and slipped off her sandals to let her bare feet sink into the sandy path that meandered through a patch of ice plant to a private beach.

Overhead, the sky had turned a brilliant red. She breathed in the fresh salt air and noted how the sun seemed to hover over the amber-colored sea like a big scarlet beachball caught by a playful wind.

She found the little one-legged seagull she'd rescued earlier that week waiting for her just beyond the growth of ice plant that marked the boundary of their property.

"Hi, there, Pogo," she cooed softly, setting the saucer a few feet away from the bird. She'd named him Pogo on the day she'd brought him back from the pet hospital. Not wanting to return the injured bird to the wild so soon, she had let him loose in the kitchen and he had hopped on his remaining foot across her floor with the ease of a child on a pogo stick.

Pogo stood perfectly still for a moment, then turned his head slowly, before bopping up and down toward the saucer. His pearly gray head darted forward and he picked up a kernel in his long stout beak that curved downward and ended in a sharp hook. Janette smiled as the little fellow quickly swallowed the corn and dived eagerly for the next kernel.

"Who ever heard of a seagull who likes corn?" A smile touched her mouth a she regarded her "baby" with maternal pride. Just as quickly the smile left her face as she thought of another baby.

The seagull finished off the rest of the kernels and hopped away just as a jogger ran by. Janette waved at the runner, gathered up the empty saucer and returned to the house.

"You're right," Janette said moments later as she walked into the living room where Stella sat reading the *Wall Street Journal*. "About the birth date not being such a coincidence."

"Of course I'm right," Stella mumbled, peering at Janette through orange-framed glasses.

Janette glanced toward the ceiling to the exact spot where the portrait was stored in the attic. She hadn't looked at the painting in five years, not since she'd found it unexpectedly tucked away in her father's studio after his death. Upon discovering it, she hadn't been able to believe her eyes. After all those years, why would he keep a portrait he so obviously despised?

Her first instinct had been to destroy the portrait. But she'd kept it, mainly because it was the only picture she had of herself as a child. Her mother, a photographer, had left the family when Janette was six. Following her mother's desertion, her father had refused to allow a camera in the house, and hadn't even bothered to order Janette's annual school photos.

"Come to think of it, I'm not even sure that Amy resembles me all that much," she added, knowing how the mind can play tricks with one's memory. Maybe Stella was right; maybe the resemblance went no further than the color of Amy's eyes and hair. Of course, there was one way to find out for certain, she thought, and that was to march right up to the attic and take a look at that portrait. She would have to anyway, if Amy agreed to model for it.

She wished that she hadn't presented the idea to Amy's father. She suspected that the portrait was one of Cameron Taylor's best works of art, but she found that dealing with it was far too painful. If she'd had a sensible bone in her body, she would have destroyed the painting on the day she'd discovered it.

Stella folded up the newspaper. "Why don't you get the portrait and bring it down here? Obviously, you're not going to rest until you see for yourself." She studied Janette's face before adding, "Do you want me to go up to the attic with you?"

"Certainly not," Janette said, straightening with firm resolve. There were enough ghosts in her past without allowing herself to be haunted by a mere portrait. "I'll be back in a jif."

The house had two staircases, one leading up to the second-floor bedrooms and the other, built originally for servants, that led to the third-floor attic. This staircase was located in the anteroom off the kitchen, which she and Stella had converted into a laundry room. Janette walked through the kitchen, finding a semblance of comfort in the soft hum of the dishwasher as she opened the door to the laundry room. She flipped on the light and started up the spiral staircase that forged upward inside the Queen Anne's tower to a small landing above that opened up to the attic.

The attic, light and airy during the day, was now cast in a red-purple glow as the last strains of the sunset filtered through the wavy glass of the gable windows. Janette reached up over her head and tugged on the chain that hung from the light fixture in the center of the ceiling. Instantly, the room filled with the soft glow of a yellow light.

Janette glanced around. Boxes filled with Christmas decorations and overflowing scrapbooks, old clothes and an odd combination of shoes were stacked everywhere. To her knowledge, Stella had never thrown away a pair of shoes in her life, or anything else for that matter. An ancient Singer sewing machine stood in one corner. A pair of Mickey Mouse ears hung from an old oak hat rack. In one dark shadowy corner stood a bassinet.

Janette felt her composure begin to shatter as she tried to keep herself from glancing at the corner. The bassinet had been the one thing that Stella had wanted to throw out, but Janette had objected. Tearing her eyes away from the faded pink bow on the hood of the bassinet, she forced herself to concentrate on the reason she'd come to the attic.

The portrait stood facing the wall and Janette felt her throat grow dry as she gingerly grabbed hold of its frame and gently eased it out of its resting place from behind an old dressmaker's form that had come with the house.

She set the portrait against the sewing machine and then stepped back for a look. Much to her surprise, she found the pain evoked by the painting had not diminished over the years.

Despite her father's strict rule forbidding anyone to see a painting in progress, she remembered creeping into his studio late one night, just before her tenth birthday, to view the portrait of herself. She'd been anxious to see how her famous father, who had been commissioned to paint kings and queens as well as movie stars, had captured her image. To her horror, she'd discovered that her likeness had been disfigured by an angry black streak of paint. The strip that seemed so like an ugly scar started in the corner and continued diagonally across the portrait, covering one eye, her nose and half her mouth. Even now, all these years later, she still remembered the devastation she'd felt that long-ago night; dressed in a linen nightgown, weeping softly, she'd stood in front of her father's easel, wondering what she had done to make her father so angry.

She never understood what feelings of rage lay behind the marring of her portrait. Neither she nor her father ever mentioned the painting after that, and not until his death had she even suspected that he still kept it.

She forced herself to put aside the hurt and concentrate on the image behind the black streak of paint. She only had one eye to work with, but it was enough. For it was the exact color of Amy's eye, there was no mistaking it. Green as all get-out!

And the hair! Why it was the same shade of blond. Amy's had been longer, of course, but not much longer, and Janette had worn a side part while Amy wore hers brushed back from her face. But other than the hairstyle, the likeness was uncanny.

Then she concentrated on the mouth. It was hard to tell much here, for her mouth was so serious in the painting and Amy's had been turned upward most of the time in a smile or, at the very least, the beginning of one. The nose was completely covered by the black paint, as was the chin.

She studied the rest of the painting her father had called *Girl with Gull*. Her eyes lingered in surprise on the seagull she was feeding that looked so real she couldn't help but reach out to stroke its lifelike feathers. She'd forgotten about the seagull, but she recalled that it had been her idea to pose with one.

Even as a child she'd been fascinated with the birds that most people considered a nuisance. She had found out something rather astounding about seagulls in her youth; they recognized people by their faces. She learned this one day while playing on the beach after a seagull had picked her out of a crowd of people and landed on her shoulder, recognizing her as the one who had fed it earlier.

But it wasn't seagulls that were on her mind as she carried the portrait downstairs and set it on the floor in front of the TV; it was the past and the present, and the strange way the two had suddenly become intertwined.

Janette stepped back and tilted her head in concentration. "I'm not mistaken," she said, after Stella had tossed her paper aside and joined her in front of the painting. "Amy could have sat for that portrait herself. I wish I could see the nose, though. A nose can make a lot of difference to a face."

"Why don't you take the portrait to an art restoration company?" Stella suggested. "There's one over on Seaside Avenue. I bet they can remove that black paint."

"I don't know," she began dubiously. "That paint..."

"You'd be amazed what they can do nowadays. If I remember correctly, they're the ones who were able to restore the mural at city hall that was sprayed with paint last Halloween. Do you remember?"

Janette nodded. "I guess it wouldn't hurt to give it a try." She glanced back at the painting, surprised to find that instead of pain, she felt a warm glow come over her as she remembered a certain charming ten-year-old girl and her extremely attractive father.

She closed her eyes dreamily and was immediately rewarded with a vision of Adam Blake as he had looked when she was at his feet, wrapping his sturdy thigh with her tape measure.

With a sigh, she let her fingers brush against her jean-clad leg and wondered what it would be like to wrap more than just her tape measure around him.

"Is THERE SOMETHING wrong with your leg, Daddy?" Amy asked from where she sat doing her homework at the desk in the corner of the living room.

Adam looked up from the newspaper and gave her a puzzled look. "My leg?" he asked.

"Yes. I saw you rub it," Amy replied, wiggling her yellow pencil back and forth. "Did you hurt it?"

Adam folded the newspaper with an exasperated sigh; for some reason he couldn't remember a thing he'd read, not even something as simple as the weather forecast. "Not that I know of."

Amy studied him for a moment, wondering why he seemed so faraway. He'd said little during dinner and afterward had headed straight for his favorite leather chair where he'd sat staring at the same exact spot on the front page of the newspaper ever since. She was puzzled. Usually after dinner, they'd go outside for a few rounds of basketball or a jog along the beach. A hurt leg might explain why he didn't want to do anything physical, but it hardly explained his silence.

She glanced at him suspiciously wondering if he was keeping something from her. Since her mother's death, he had never been sick—at least he never complained to her. He knew how she worried about his health and the possibility of losing him as well.

She decided finally that he probably had a problem at work and she turned her attention back to her math book.

She only had ten long division problems left to finish. If she hurried, she could watch the Dodgers' game on TV before going to bed. Needing no further motivation, she tackled the next problem with renewed energy.

Adam lifted his eyes toward his daughter and realized that his hand had once again started to rub the spot on his upper thigh where Janette Taylor had wrapped her tape measure. More surprising was the realization that the appealing blue-green-eyed woman with blond-red hair had been in his thoughts almost nonstop since they'd met earlier that day. He had carried the vision of her to his meeting with city officials that afternoon. While the others had stared intently at the city map of streets and subdivisions, he had seen only wide dreamy eyes and ruby-red lips. He could still feel the pressure of her fingers on his thigh. Damn it, he thought. What he was really remembering was the light touch of her hand brushing against the part of him that had lain dormant since Carolyn's death.

As if his fingertips had suddenly caught fire, he pulled his hand away from his lap and tucked it beneath his arm. He glanced at Amy, relieved that she hadn't noticed his sudden jerking away. As perceptive as she was, she would be convinced that he was in pain and would insist upon playing nursemaid or worse yet, calling her grandmother. That's all he needed—his mother-in-law barreling over with her old-fashioned remedies and advice.

He was in pain but it wasn't the sort of pain that you could explain to a ten-year-old, not even one as mature and sensitive as Amy. It was the kind caused by deprivation, loneliness and longing, the kind that had throbbed inside like a toothache for so long, he'd almost grown accustomed to it.

Despite the aching, he had managed to fill his life with his work and his daughter, telling himself that if he ignored the pain long enough, it would disappear. But today, after meeting Janette Taylor, the pain had become too strong to ignore. More surprising still, he'd suddenly wanted to acknowledge the pain, not ignore it. Now he suspected that maybe, just maybe, a cure did exist.

It seemed strange to think about a woman other than Carolyn. Since her death, he hadn't even looked at another woman; he hadn't wanted to. He'd been content, or so he'd thought, to spend the rest of his life knowing that he'd experienced one happy marriage, with one beautiful and remarkable woman. It never occurred to him that a person could be lucky twice.

Amy finished the last of the math problems, and slid her notebook into her Los Angeles Dodgers backpack ready for Monday morning. "The Dodgers are playing Cincinnati," she said.

"Is the game on TV?" Adam asked.

"Yes," Amy replied, surprised that her father would have to ask. "Starts at seven-thirty." She walked over to the TV and reached for the remote control.

"Before you turn that on, I'd like to talk to you for a moment."

Amy turned. "I finished my homework and took out the trash and..."

"Hey, slow down, sport. That's not what I wanted to talk to you about." He patted the arm of his chair. "Come over here."

Amy didn't need a second invitation. She crossed the room, slid down on her knees and rested her elbows on the arm of his chair.

Adam's eyes softened as he took in her loving face. "Do you remember Janette...ah...Miss Taylor, the lady who gave your class a tour of the Living Masters?"

Amy nodded, her face as bright as the sun as she recalled the nice lady whose kind eyes and gentle smile had made her feel so warm and safe. Afraid her father might think it disloyal of her to feel such things toward a woman who was not her mother, she thought it best not to tell him how she had dreamed of Miss Taylor every night since; happy wonderful dreams of them hugging each other, going shopping together, making cookies. In her dreams, she had shown Miss Taylor her secret cave on the private beach near her house, and the two of them had had a picnic right there on the rock, just outside the entrance.

Feeling guilty for the way Miss Taylor had replaced her mother in her dreams, Amy gave her father a troubled look. "Miss Taylor saved me from Mrs. White."

Adam frowned. "Well, I'm not sure she did you any favor there. If you deserved a dressing-down..."

"Oh, Daddy!" Amy's face crinkled into a loving moue. He knew as well as she did that she never did anything seriously bad at school.

"To get back to Miss Taylor," Adam said, not wanting to argue the point. "I saw her today."

Amy sat back on her heels in surprise. "You did?"

Adam nodded. "Your teacher called and said that Miss Taylor wanted to see me. So I dropped by her office during my lunch hour."

Amy's eyes widened. "What did she want to see you about?"

"She wants you to model in one of the paintings."

Amy stared at her father in disbelief. "Really? Me? But I'm not an actress or anything."

Adam watched his daughter's face as she considered Miss Taylor's offer. "I don't think any of the models are professionals. Didn't you tell me they were all volunteers?"

"Yes, but..." She imagined herself all made up and wearing one of those costumes made from muslin and being on stage and maybe getting her name in the paper and...

"You know this would mean that you might have to give up some of your softball games," Adam pointed out.

"I know..."

"And you'd still have to keep up your school-work."

"But I thought the show doesn't open until July."

"Yes, but from what Jan...Miss Taylor said, I gather the rehearsals are already underway. You still have a few weeks left before school lets out. And don't forget finals."

But nothing he said could dampen her enthusiasm. She clapped her hands together, her eyes shining. "It's so exciting. Me a model!" She jumped to her feet and danced around the room. "Introducing Miss Amy Blake, the world's best model."

Adam couldn't help but laugh. "I hope this isn't going to go to your head," he teased. "I still have to live with you."

Amy leaned over his chair to plant a loving kiss on his forehead. "Oh, Daddy," she said softly. "I know I can model and still keep up my grades."

"Are you sure?"

She straightened. "I'm absolutely, positively sure!" She paused for a moment and was warmed by a sudden thought. "Does this mean I get to see that nice Miss Taylor again?"

"It means we both get to see that nice Miss Taylor again," Adam said, his spirits soaring. He reached over and chucked Amy's chin. "How about switching on that ball game?"

Amy bounded across the room and flipped on the TV. She grabbed her Dodger baseball hat and settled down on the floor. Watching her, Adam felt a warm glow. She was everything he'd ever wanted in a daughter. And to think, he'd been so close to not having her.

He and Carolyn had wanted a child so desperately, but Carolyn's heart problem made it dangerous for her to carry a baby and an unlikely candidate for adopting one. For a while it appeared that his lifelong dream of having children would be denied him.

When Carolyn announced she was pregnant, he'd been so afraid for her. Despite the precautions they'd taken, he felt guilty and blamed himself. The months until Amy's birth had been the longest of his life.

Amy yelled out, her excited young voice drawing a curtain between the past and present. "Way to go, Dodgers!"

Her enthusiasm made him smile again and he drew his attention to the screen long enough to see that the Dodgers had scored three runs in the first inning despite having three of their best players benched with injuries.

Impossible odds is how the doctor had described Carolyn's chances of giving birth to a healthy child. But Adam hadn't cared about that, not then. All he could think about was Carolyn.

He'd been called to the hospital as soon as she'd begun labor. He'd left work and rushed to the hospital only to find the lobby jam-packed with violently ill patients, victims, he'd found out later, of food poisoning. The hospital, a small community facility outside of town, was ill-equipped to handle so many patients at once, especially over the Labor Day weekend when it was short-staffed.

By the time he'd located Carolyn she had gone into cardiac arrest and he'd stood helpless and terrified outside her room watching doctors and nurses and an amazing assortment of medical apparatus pass through her door.

He hadn't been able to believe his luck when she pulled through. Not only pulled through, but grew strong enough to take care of Amy with the help of a live-in nurse. Amy soon became the joy of Carolyn's life. Of both their lives. For the next several years, his world had been perfect.

But his perfect world had come to an abrupt end when Carolyn died. It had all happened so suddenly. A cold—a simple cold—had settled in her lungs, putting too much strain on her damaged heart. She was admitted to the hospital, but only as a precaution. Adam had been stunned upon receiving the call. "I'm sorry to have to inform you that . . ."

After Carolyn died, he thought his life would never be complete again. Amy filled a lot of his life in warm and wonderful ways, but there was a part of him that ached with loneliness. And it was this cold, empty part of him that he'd thought a lot about in the hours since Janette Taylor had attacked him with a tape measure.

A BABY CRIED. Slowly, Janette climbed out of bed and walked over to the bassinet. As she neared, the crying stopped abruptly. Janette halted her steps, too terrified to move. Then, a tiny hand with five perfect fingers and skin as smooth and soft as the skin of a peach reached out to her . . .

With a deep anguished moan, Janette's eyes flew open. She lay motionless, staring at the dark ceiling, her heart pounding like drums beating out a warning in her chest.

The nightmares that had begun shortly after she'd lost the baby had become less frequent in recent years, but still they'd haunted her. Even so, all the times she'd had the same nightmare, never had it seemed as real as this last one.

It was as if she'd traveled back in time and had experienced every moment of that long-ago day, the onset of labor, the woman at the reception desk who so pointedly asked Janette if she was alone. The waiting room that had been packed with countless men, women and children who'd been taken sick following a company picnic. Their moans had accompanied her all through labor, half of which she endured in a busy corridor before finally being wheeled into a makeshift delivery room.

Here the dream had grown foggy, vague, filled with frightening shadows. She remembered so little after that. Except for the cry of a baby. After delivery, she'd been moved to make room for a heart patient.

She'd asked to see her doctor, not the one who'd delivered her baby, but the one who'd taken care of her for the previous six months. But she was told he'd gone away for the weekend. She'd been surrounded by strangers, not one familiar face among them. And not one of them could explain the baby's crying.

Stillborn, they'd said. And everyone knew that stillborn babies don't cry.

Janette got out of bed just as the silver light of dawn touched the fringes of her room. She reached for her robe and threw open her window hoping that a good whiff of early-morning air would chase away the dark gloom left by the nightmare.

Why now? she wondered. Why have the nightmares returned at this particular time of her life? Because Amy had the same birth date as her baby? Was that the reason? Because she had dug out her portrait and been reminded of the arguments she'd had with her father about whether or not she should keep the baby? Because she'd come across the empty bassinet in the attic?

She was still shaken by the nightmare when she walked outside later to feed the seagulls. Pogo hopped to her side and dived eagerly for the pieces of fish she threw him, bringing a smile to her face. The smile left abruptly when a seagull glided overhead, and let out a long wailing cry.

Janette flinched at the sound. It suddenly occurred to her why the nightmare had disturbed her more than usual; her baby always cried in her dreams, but never before had her baby reached out to her.

CHAPTER FOUR

AMY ARRIVED at Janette's office with her grandmother at precisely four o'clock the following Monday afternoon.

Janette was both surprised and delighted when Amy greeted her with an exuberant hug. The instant Amy pressed her warm smooth cheek against hers, Janette's disappointment at not seeing Adam was all but forgotten and for a moment, so was Amy's grandmother.

It wasn't until Amy backed away that Janette realized her embarrassing oversight. She turned to the older woman in apology and offered her hand. "I'm sorry. I'm Janette Taylor, the coordinator of the pageant."

The woman regarded Janette with cool reserve. She was dressed in immaculate white pants with a red-and-white striped top. She lifted a jeweled hand and dropped it limply into Janette's. Her face was as hard as the rigid white waves that made up her perfect coif. Lids thick with blue mascara guarded eyes void of warmth or friendliness. "I'm Mrs. Spencer," the woman replied woodenly.

"I can't believe I'm going to be a model," Amy said excitedly, her face flushed. "I never modeled before but I was a mushroom once in a school play."

Turning back to Amy, Janette couldn't help but smile. "A mushroom? A real honest-to-goodness mushroom?"

Amy's green eyes twinkled in merriment. "My teacher said I moved too much. But I think mushrooms like to move, especially if the wind is blowing."

Wanting to include Amy's grandmother, who was standing staunchly on the sidelines, Janette smiled at her. "I think mushrooms do sway in the wind, don't you agree, Mrs. Spencer?"

Mrs. Spencer met her smile with a glaring look that sent cold icy chills all the way to Janette's toes.

Her smile dying, Janette turned back to Amy, wondering what she could have possibly done to deserve such a hostile reaction.

"Do I get to wear makeup?" Amy asked. "And what about my hair? I'd like to wear it on top of my head but Daddy says that I'm too young. Do you think I'm too young to wear my hair up like this?" She gathered her hair and pulled it upward. Moving around the office in an exaggerated strut, she pushed out her lower lip in a practiced pout.

Laughing aloud, Janette glanced at Amy's grandmother, who obviously didn't appreciate Amy's attempt at imitating a high-fashion model.

"Amy," her grandmother scolded, "I'm sure Miss Taylor has work to do." She glanced at Janette as if she held her personally responsible for any laxity in Amy's conduct, the contempt evident on her face.

Thinking Mrs. Spencer was afraid that Amy was growing up too quickly, Janette reached out and touched Amy's hair, wrapping a golden strand around her finger. "I'm afraid you'll have to wear your hair down. Besides, it looks perfectly lovely this way." She reached for her tape measure. "I need to take some measurements. Then we'll go to makeup."

"I get to wear makeup?" Amy squealed, clapping her hands together.

"We have to make your face look exactly as the artist painted it in the picture," Janette said. She met the older woman's cold eyes. "I wish I had the portrait here. I think you would be amazed at how much Amy resembles the girl in the portrait." Janette thought it best not to mention that she herself had modeled for the portrait.

"Miss Taylor, if you don't mind, Amy has schoolwork to do. I think it best if we get on with this."

"Yes, of course." Janette turned to Amy and draped the tape measure across her shoulders.

Amy's exuberance more than made up for the negative vibrations her grandmother generated from the corner of the room; Janette was not only charmed by Amy's constant chatter but grateful for it.

After writing down Amy's measurements, Janette led her to makeup, feeling profound relief when Amy's grandmother chose to stay behind and wait.

Sally greeted Janette and Amy with a smile. "Sit in my magic chair," she said, turning on the overhead light to study Amy's skin. She jotted down a few notes, then ran her fingers through Amy's hair. "She's perfect."

Janette grinned. "What did I tell you?" After Sally was finished, Janette took Amy back along a different, longer route, which allowed them to walk across the stage. Janette was unwilling to release Amy to her dour grandmother. Actually she was unwilling to let Amy go, period.

"Ohh," Amy said, her voice suddenly hushed. She glanced about the dimly lit stage. During the school tour, the stage had been lighted, but in the shadowy darkness it took on a mysterious aura that offered all sorts of possibilities to a mind as fertile and imaginative as Amy's. "This looks like my own private cave," she said in a hushed voice, her eyes bright with excitement.

"You have a private cave?" Janette asked.

Amy nodded. "You won't tell anyone, will you?"

Feeling a childish delight that the girl would entrust her with her secret, Janette squeezed Amy's small hand. "I wouldn't think of it. It must be fun having a special place of your own." She thought back to her own childhood. When she was growing up her secret place had been a corner of her father's attic.

"Sometimes I pretend to be all my favorite movie stars," Amy said. "I can stand inside the cave and sing as loud as I want and no one can hear me."

Janette's heart nearly stopped beating. Acting, singing, those were the same things she'd liked to do as a child. Some of her fondest memories were of dressing up in her grandmother's old clothes, singing all the popular songs of the day. There was a time she thought about being a singer but that was before she realized she was tone-deaf. "Do you like to sing?"

Amy nodded. "My mother used to sing." Her animated face grew still. Janette longed to reach out and chase the shadows away that had suddenly dimmed Amy's face.

"I always admire anyone who can carry a tune," Janette said lightly. "I like to sing, too, but I'm afraid I sound like a frog with a sore throat."

The weak attempt at a joke was rewarded with a brilliant smile. "Mommy used to say that Daddy sang like a giraffe who swallowed a tuba." Amy covered her mouth to hide a giggle. "He sings every day in the shower and it's awful."

Janette smiled. Just thinking of Adam in the shower made her skin tingle.

"What's this going to be?" Amy asked, moving toward the back of the stage to examine a piece of canvas stretched taut across an enormous wooden frame.

"That's the backdrop for the portrait you're modeling. By the end of the week I'll have the portrait here so you can see it. You'll have to stand to the right and hold your hand out like you're feeding a seagull." Janette demonstrated, holding her arm exactly as she had those many years ago in her father's studio. "Do you want to try it?"

Amy nodded, and took her place in front of the canvas. "Like this?"

"Yes, but you can't move your arm. You have to keep perfectly still."

"But what if I have an itch?" Amy asked.

"I'm afraid you'll have to wait to scratch it until the curtain comes down," Janette said.

Amy looked at her, her green eyes shining with mischief. "What if I have to sneeze?"

Janette smiled. "You'll have to hold it in, and," she added, anticipating the next question, "the same goes for having to go to the bathroom."

Amy's face grew thoughtful. "How long do I have to keep still?"

Janette tilted Amy's chin upward and smiled into the lovely young face. "Ninety seconds," she said. "You have to keep perfectly still for ninety seconds."

"If you can manage to keep Amy still for ninety seconds," a male voice rang out, "then I'll personally reward you."

"Daddy!" Without a moment's hesitation, Amy dashed across the stage to greet her father. "You came!"

Spinning around to face Adam, Janette was grateful that his attention was momentarily diverted by his daughter who had unabashedly thrown her arms around his neck. If it hadn't been for Amy, he might have noticed Janette's flushed face. The only problem was that when he finally disengaged himself from his daughter's embrace and straightened, she was no closer to pulling herself together than before.

"Miss Taylor," he said, flashing her a devastating grin that practically lit up the stage.

"Don't you remember I asked you to call me Janette?" she managed to squeak out, wishing that Amy hadn't evoked the image of giraffes choking on tubas.

Adam walked across the stage toward her. I remember, his eyes seemed to say. Amy walked by his side, talking nonstop. "And Daddy, I can't even sneeze or scratch or..."

He was more handsome than she remembered. Taller. Darker. One arm was draped lovingly around Amy, and Janette felt a sudden pang as she watched with admiration and yes, envy, the warm comfortable relationship between father and daughter. Once again, she was reminded of all that had been denied her as a child.

Adam couldn't begin to guess what was going through her mind, all he knew was that looking at her made every nerve in his body feel alive and vibrant. In the dim light of the stage, her hair was more red than blond. It was too dark to see the details of her dress, but her feminine curves were all too obvious, all too tempting.

"And I get to feed a seagull," Amy continued, without missing a beat. "Only it's not really a seagull because a seagull can't keep still for ninety seconds. It will be painted on the canvas and..."

It wasn't until Amy stopped talking and glanced from one to the other that Janette realized with a start that she and Adam had been gazing at each other. Embarrassed and confused by an onslaught of emotions too intense to sort out, Janette glanced down at Amy who was watching her father's face with interest. "Don't worry about the ninety seconds on stage," Janette said softly, her voice catching. "We'll practice until you can do it without any problems at all."

Janette glanced up at Adam only to find his eyes still on her, his gaze showering her with warmth.

"I don't know why," he said, his smooth baritone voice melting over her. "But I have the strangest feeling that we've met some time in the past."

Swallowing a wave of disappointment, Janette shook her head slightly. Was that why he stared at her so intently? Because he thought they'd met? "I'm sure we haven't..." her voice dropped.

She glanced at Amy who had discovered a kitten hiding in a corner behind some props. The gray-and-white kitten was from the litter of a huge tabby named Sarah Bernhardt who was in charge of rodent control. "Maybe we should go back to my office," Janette suggested, moving away from Amy. She was allergic to cats and the last thing she wanted to do in front of Adam was to have one of her famous industrial-type sneezing attacks. "Amy's grandmother is waiting in my office."

Adam shook his head. "I sent her home."

"Oh..."

"I was lucky enough to sneak out of work early today, and I couldn't see any reason that both of us wait for Amy." He glanced at his watch. "You wouldn't by any chance be free tonight, would you? I thought we could have dinner together and get better acquainted."

Amy broke into a delighted smile, but whether it was because she held the kitten in her arms or because of her father's suggestion, Janette wasn't certain. "Oh, let's go to La Fiesta. Please, Daddy, please." Not waiting for his answer, she turned to Janette. "Mexican food is my favorite. They have the best enchiladas you've ever tasted and—"

"Slow down," Adam said good-naturedly. "Must I remind you that this is a school night? If I recall you have a math test tomorrow."

Amy looked disappointed. "Does that mean I can't go?" She glanced at Janette beseechingly as if she thought that Janette had some persuasive power over her father that she lacked.

Adam pressed his finger on his daughter's upturned nose. "Bingo."

Amy looked so disappointed that Janette was tempted to plead with Adam on her behalf. But not wanting to share Adam that night, she tried another approach. "Tell you what. As soon as school is out, how about you and I go there for lunch and order a plate of enchiladas as big as... all get-out."

The corners of Amy's downcast mouth inched upward. "Do you mean it?"

"Of course I mean it," Janette said.

Watching Janette over Amy's head, Adam's eyes flickered with warm lights. "Thanks," he said softly, so softly that she doubted Amy had heard it.

"What do you say I pick you up at seven?" Adam asked.

"Seven would be perfect," she said, and then suddenly remembered she'd scheduled a rehearsal that night. She quickly decided that just this once the company would have to rehearse without her and before she could change her mind, she gave him her home address and telephone number and would have given him her social security number if she thought he was the least bit interested.

"Come on, sport," Adam said to Amy. "Put the kitten back."

"Oh, Daddy, do I have to?" Amy rubbed her cheek against the kitten's fur. The kitten mewed softly and began to purr.

"Yes, you have to," Adam said.

"If you happen to know anyone who wants a kitten, let me know," Janette said.

Amy's eyes widened. "Oh, let me keep her. I'll take such good care of her." She turned to her father beseechingly. "Please, Daddy, please. I don't have a pet and you know how much I want a pet and..."

"You remember what happened the last time you brought an animal home?" her father reminded her. "You sneezed constantly."

"You're allergic to animals?" Janette asked, her voice catching.

"Only to dogs," Amy explained. "I had a puppy once that made me sneeze so much we finally had to find it another home."

"We don't know whether or not it's just dogs that make you sneeze," Adam said. "You've never had a cat."

"Let me try, Daddy, please. If the kitten makes me sick then I'll find another home for it. Please."

Adam hesitated a moment before he relented with a reluctant nod. "All right, we'll give it a try." Adam gazed over Amy's head at Janette and shrugged in good-natured defeat. "If it's all right with you."

Janette nodded. "I'm just so glad to find a good home for the little thing." She watched Amy hug the tiny kitten close, and thought about how alike she and Amy were. Not only did Amy look identical to her at the same age, but she liked to do many of the same things. Now it turns out she's allergic to animals, as well. Janette couldn't be near a furry animal for long without her throat tickling and her eyes watering. Already she felt the need to sneeze. Fortunately the need grew less urgent once Adam had corralled Amy and the kitten and ushered them toward the stage door.

"See you at seven," he called, giving her one last lingering look before he disappeared altogether. It took all her control to keep from doing somersaults like a lovesick teenager right there on the stage. Instead, she had one of her famous sneezing attacks.

She was still sniffling a short time later when she walked into her kitchen and found Stella standing in front of the open refrigerator, staring at the empty shelves as if they held a mystical meaning.

"I think I'm in love," Janette announced matter-of-factly.

Stella reached for a plastic dish and eyed it with suspicion. "Are we talking about those size twenty-eight thighs again? Owned by a man you met three days ago?'' She gingerly lifted the lid, sniffed the contents and made a face.

''That's Pogo's dinner,'' Janette explained, kicking off her shoes and sinking gratefully onto a chair. ''And I'm talking about Adam Blake, the handsomest, most desirable man I've ever met.''

Stella slipped Pogo's dinner into the refrigerator and flung the door shut. Turning, she gave Janette a sharp penetrating look that was usually reserved for miscalculated ledgers or bank statements that refused to balance. ''Before you go off the deep end, would you at least remind yourself that mature, successful women do not get swept off their feet.''

The thought of being swept off her feet brought a smile to Janette's face. Pulling her feet up to the seat of her chair, she wrapped her arms around her legs and wiggled her toes. ''And why not?''

''Because,'' Stella said, ''when they get swept off their feet they get forgetful. The next thing you know they forget to stop at the market and that means that their dear, sweet roommates get to starve to death.''

''Oh, no!'' Janette groaned, slapping a palm to her forehead. ''It was my day to stop at the market. I'm sorry.''

''Think nothing of it,'' Stella said, brushing her hand down a hefty thigh. ''I hate to admit it but you probably did me a favor.''

''I'll make it up to you,'' Janette promised. ''I'll cook the rest of the week.''

Stella groaned. Janette's specialty was Italian food—buried beneath rich sinful sauces that never failed to pack on another layer of insulation. ''Forget about the rest of the week,'' Stella moaned. She studied Janette thoughtfully, her face uncharacteristically serious. ''Do me a favor, will you? Ask yourself how much of your attraction to this Adam Blake has to do with the fact that he has a daughter who coincidentally happens to be the same age that Stephanie would have been?''

Just hearing Stephanie's name brought that old familiar ache. But it wasn't just the pain of loss that Janette felt, there was also resentment that her dearest friend would accuse her of using Adam to get to Amy. "I assure you that one has absolutely nothing to do with the other."

"Maybe, maybe not," Stella said. "But at least give it some thought."

To be fair, Janette did ask herself the question later that night as she sat across from Adam at a table facing a trickling waterfall. She asked herself the question and tried for all the world not to stare at him. But it was hard to pull her eyes away from his face, harder still not to show too much interest in the way his hands held the menu, hardest of all not to think about the slight brush of his legs against hers. Stella was wrong, she thought. Even if Adam had no children, she would still find him the most attractive and appealing man she'd ever met.

Adam closed the menu and set it aside. Steepling his fingers together he studied her in the soft glow of candlelight that drew an enticing circle of intimacy around them. "Amy thinks you're very special," he said.

Janette smiled. It was difficult not to smile when thinking of Amy. It was even more difficult not to smile in response to the beguiling way Adam looked at her. "I think she's pretty special herself. She has so much enthusiasm and excitement. You must be very proud."

Adam grinned and his eyes shone with a fatherly pride that only endeared him to her all the more. "I *am* proud. But of course, I can't take all the credit. She was very close to her mother." His face grew serious and for a moment a shadow seemed to cross his forehead. The pain she saw in his face matched her own hidden pain. Everything inside her reached out to him.

"How long...since your wife died?" she asked gently.

"Three years ago." Just then the waiter arrived to take their order. Janette resented the intrusion. But as soon as they were alone again, Adam continued where he'd left off. He told Janette about his wife's heart condition, describing his shock when his wife had died following a simple cold. He talked about the days that followed her death, the years.

"It must be very difficult to raise a ten-year-old girl by yourself," she said, remembering her own lonely childhood.

Adam nodded. "I'm afraid it's getting more difficult now that she's so grown-up. I try to talk to her about the things that a mother would normally discuss with a daughter. You know, body changes, boy/girl stuff." His unexpected blush brought a smile to her lips. "So you think it's funny, do you?" he asked, humor shining in his eyes.

Regretting her thoughtless gesture, she leaned forward in earnest. "You must be doing everything right. You have a remarkable relationship with your daughter."

Adam's gaze drifted down to her lovely graceful hand that rested on the table so close, so temptingly close to his, it would take only the slightest move for their fingers to touch. "It's not easy, and I think when we have one of our serious talks, we both end up feeling more embarrassed than enlightened."

Janette nodded in sympathy. She admired the honesty with which he acknowledged his shortcomings. Although her own mother had deserted the family when she was six, her father never concerned himself with her sex education. She had been left to figure things out for herself with the help of inadequate school movies and information gleaned from her friends. Things like you can't get pregnant if you kiss with your mouth closed or turn around three times afterward. You can't get pregnant the first time... Her ignorance cost her dearly.

"I'm sorry, I didn't mean to bore you with all this," he said, sensing her withdrawal.

"You're not," she said, annoyed that she had let her mind drift backward in time. She wanted to concentrate on Adam, not the past. "I was just remembering how it was with me. My mother... left when I was young." Even now, all these years later, it was difficult to talk about a mother who would put her own needs before the needs of her child. The fact that her mother had died less than two years after leaving the family didn't make it any easier to overcome her resentment. "And my father..." There it was again—the bitterness, apparent in the sudden harsh tone of her voice. She softened her voice and began again. "My father didn't think about those things. It was difficult." Disastrous was more like it.

"I can imagine," he said. Succumbing to temptation, he lay his hand on top of hers, but resisted the urge to squeeze it. "Back then I guess the main concern was birth control. Today, there's AIDS to worry about, as well. A young person's education is now a matter of life and death."

But it was back then, too, she wanted to cry. Her baby had died. Her Stephanie . . . She bit her lower lip, surprised and dismayed by the lump that had suddenly risen in her throat. She sensed that he would be a sympathetic listener, but something held her back. A sense of fear, perhaps. Or was it the feeling she had that if she verbalized her pain, a hole would appear in her armor? She knew from past experience how disastrous the smallest opening in her resolve could be.

Fortunately, their dinner came before she had a chance to change her mind and confide in him. Gratefully, she concentrated on her large plate of steaming Spanish rice and refried beans and the enchiladas that lay buried beneath generous layers of melted cheese—Amy's favorite dish.

"Can't Amy's grandmother help out in the womanly talks?" Janette asked between bites.

"Virginia? She's a bit . . . well . . . old-fashioned. Carolyn was a sickly child. I guess it's only natural that Virginia became an overprotective mother. The problem is she's an overprotective grandmother as well. She never learned how to let go."

Janette considered the woman's hostility in this new light, but it didn't help her like the woman any better. "Does Virginia have any other children?"

"Carolyn was her only child. I don't think she'll ever get over her death. The only thing that keeps her going is Amy. I'm afraid that's all she lives for."

After dinner, they strolled along the wooden pier outside the restaurant, and watched the lights from the anchored boats flicker in the velvet softness of the night. The clang of a swaying buoy echoed in the distance. The soft lapping sound of water drifted up from beneath the pilings.

Somewhere between the restaurant and the dock, Adam reached for her hand, his eyes searching hers for a moment as if to seek her approval. She felt her heart march to double-time. This was far more than the friendly gesture in the restaurant, and yet it felt so right to be holding hands with him. Apparently satisfied by what he read in her eyes, he tightened his grip and led her along the water's edge.

Although Janette wore a summer dress with spaghetti straps, not even the cool breeze blowing off the ocean affected her. All she could feel was the warmth of her hand in Adam's and the blazing look he gave her as they stopped to watch an oil tanker glide past.

"Thank you," he whispered softly.

She looked up at him in surprise, surprised by how close his lips were to hers, surprised that he had anything to thank her for.

"Whatever for?" she asked, her heart fluttering. The look he gave her said he was going to kiss her. With that realization came the knowledge that she was going to let him. Her lips burned with sudden need. Don't wait, she wanted to tell him, don't hold back. Suddenly she had no patience for the rules of propriety.

"Thank you for listening to my parental frustrations. For being kind to Amy."

Feeling his sudden mood change, she took in a deep breath. Maybe he wasn't going to kiss her. Dear God, don't let Amy be the only way to his heart.

Taking both her hands in his, he let his forehead touch hers. "Thank you for making me look forward to the future for the first time in a very long time."

Her heart sailed. These were the words she wanted to hear. Not a commitment, for it was too soon, but an opening, a beginning, an invitation.

Not wanting to wait for the kiss he was holding back, she tilted her head upward until their lips were so close they were all but touching. Stepping on tiptoes, she pressed shamelessly against him.

His lips moved against hers tentatively at first, as if he thought she might pull away. His arms encircling her waist, he pulled her closer. Finally, his mouth pressed deeper, his lips merging with hers as easily as a whisper on a breeze.

Her lips parted slightly allowing his tongue to flick in and out of her mouth in an erotic dance that made her heart respond in a dance of its own.

He felt her heart beat wildly next to his chest as he filled her mouth completely with gentle thrusts, each one designed to gather up as much of her sweet nectar as was possible. His lips, his mouth, his tongue caught fire, her quivering lips spreading the flames downward until his body was consumed.

Janette felt as if she were floating through space, anchored only by his warm wonderful lips, and caressing hands that were pressing into her back with such urgency.

When at last their lips parted, they could only gaze into each other's eyes as if to seek confirmation that both of them had been affected in the same way. Adam didn't want to push her, to hurry her. Everything told him she wanted him every bit as much as he wanted her, but where women were concerned, he was woefully out of practice. Maybe he was reading more into her kiss than she meant to convey.

"I better take you home," he whispered softly, knowing that he couldn't keep her out all night trying to decide what to do next.

They spoke little on the way home. Adam could hardly concentrate on his driving and managed to make a wrong turn in the part of town he knew by heart. He felt an ache in his loins for the woman by his side. His arms longed to hold her again, his lips burned with the need to kiss her. He pulled in front of her house and held onto the steering wheel with damp hands.

"Janette, I..." He stopped. Everything that came to mind sounded corny. "I want to see you again..." Damn, he thought in annoyance, *I want to make love to you, here, now, this very minute. Why can't I just say it?* he wondered. Why at the age of thirty-five was there still this need to play games? He was at a time in his life when the old rules should no longer apply. He wanted to take hold of life and run with it. His life had been static for far too long.

Janette felt as if the happiness inside would explode. "I want to see you again," she whispered. *But tonight, tonight, I want you to hold me, make love to me. How can I tell you that without your thinking I'm promiscuous?*

He leaned toward her, touching a strand of her hair. "May I call you?"

She nodded, but only because she was afraid of what she might say if she allowed herself to speak. To her profound joy, she didn't need to speak. He kissed her lips tenderly in the car, and after walking her to the front door, kissed her again, this time more passionately.

He gazed at her with wonder and awe in his eyes. "I don't know why I thought at first that we'd met. I've never met you before. I've never met anyone like you before. I can't believe we've lived in the same town all these years without crossing paths."

She leaned back against the railing of the porch, grateful for the dark that kept her flaming cheeks hidden, for the cold hard feel of the wrought iron that cooled down her burning palms. "How long have you lived here?"

"Since before Amy was born."

A sudden thought occurred to her; a hard cold wave of reality washed over her. "Then...then Carolyn gave birth to Amy here, in Crystal Beach."

Adam nodded. "As a matter of fact, she did. At the Crystal Beach Community Hospital."

An icy chill touched her heart. A faint feeling came over her. It was all she could do to keep her emotions hidden as she bid him good-night, and hastened into the house. Shaking, she stood behind the closed door listening for the engine of his car to start, before lowering her body numbly onto a velvet love seat. One more bone-chilling coincidence clawed at her emotions. Could it possibly be more than a coincidence! No, never! Stephanie had died at birth. Janette closed her eyes, hoping she could keep the impossible idea from entering her mind.

CHAPTER FIVE

POGO DIVED HUNGRILY for the tiny pieces of fish Janette tossed him, then hopped across the sand, away from the other seagulls, to enjoy his meal in peace. Overhead, a seagull let out a cry of protest and landed on a nearby rock to eye Pogo with disdain. Refusing to be intimidated, Pogo finished his meal and hopped toward the gently rolling surf.

Janette slipped the lid back onto the plastic dish and followed the narrow sandy path toward the house.

The smell of coffee and burned toast greeted her as she stepped into the kitchen. Stella, dressed in an old pink chenille robe and purple mules, shuffled between the toaster and the coffeepot. "How do you want your toast?" she asked, looking at Janette through half-open eyes. "Burned or cremated?"

"Don't tell me the toaster is acting up again." Janette reached for a mug. "What do you say we pool our money and buy a new one?"

"What?" Stella looked offended. "And take all the excitement out of my life? I think I finally have a handle on it. I just need the right screwdriver. I'll stop by Larry's on the way home tonight." Larry Hodges owned the hardware store on the edge of town. If the truth were known he probably owned the mortgage on their home, as well. Hardly a week went by without the house needing some major repair. Last week, Larry had sold Stella a water heater on account. The week before, it was a garbage disposal.

Janette knew when she bought the house that it was a fixer-upper, but she hadn't counted on it being more of a fixer than an upper. She wouldn't mind the constant repairs so much if only the appliances would die a quiet dignified death or if things would fall apart in a more subdued fashion. But that was never the case. The water heater exploded with a boom that shook the neighborhood and left a six-foot gap in the garage wall. The garbage disposal plugged up every drain in the house and a brick cap fell off the chimney, breaking an upstairs window in the process.

Stella set a plate of charred toast on the table and studied Janette through sleep-laden eyes. "You don't have to look so depressed. I said I was going to fix the toaster not jump off the roof."

Janette filled her mug with coffee, and leaned her back against the counter. "I didn't sleep last night. Lately, those nightmares have been coming back."

Stella's forehead creased. "Nightmares? You mean the ones about Stephanie?"

Janette nodded and took a sip of coffee.

Stella squeezed Janette's shoulder. "Why do you suppose they've come back after all this time?"

"That's what I don't know. I mean...Oh, Stella, I'm so confused. Last night with Adam was perfect until..."

"Don't stop," Stella pleaded half-jokingly. "Don't keep us cloistered nuns in suspense."

"You're not going to believe this." Janette walked over to the table and sat down. "Not only was Amy born on the same day as Stephanie, but she was born in the same hospital."

Stella's face dropped in disappointment. "Don't tell me you spent the evening with a gorgeous man talking about babies. Good grief, girl, where is your head?"

Janette frowned impatiently. "Stella, did you hear what I said? The same hospital!"

"So?" Stella shrugged. "Ten years ago, there was only one hospital in Crystal Beach. Unless you drove twenty miles..."

"Don't you understand?" Janette cried. "They were there at the hospital with me. Amy, Adam and his wife, Carolyn. Don't you see what that could mean?"

Sitting down opposite Janette, Stella regarded her seriously. "Either it's too early for my mind to click or you've lost me. I don't see that it means anything."

"It's crazy, but I have this feeling, this terrible, terrible feeling..."

"Hey." Stella reached for Janette's hand. "I've never seen you like this. What feeling? What are you saying?"

Janette swallowed. In the still of the night, her thoughts had made some sort of crazy mixed-up sense. Too much sense. She needed Stella's logical mind to point out the flaws in her thinking, the improbabilities.

"While we were having dinner last night, Adam told me that his wife had a congenital heart problem. It wasn't until later, after I learned that she was in the same hospital as I was, that I remembered being wheeled out of my room because it was needed for a heart patient. Don't you see, Stella? That heart patient must have been Adam's wife!"

"I suppose that's possible," Stella said thoughtfully. "It was a small hospital. I don't imagine it had a very large obstetrical area. But even if it were true, why does this have you so upset?'' Stella's face took on a knowing look. ''Unless you don't want Adam to know that you had a baby at seventeen. Is that it? Look, these are the nineties. If this man is so old-fashioned that a mistake in your past is going to change his feelings toward you, you're probably better off without him.''

''What Adam thinks or doesn't think has nothing to do with this,'' Janette said. ''The doctors said that Stephanie died because of an enlarged heart. Stella, there is no history of heart problems in the family, none.''

''You don't know that for sure. What about Stephanie's father?''

''I know,'' Janette insisted. She'd never told Stella that she had contacted Stephanie's father following the baby's death, thinking he might like to know. What a mistake that had been! Not only was he unaffected by the news, he denied that there was any history of heart problems in the family. He went so far as to voice his suspicion that maybe he wasn't the father. To a young woman desperate to share her grief with someone, it was a bitter blow. Biting back the anger that the memory aroused, she squeezed her fingers around her mug. ''There is no history of heart disease in his family, either.''

Stella stood, poured herself some coffee and took a long sip, watching Janette over the rim of her mug. ''Okay, so what do you think all this means? Obviously, you've something going on in that head of yours.''

''Doesn't it seem strange that my baby would die of a heart problem? I mean, Adam's wife gave birth to a healthy child. Doesn't that strike you as odd?''

Stella shrugged. "I suppose. But strange things happen. Medically speaking, I suppose anything's possible."

Janette leaned toward Stella. "But what if there was a mistake? A ghastly mistake. What if my baby didn't die. What if Amy is really my child?"

Stella looked at Janette as if she had suddenly gone mad. "That's crazy talk. Good Lord, Janette! Listen to yourself."

"I am listening to myself!" Janette exclaimed. "I listened to myself all night."

"I can't believe this. You've always had an overactive imagination. But this is too much even for you!"

"All right. Let's examine the facts. Amy looks the spitting image of me when I was that age. She even likes to do some of the same things I liked to do as a child. She sings, acts."

"Which proves nothing!" Stella said stubbornly. "Most girls that age like to perform."

"She's allergic to animals."

"And so is 18.9 percent of the population."

Janette took a deep breath, trying to control the rush of emotions inside. When she spoke, her voice was but a broken whisper. "I heard my baby cry."

Stella sat back down. "We've been over this before. You were under anesthesia. You were confused."

"No! I was not confused. I heard my baby cry that day." Not just that day, but every day since. "Don't look at me like that Stella. I'm not crazy."

"I don't think you're crazy." Stella picked up a piece of burned toast, stared at it and tossed it back on the plate. "Maybe it would help if you talk to someone. You know..."

"A psychiatrist?" Janette's hands gripped her mug. "No psychiatrist is going to change how I feel when I look at Amy. No one in the world is going to convince me that I didn't hear my baby cry that day."

Stella studied Janette's face worriedly. "What are you planning to do?"

"I don't know." Wrapping her arms around her body she tried to ward off the cold shiver that crept along her flesh. "I've got to do something. I can't live with this suspicion without exploring it further."

"And what about Adam? How do you think he's going to react upon learning that you have some wild idea that his daughter might not belong to him?"

Janette closed her eyes, dreading the thought of how this would affect her relationship with Adam. She couldn't keep something as serious as this from him. But how could she tell him? If her best friend thought she was crazy, how could he think any less? Chances are he would never want to see her again. Just as devastating was the possibility that he would never again let her see Amy.

A TALL VASE of baby roses nestled in a cloud of Queen Anne's lace was sitting on her desk when she arrived at her office. Her heart fluttered wildly as she reached for the tiny card and read the simple message. "Thanks for a wonderful evening. Adam."

She closed her eyes, inhaling the sweet fragrance of the roses, and thought about the evening they'd spent together. She'd wanted him so much, still wanted him. It had been so long since she'd felt like a woman. There'd been men, of course, in her past. But nothing serious, nothing like this. Maybe Stella was right; maybe she was crazy. Crazy in love. Suddenly her spirits lifted. She had an explanation for the strange way her mind had been working recently. She was in love. That was all there was to it.

With this overwhelming thought, she pulled out the permission slip that Adam had signed and put her finger on his work phone number. Humming a tune to herself, she punched out his number and pulled the receiver to her ear. Expecting a secretary to answer, she was pleasantly surprised to hear his deep voice come over the line.

"Adam?"

"Janette?"

Did she only imagine the smile in his voice, the warmth as he said her name? Perhaps. But she didn't imagine the glow that radiated from her as soon he spoke.

"The roses . . . they're absolutely beautiful."

"I hope you don't think I lack imagination," he said.

"They're perfect," she assured him, letting her eyes linger on a tiny bud that was beginning to unfold. "And I don't think you lack imagination at all."

"Will you let me prove that?" he asked.

"What?"

"That I can be imaginative."

She ran a finger across a velvety petal. A shiver of anticipation ran through her body. "What do you have in mind?" she asked through trembling lips.

The slight hesitation told her exactly what he had in mind. "Can I see you this weekend?"

"Friday?" she suggested, wondering how she would ever manage to wait until Friday to see him.

"How about Friday, Saturday and Sunday?" he asked and when she didn't reply, he quickly added, "I'm rushing you, aren't I?"

"No. I want to see you." It was a strain not to add, I need to see you. I have to see you. "I have to work on Saturday, but I'm free that night."

"Great! I'll see you Friday and Saturday. What about Sunday? All right, I know, I'm being too pushy." His low apologetic laughter rumbled along the line. "We'll discuss the rest when I see you." Explaining that he was late for a meeting, he hung up, leaving her feeling unsettled in the nicest possible way.

For the first time in her life, work actually held little appeal. All she wanted to do was to sit and remember how Adam's lips made her feel, and how they were going to make her feel come Friday.

Pat poked her head into the office, an arm full of bracelets jingling when she knocked. "Is there something wrong with your buzzer?"

Embarrassed to be caught daydreaming, Janette blinked. Glancing at the intercom, she shook her head. "I don't think so, why?"

Pat pushed the door open and walked into the room. "I've been buzzing for at least five minutes. The art restoration company called and said your painting won't be finished until Friday, the earliest."

Janette grimaced. She was hoping they could get the initial sketches for Amy's tableau completed this week. "Anything else?"

"I need a final list of cast members and an okay on the program design."

"I'll work on that today."

Pat made a note on her notepad. "Lester says he'll have *The Fishermen* ready for review tonight."

"That's a relief," Janette said. *The Fishermen* was one of her father's paintings. As late as last Friday, Lester had expressed doubts about the painting working on stage. Much to her disappointment, he hadn't changed his mind when she saw him later that night.

She sat in the front row of the amphitheater, watching the stage with narrowed eyes. *The Fishermen* was far from being her father's most notable work, but it was one of the few pieces her father had painted that didn't have a painful memory attached to it. For that reason she'd chosen it, but she honestly thought the sweeping sky in the background, and the turbulent sea that rocked the fishermen's boat would make for a stirring presentation. It was a classic example of man against nature. Even so, Lester was right; the tableau lacked drama. She scribbled some notes about lighting and music, not certain whether changing one or both would make a difference.

"Dim the lights," she called backstage, then sought another seat hoping to get a different angle. Softer lights made the blues and grays blend together too much, muting the battle between the raging storm and the turbulent sea. "Up the lights," she called out again. Almost instantly the stage grew brighter, and the intensity of the two men battling to stay afloat was washed out. It wasn't the lighting.

She glanced helplessly at Lester, who ran a hand through his shoulder-length hair and shrugged.

"Let's all go home," she called wearily. Maybe in the morning when she was fresher, she and Lester could put their heads together and come up with a solution.

"You guys did a great job," she called to Moe and Josh, the two male models. "See you Monday."

"No rehearsal Friday night?" Moe called.

"Yes, for you, no, for me," Janette said, thrilling to the thought that in a few days' time, she would be with Adam. After the two men left, Janette walked on stage and examined the backdrop.

She trailed her hand along the length of the painted muslin, which took up the entire stage. In past years she had managed to successfully orchestrate the world's most renowned painters, from Rembrandt to Picasso, from Leonardo da Vinci to David Hockney. But she had never successfully captured her father's work. Not completely. This year, she told herself, would be different. This year she had *Girl with Gull*. This year she had Amy.

"ARE YOU GOING to take Janette to La Fiesta?" Amy asked, straightening her father's tie. She sneezed and cast her father a guilty look. She drew a tissue from her jeans pocket and wiped her nose.

"Not this time, sport." Adam studied his young daughter, noting how tall she was getting. In another year, she'd be up to his shoulder if not higher. "Is that kitten bothering you?"

Amy diverted her eyes. "I don't think so. It's just a cold."

"I'm not so sure." He touched her forehead with his hand. "You've been sneezing up a storm ever since we brought that cat home."

"I'm okay, Daddy." She ducked from beneath his hand and quickly changed the subject. "Where are you going?"

"I'm taking Janette to Pelican's Inn."

"Isn't that rather expensive?" Virginia said, looking up from the couch where she sat reading a magazine.

Adam met his mother-in-law's eyes. Although Amy insisted that she was "ten and three-quarters and didn't need a baby-sitter anymore," he was grateful that Virginia agreed to spend time with Amy while he was out. He wondered if he would ever get to the point where he could feel comfortable leaving Amy home alone. He was having enough trouble getting used to the idea that he no longer had to stoop to hug her. "The food is excellent and they have a great band."

"Is there dancing?" Amy asked. Her best friend, Tammy, had told Amy that you could tell when couples were in love by how they danced. She watched her father curiously, trying to imagine him playing the role of romantic hero.

Seeing Virginia frown, Adam glanced at his daughter's intense face. "Come to think of it, I do believe there's a dance floor," he said. Dancing had never been on his list of priorities before. It was a good thing since Carolyn had never been able to manage anything that taxing.

Suddenly, though, the thought of holding Janette in his arms and leading her around the dance floor held an appeal he could hardly deny. He checked his pockets. "How about doing your dear old dad a favor and running upstairs to get my car keys off the dresser?"

Amy hurried from the room but not soon enough to hide another sneeze.

Virginia tossed her magazine aside. "I didn't know you were dating someone."

Adam lifted an eyebrow. "I told you I was taking Miss Taylor out to dinner."

"Yes, you did say that," she said pointedly. "But I didn't know you were going to take her dancing."

Adam ran a hand over his smooth chin. He didn't miss the accusatory tone in his mother-in-law's voice, nor the look on her face that seemed to suggest he was committing some unpardonable sin. "Virginia, Carolyn's been gone for over three years."

"You don't have to tell me how long my daughter's been gone," Virginia said, her voice tight with emotion.

"The point I'm trying to make is that three years is a long time. A man can get lonely."

Virginia bit her lower lip and glanced over at the framed photo of Carolyn and Adam on their wedding day. Next to the silver frame was a picture of them bringing Amy home from the hospital. Virginia remembered taking that picture herself. Carolyn had looked so radiant that day, holding her baby in her arms and looking healthier than Virginia had ever seen her look, despite the scare she'd given them when her heart had stopped shortly after delivery. "You have Amy."

"You know as well as I do the kind of loneliness I'm talking about," Adam said in irritation. He was not going to allow Virginia to make him feel guilty. He had a right to live, to reach out for happiness. They all did.

He sat on the couch next to Virginia. "I think it's time we put the past to rest and start to pick up our lives again."

"My only daughter is dead and you think I can forget just like that."

"Damn it, Virginia. I haven't forgotten Carolyn. I can never do that. I loved her very much. She was the mother of my child. But Carolyn wouldn't want me to spend the rest of my life alone. She was too loving and caring to want us to live in grief."

"Don't tell me what Carolyn would want," Virginia said, bursting into tears.

Surprised by this sudden display of emotion, Adam handed her a clean handkerchief. Was his taking a woman to dinner really so awful? "What do you want me to say? That I'll spend the rest of my life, here, night after night..." *Aching*.

"No!" Virginia wiped her eyes with a handkerchief. "No, that's not what I'm saying. Oh, Adam, I want you to be happy. But I'm so afraid. I'm so afraid that I might lose Amy."

Virginia's sudden honesty dissolved the anger and resentment he felt toward her. He took her hand in his and squeezed it affectionately. The two of them had been through a lot together. "You're not going to lose Amy. I give you my word. No matter what happens in the future, Amy will always be a part of your life."

"Here's your keys, Daddy," Amy said bounding into the room. Upon seeing her grandmother in tears, Amy hurried over to her. "What's the matter, Grandma? Why are you crying?"

"Because I'm a foolish old lady," Virginia said, sniffling and wiping her eyes with Adam's handkerchief.

"Take care of her, will you, sport?" Adam stood and took the keys from Amy. He narrowed his eyes as he studied his young daughter. Her eyes looked red and watery. He was almost positive she didn't have a cold. He dreaded the prospect of having to find the kitten another home, and cursed himself for giving in and letting her have the damned cat in the first place. "Have fun, you two."

After Adam left, Virginia and Amy played cards. Watching her precious grandchild, Virginia kept thinking of Adam's promise. From the first moment that Adam had walked into her dear sweet Carolyn's life, Virginia had loved him as if he were her own flesh and blood. She had no doubt of his sincerity when he said she would always be a part of Amy's life. But things change and she couldn't forget the feeling of being excluded as she stood in Janette Taylor's office and watched the unexpected rapport between Amy and that near perfect stranger. From the first moment she met that woman she couldn't shake the feeling that Amy was beginning to slip away from her.

And there was no way she would let that happen.

FROM THE MOMENT Adam came to the house to pick her up, Janette was blissfully aware that he couldn't seem to keep his eyes off her. Admiration blazed from the depths of his deep blue eyes as he took in her white dinner dress, with its full graceful skirt and elegant beaded top that plunged to her waist in back.

It was hard not to bask in the glow of his warm admiring gaze. The way he looked at her not only made her forget any questions about Amy, it made her practically forget her own name. His hand, warm and gentle on her bare back as he helped her into the car, sent ripples of warm sensations shooting up her spine.

The inn was ablaze with candlelight when they arrived. They were seated by a window overlooking the harbor, at a tiny table that made even breathing seem as intimate as a kiss.

All too aware of his leg brushing against hers, Janette forced herself to look away from him long enough to glance outside. The ocean shimmered beneath a near full moon. In the distance, amber lights flickered from the ghostly shadows of passing ships. Janette couldn't imagine a more romantic setting.

She could hardly concentrate on dinner, though a part of her knew that it was wonderful, delicious and perfect. Nor could she begin to imagine how they found so much to talk about. He told her about his job and he somehow managed to make an oil company sound like the most exciting place in the world. What surprised her the most was his concern for the environment.

"What the public doesn't realize is that drilling off the California coast can actually protect the environment," he explained in response to her question about the danger of tanker spills. "Everyone wants to restrict the tanker traffic. The only way to do that is to produce more oil domestically or to figure out a way to live without it."

She smiled, a slow sensuous smile that made his heart do flip-flops. "Do you think we'll ever come up with a way to live without oil?"

"When we run out of oil, we'll learn to live without it." With a smile like hers, who needed oil? he wondered. And why was he even talking about oil? What he wanted to talk about was how the candlelight danced in her eyes, how the flickering flames showered golden stars in her hair, how... "Enough about me. I want to know about you."

Blushing, she told him about her job and was flattered that he took such an interest in her daily routine.

"I would think working with so many people would be quite a challenge," he said.

Janette smiled. "Actually, the challenge comes from the little things. This year, for instance, we had to figure out a way for a ballerina to stand on her toes for nearly two minutes.''

It wasn't until their dessert came that talk turned to Carolyn, and again she was reminded of the nightmares that had hounded her in recent nights. Again her mind tabulated the strange coincidences between Amy and her own baby. Again she felt like her entire world was about to come toppling down.

''Are you all right?'' Adam asked suddenly.

Janette blinked. ''I'm sorry?''

''I thought I saw you shiver.'' He lifted a dark eyebrow, his warm gaze sliding across her lovely bare shoulders as easily as rain on glass.

''I'm perfectly fine.'' Janette smiled to reassure him.

After dinner, Adam led her outside to a small private beach at the back of the restaurant. The beach was sheltered by tall palms, the broad leaves illuminated by soft colored lights. A slight ocean breeze ruffled the palm leaves and played with the hem of her skirt, giving Adam a tantalizing glimpse of a shapely thigh.

Soft violin music floated from the windows of the restaurant. Slipping off her high heels, she danced with Adam in the sand, his hands on her waist, her arms around his handsome neck.

Adam sang to her as he led her around their own private dance floor, their feet sinking into the cool softness of the sand. The haunting tune of ''Moon River'' wafted through the air and Adam crooned the words into her ear.

When he finished, Janette gave him a teasing smile. ''Amy's right,'' she said. ''You do sing like a giraffe with a tuba in its throat.''

Adam's eyes sparkled with laughter. ''Did Amy really say that? Why, that little...'' He pulled her closer, and began humming the next tune. Despite Adam's tuneless rendition, she recognized the song as "Smoke Gets in Your Eyes." Janette joined him, and was amazed at how well their voices blended together, drifting in an unmusical, yet strangely harmonious tune across the sand to be swallowed up by the churning surf.

At the end of the song, Adam dipped her and then pulled her body firmly next to his. With a contented sigh, her lips parted. She was all too aware of how her breasts were pressed against his chest.

"I'm afraid that with very little persuasion," he said huskily, "I am going to fall hopelessly and madly in love with you."

Janette studied the dark eyes that shimmered in the moonlight, expecting to see the humorous teasing lights she so often saw there. She was surprised, instead, by the seriousness of his face, and the flip answer she was about to form died on her lips. He wasn't teasing. Not knowing what to say, she stared at him in disbelief and wonder. "So soon?" she asked, feeling both deliriously happy and a little alarmed. There had been no reservations in his voice, not a hint of uncertainty. "You hardly know me."

"I know you," he said, pulling her down on the sand. "And I know how I feel." He nuzzled against her neck. "What I want to know is how you feel."

The look he gave her told her it was not only probable he would fall in love, but it was extremely likely. She felt confused, off balance. It was all happening too quickly. Only in the movies or in books did people fall in love so quickly.

Besides, there was Amy. She couldn't allow love to complicate matters. Not as long as there were so many unanswered questions about Amy. Torn by the need to be in his arms and the need to be honest and open with him, she made a halfhearted attempt to pull away.

"Falling in love is a big step for me," she said.

He lifted her chin, forcing her to meet his quizzical eyes. "I hope you don't think it's any less of a step for me."

"Of course not," she whispered. "I'm just afraid to believe that something as wonderful as this could happen so quickly."

"I know." His voice, soft as moonlight, filled her heart with music.

Looking into his magnetic eyes, and seeing flares of desire dance within their depths, she told herself that thinking Amy was her child was insane. His lips settled on her mouth and she told herself that Stella was right: Amy's resemblance to her as a child had stirred up old memories, nothing more.

He kissed her gently at first, savoring the taste of the warm night on her lips, the taste of the sea that had somehow settled on her cheek, the taste of her that was so deliciously unique. His hand drifted down her arms and crossed to her breasts. He felt the soft curves strain against the beaded fabric of her dress as he pressed his hands against her breasts. With a cry, she arched toward him and his hand reached down to pull up the skirt of her dress.

He wanted to make love to her there on the beach, the surf at their feet, the sound of music floating over them, the silvery mist of moonlight their only protective cover, and he knew with a boundless joy that she would not stop him. What did stop him was the sound of voices.

His hand stilled for a moment at her thigh, then he quickly jerked the hem of her skirt down. He sat up just as a couple walked past, hand in hand, their laughter fading away as they disappeared into the velvety darkness.

Adam lifted his mouth and flicked her earlobe with the tip of his tongue. "I want to make love to you, but not here. And we can't go to my place because of Amy."

She smiled dreamily, feeling a warm satisfaction that he worried about entertaining a woman in the presence of his daughter. It told her a lot of things about him, a lot of *nice* things about him. "My roommate is out tonight," Janette whispered.

He kissed her deeply, his hard body pressing next to hers until she thought she would explode with the sweet exquisite frustration that comes with unfulfilled need. "Let's go," he said, his voice thick with desire.

As if by mutual consent, they said little in the car, content to let their emotions fill up the space between them. Adam drove faster than was usual for him, making it back to her place in no time at all.

He led her up the walk in a slow sensuous dance, kissing her with every turn. Finally, he carried her up the steps of the porch, his mouth lingering on hers before letting her body inch downward along his until her feet touched ground again.

Trembling, she held out her key and he took it from her, kissing her before unlocking the door, kissing her during and after he turned the key. Holding her, his lips devouring hers, he managed to lead her to the foot of the stairs. "Which room?" he asked between kisses.

"The one to the left," she answered. "Oh, Adam!" His name was a moan of wanting, of longing. She sat on the bottom stair, her body enslaved by his hands and his mouth.

"Adam, please . . ." She pushed against him.

Adam pulled back, and looked at her with warm blazing eyes. "I'm sorry, Janette, I'm moving too fast."

"You're not!" she assured him, sitting upright.

"Are you sure? I want it to be right for you. For us."

"So do I," she smiled. "And I think it would be perfect if we went upstairs."

He glanced at the stairs and laughed. "Oh, so that's it." He pulled her up and gazed into her eyes. "I just don't want us to waste one moment more than necessary."

She studied his face questioningly, knowing that people who had spent years in grief and mourning often became obsessed with making up for lost time. She didn't want anything that happened between them that night to be a result of the past, of Carolyn . . .

And with thoughts of Carolyn came the rest: the nightmares, the fear that Amy . . . The horrible nagging suspicion. Feeling suddenly as if she had been caught in the path of an overflowing dam, she reached for the newel post and held on.

"Janette! What is it? What's the matter?"

She shook her head. "Nothing. I . . ." How could she tell him about the thoughts that kept her tossing and turning into the night? How could she not?

"I just felt dizzy for a moment."

Alarmed, he slipped his arm around her waist, afraid for her, afraid for him. He remembered all too well that Carolyn had suffered from dizzy spells, and with this memory came the feeling of helplessness.

"Sit down for a moment," he said, coaxing her away from the post.

She slipped down the post until she was firmly seated on a step. Adam sat next to her, taking her hands in his and gazing into her face with grave concern. "Do you have dizzy spells a lot?"

The anxiety in his voice made her feel guilty for her little white lie. She should have known that Adam would be concerned for her health. But how else could she explain her sudden withdrawal? She shook her head no, but when he continued to look shaken, she felt the need to offer a better explanation. "I haven't been sleeping well lately."

"I'm sorry... Have you tried all the usual remedies? You know, hot milk."

She glanced into his face, and saw only honest concern. Most men would have resented her pulling away. If she hadn't already fallen madly in love with him, she would have fallen head over heels in love with him at that very moment. His understanding made her feel vulnerable and she did something she seldom did, she burst into tears.

Alarm crossed his face and before she could think of a logical explanation for her illogical behavior, she was in his arms, her head on his chest. Before she could stop herself, she'd blurted out the entire story of Stephanie and how she'd felt upon learning that Amy had the same birth date.

"I couldn't believe that Amy was born on the same day as my Stephanie," she said, accepting his handkerchief and wiping away her tears.

"I can't either." Adam's voice was a mixture of disbelief and awe. "I can't tell you how sorry I am that you have to go through it all again because of me."

"It's not your fault," she hastened to assure him. "If it wasn't for these nightmares..."

Nodding in sympathy, his face grew grave. "I have firsthand experience of how nightmares can work on a person's psyche. Carolyn used to have nightmares."

Janette dabbed at her eyes. "Oh?"

"It's the craziest thing. For years after Carolyn had Amy she had nightmares about giving birth to a baby who didn't cry."

Janette suddenly went cold. "But...why?" she stammered. This time the room really did seem to spin. "Her baby lived."

"Carolyn had been highly medicated during labor and in her haziness, she apparently didn't hear Amy cry. No matter what the doctors said, she was convinced that her baby hadn't cried. Later when she saw with her own eyes how healthy Amy was, she insisted that it was a premonition of things to come. She suffered from those same nightmares for years."

Janette closed her eyes. Oh, God! This can't be happening! "Do you mind if we call it a night?" she whispered. "I need to be alone."

Adam's eyes deepened with hurt. "Don't turn away from me, Janette. The only way to make the nightmares stop is to talk about them. Tell me about your baby. Maybe between the two of us we can figure out why you're still having nightmares."

"I can't talk about it now." She gently, reluctantly, pushed his arms away. It was a difficult thing to do, but she had no choice. His arms made thought all but impossible and she had to think. Somehow she had to make sense of everything that was happening. "Adam, please don't misunderstand. I appreciate your willingness to help. But...I really need to be alone."

The desperation he saw in her eyes filled him with alarm. He touched her forehead, hoping the shadow centered there would give him a clue as to why she looked so afraid. He wished he knew what to do to help her. He felt so terribly, terribly helpless and it was this feeling that made him reach out to her when it was so obvious his touch only distressed her more.

He held her by the arms, his fingers wrapping around her flesh in a way that revealed his fear of losing her. He sensed something working against him that he didn't understand. "Call me if you want to talk. Please, Janette, I don't care how late it is."

She nodded. "Thank you, Adam."

He lay a hand against her cheek and she found herself pressing her face into his palm. Lowering his head, he brushed his lips against her forehead. She lifted her head and he glanced hungrily at her lips.

The front door flew open, and Stella walked in. She glanced toward the stairs, where Adam and Janette sat staring at her as if she were a ghost.

Stella glanced up at the ceiling and began talking to herself. "Stella, you're a great kid but you've got lousy timing." With an apologetic shrug, she inched toward the kitchen. "Pretend like I'm not here."

"My roommate," Janette explained, after Stella had disappeared through the swinging door of the kitchen.

Adam pulled his hand away. "At least you won't be alone tonight."

He was wrong, for as soon as he left, Janette felt more alone than she had ever been in her life.

No sooner had Adam driven away, when Stella rushed out of the kitchen, curiosity written all over her face. "What an absolute dreamboat! Don't tell me, he wanted to take you to bed and you said no. Please, don't tell me that."

Janette clutched the newel post, her face drained of all color. "No."

Stella palmed her forehead. "Don't tell me you told him your ridiculous baby-switching theory. Please, *please* tell me it isn't so."

Janette shook her head. "I didn't tell him."

Stella raised her hands upward. "Thank God for small favors." She narrowed her eyes. "I hope this means you've had time to realize what a ridiculous notion that is." When Janette failed to concur, Stella groaned. "You don't think it's a ridiculous notion."

"Her baby didn't cry," Janette whispered.

Stella gaped at her. "What?"

She repeated herself, louder this time, each word striking new terror in her heart. "Carolyn Blake's baby didn't cry."

CHAPTER SIX

THE FIRST THING Janette did upon arriving at her office the following morning was to call her attorney friend, Merv Davidson, apologize for disturbing him on a Saturday, and ask him to meet her for lunch. Little more than three hours later, she arrived at the Seaside Inn ahead of Merv and was shown to a little table for two outside on the brick patio, beneath a trellis covered with purple bougainvillea.

After a few minutes, she spotted Merv, and waved. Merv nodded his head in return and headed toward her table, ducking his head beneath a hanging Boston fern.

She stood and kissed the older man on his cheek, smelling peppermint on his breath. It brought back memories of her childhood when Merv never failed to offer her peppermint candy whenever he came to the house. "Thanks for seeing me."

Merv sat, pulled off his sunglasses and stuck them into the top pocket of his suit jacket. After they exchanged the usual amenities, he studied Janette with a quizzical look. "I was hoping this was a social lunch, but something tells me it's not."

Janette wrapped her linen napkin around her finger. "I need you to tell me I'm crazy."

Merv watched her thoughtfully, his gray eyes narrowed beneath his bushy eyebrows. "I can't imagine telling you any such thing."

"Stella thinks I'm crazy," she said. "I've known you a lot longer." All her life, actually. Merv had been Cameron Taylor's lawyer for years, and was probably the closest thing to a friend her father had ever had. "It's about my baby..." Merv knew about Stephanie. Her father had summoned him over to the house on several different occasions during her pregnancy to discuss the situation. Janette would always feel grateful to Merv for providing legal counsel without trying to force her father's will on her. In those days she had needed an ally and Merv had certainly met that need. In the years since, he had become a friend.

She explained how she'd met Amy and the astounding conclusion she had drawn as to why, after all these years, she was positive that the doctors were mistaken about her baby.

"Merv, I know that I heard my baby cry that day. I don't care what the doctors said. I know what I heard."

Merv stroked his brownish-gray beard. "Maybe you're right about what you heard. Maybe the baby lived for a moment or two. Isn't that possible?"

"The doctors said the baby was stillborn." She leaned forward earnestly. "There's more. Amy's mother, Carolyn Blake, swore that her baby didn't cry. Her husband told me himself that she suffered nightmares for years after Amy's birth. She dreamed her baby didn't cry and I dreamed my baby did cry. Don't you think that's strange?"

Merv rested his elbows on the table, clasping his hands together. "Maybe it's maternal or something. I don't know. Janette, do you honestly believe your baby was switched with someone else's child?" He waited, his face drawn in a look of disbelief.

Hearing her worst fear coming from someone else's lips was comforting in an odd sort of way. It *did* sound crazy. On the bright bustling patio, the nightmares of the previous nights began to fade. She relaxed. "You don't think it's possible?"

He spread his hands out. "I'm sorry, Janette."

She frowned in annoyance. "Sorry? Merv, do you think I *want* to believe that my baby was taken from me at birth? That I lost ten years of my child's life? That my child belongs to someone else? My God, Merv, I don't know how I could live with that!"

"I'm still not clear as to how you came up with this notion in the first place. We're talking nightmares, a birth date and a certain physical similarity. It's not like you to jump to conclusions based on so little."

"I know." She bit her lower lip thoughtfully. She hadn't told him everything; she wasn't even sure if hearing the rest would change his mind. "What I haven't told you is the feeling I have. From the moment I met Amy it was like a part of me had been restored. I can't stop thinking of her."

"That's not too hard to understand," Merv said gently. "Some women have very strong maternal feelings. Maybe what we're talking about here is that old biological clock thing. Have you thought about adopting a child?"

She stiffened. If he had slapped her face he couldn't have hurt her more. "Adopting a child isn't going to change how I feel about Amy. This isn't about my wanting a child." She closed her eyes and recalled the nightmare of the previous night. Her baby had called to her, and this time she had looked into the bassinet. The baby had been Amy.

Despite the warm sun that filtered through the overhead trellis, her body turned ice-cold. She opened her eyes to find Merv watching her with grave concern.

"What if the idea isn't crazy?" she asked. "I've heard of cases where mistakes like this occurred."

"That's true. But usually the mistake is caught quickly. Within days or a week of a child's birth. Hospitals have all sorts of safeguards against such things occurring."

Janette sat back. It *was* a crazy idea, there was no doubt about it. And yet, she couldn't ignore the feeling she had whenever she looked at Amy. She couldn't ignore a lot of things. "Merv, you weren't there the day my baby was born. It was bedlam. There were people everywhere. The hospital was understaffed and overcrowded. They didn't even have a room to put me in. And Merv, I didn't tell you that a woman had gone into cardiac arrest shortly after I gave birth." Adam's wife; it had to be. "Everyone was gathered around her. Doctors, nurses. They completely forgot about me. And if they forgot about me, isn't it entirely possible that during the confusion, safeguards were ignored?"

Merv studied her face. "You're serious about this, aren't you?"

"I don't know," Janette said honestly. "It's this feeling I have deep down inside that I can't explain."

"There is a way that we might be able to put this idea to rest," he said, reaching into his pocket for a peppermint candy. He watched her carefully as he peeled off the cellophane wrapper. "Have you thought about genetic testing?"

Janette's face grew still. "Genetic testing?"

He nodded. "These tests have become quite sophisticated in recent years. They will prove whether or not you're the child's natural mother. I've been involved with several cases where genetic tests were used to prove paternity."

Janette's heart began to pound. "What does a test like this involve?"

"You, the child and the child's father of record will have to be tested. It's a matter of going to a lab and letting a technician draw tissue samples. There might be some minor discomfort involved in the taking of tissue samples, but if it will set your mind at rest, it might be worth the trouble."

"I don't know if I can put Adam and Amy through all that just to set aside my own crazy suspicions," she said. For the first time it occurred to her how going public with her suspicions might affect Amy. "What if I'm wrong?"

Merv popped the candy into his mouth. "If you're wrong, you'll put this entire matter out of your mind and get on with your life."

"And if I'm right? How do I deal with the possibility that I have been denied my child all these years?"

Merv offered her a candy and when she shook her head, tucked the package back into the pocket of his suit jacket. "I can't answer that question, Janette. I hope to God I never have to. All I'm saying is that if you really believe that a mistake was made all those years ago, you do have an option."

"I'm not sure it's much of an option," she said. "Adam would never agree to the tests. Why should he?"

"He might not have to. If we can convince a judge that there was in all probability a mistake made at the hospital, we might be able to get a court order. Then this Adam won't have a choice in the matter."

Janette shook her head. It was getting too complicated. She could just imagine Adam Blake's reaction upon receiving a court order to have Amy tested. He idolized his daughter.

"If you like, I can begin the legal proceedings for you. It should only take a few days."

"No!" Feeling suddenly foolish, she shook her head vehemently. "Forget it, Merv. I really don't have anything to go on. I appreciate your help. You're a good friend."

He nodded. "I'm glad I can be there for you. Let me know if you change your mind."

She picked up the menu and opened it. She wasn't going to change her mind. All she had was suppositions, vague feelings and nightmares. Hardly enough to go on and certainly not enough reason to disrupt a little girl's life.

Nevertheless, after she and Merv parted in the parking lot, she realized that instead of putting her mind at ease Merv had managed to add yet another complication. It had never occurred to her that there was a scientific way to check out her theory. Now that she knew it was possible to prove or disprove her suspicion, it was harder than ever to let go of the vague uneasiness that plagued her.

She could think of nothing else as she drove from the Seaside Inn to the pageant grounds. She was so deep in thought, she didn't see the man and child who stood at the entrance of the staff parking lot waving to her. With a start, she glanced in the rearview mirror, shocked to discover that she had driven right past Adam and Amy.

Pulling into her assigned space, she parked and locked the car.

Amy ran over to greet her. "Miss Taylor, Miss Taylor, guess what? We brought you a surprise." Amy held up a picnic basket. She was dressed in white shorts and a pink T-shirt, her hair pulled back in a ponytail. "We brought you lunch. I hope you like tuna sandwiches. I made them all by myself. Well, almost. Daddy cut up the onions and celery and..."

Janette looked into Amy's earnest eyes and found herself grinning like a jack-o-lantern. "I love tuna sandwiches," she said when she was finally able to get a word in. "And I would love it even more if you would call me Janette." She wrapped one arm around Amy's shoulder and together they walked toward Adam, who stood watching from a short distance away. Just the sight of him standing there, legs apart, his sensuous mouth curved in a relaxed smile, his dark hair gleaming in the sunlight, filled Janette with pleasure. She wished she hadn't eaten the entire Cobb Salad during her lunch with Merv.

Adam's smile turned into a boyish grin. "I hope you haven't had lunch already. We'd hoped to make it over here earlier, but Amy's game went into extra innings."

"Great." Janette said, not wanting to disappoint Amy. She would eat again if it killed her. "How did your team do?"

"We won nine to five," Amy said, grinning.

"Thanks to our champ here," Adam added, playfully punching Amy's arm. "Would you believe she hit a grand-slam home run in the eighth inning?"

Janette felt as proud as a mother hen. "Hey, what do you know? Congratulations."

Amy lowered her head in embarrassment and, for once, was silent, but nonetheless she looked pleased.

"I once hit a grand slam myself," Janette added. "I was probably not much older than you."

Amy glanced up, her eyes wide with interest. "Did you used to play softball, too?"

"I sure did," Janette said. "I was pretty good at it if I do say so myself. In fact I was the pitcher."

"Before you two start comparing notes, what do you say we find a place to sit before our lunch grows warm?" Adam asked, glancing around the parking lot.

"I know just the spot," Janette said, leading the way. She took them to a picnic table centered amid a grove of sycamores. It was Janette's favorite spot and she often came here to sit and watch the ocean.

"Hey, this is perfect!" Adam said, helping Amy with the picnic basket. Within minutes the three of them had spread a red-and-white checkered tablecloth across a table, along with paper plates, cups and napkins.

Janette was impressed with the picnic Amy had packed. Along with the tuna sandwiches, there were carrot strips and bunches of green grapes. For dessert, they had chocolate chip cookies that Amy had baked herself, and ice-cold lemonade.

"This is a real treat," Janette said. She couldn't remember the last time she had been on a picnic, or had taken the time to enjoy the pleasures of nature. But today, she found that even the grass beneath her feet seemed miraculous and all because she was with Adam. Adam and Amy.

"How is your kitten doing?" Janette asked. Amy glanced at her father and Janette got the impression that the two were in some sort of disagreement. "I hope there's not a problem?"

"Well," Amy began, looking forlorn. "Shortstop makes me sneeze and Daddy thinks we should find another home for him. But I love him so much. I really do. I can't bear to think of his living somewhere else."

"I'm sure you do love the kitten," Janette said, blaming herself for the unhappy situation. "But an allergy can be serious. If you like you can bring him back to the pageant grounds. That way you can still see him."

"Thanks for the offer," Adam said. "But we have a family up the street from us who's interested. They told Amy she's welcome to see Shortstop anytime she pleases."

"I think that's great," Janette said. "He will still be your cat even though he'll be living in another house."

"Do you think that will work?" Amy asked, frowning with uncertainty. "I don't want Shortstop to forget me."

"He isn't going to forget you," Janette assured her. "And just think. Shortstop will have two families to love him. How lucky can a cat get?"

Amy looked from Janette to her father. "Two families. I never thought of that. Well, maybe..."

Janette smiled. "Atta girl." She glanced up at Adam and the look he gave her turned her insides to liquid.

"Thanks," he said, when Amy had wandered out of earshot. "Somehow you managed to turn the situation into something positive and that's what did the trick. I wish I could think of the right things to say to her. They seem to come so naturally to you."

Pleased by the compliment, Janette nevertheless had to take issue with him. "I have a feeling that there are not many times that you don't think of the right things to say."

"There are times," Adam said. "I couldn't seem to think of the right things to say to you last night. I hated seeing you hurt so much. I wish..."

Janette held her breath waiting to hear what it was he wished but he was distracted by Amy who was calling and waving her arm. "Come over here. Hurry!"

Adam helped Janette to her feet and, hand in hand, they hurried toward Amy who was on her knees in the grass. A few feet in front of her a cottontail rabbit stood motionless, its ears standing straight up. Almost as soon as Adam and Janette approached, the animal scampered away and disappeared into a hole.

While Amy searched for other rabbits, Adam dug into the trunk of his car for a ball and talked Janette into a game of monkey-in-the-middle with Amy being the monkey. With a mischievous grin, Adam threw the ball to Janette. Showing off her pitcher's arm, she hurled it back to him, high over Amy's head. Adam jumped up to catch the ball with athletic grace.

Grinning, he made a face at his daughter, then settled his gaze upon Janette. Feeling a warm glow, Janette prepared herself for the catch.

"Put it here, partner," she called, clapping her hands together.

Adam threw back his arm and tossed the ball again. This time the ball sailed higher and farther away than before and Janette was forced to run after it. Amy nearly beat her to it and the two ended up rolling over each other, laughing.

Lying in the grass, legs and arms entangled with Amy's, Janette lay on her back and glanced up to see Adam standing over them, his eyes as warm as the overhead sun. Locking gazes with her, he held out his hand and helped her to her feet.

"This is neat!" Amy said sitting up and hugging her legs. Grinning, she looked from Janette to Adam. "It's like we're a family." Amy jumped to her feet and slipped her hand into Janette's. Amy's hand in hers was enough to warm the cockles of her heart. Startled that she had suddenly recalled another one of her grandmother's favorite expressions, Janette smiled.

"It feels like a family to me," Adam agreed. He held onto Janette's hand and then completed the circle by taking Amy's hand as well.

A family. Janette held the thought in her heart for the rest of the afternoon. It was difficult to concentrate on work. Impossible. She stood staring at the list of things to do on her desk and thinking how it felt to be a part of a family. The time spent with Adam and Amy had gone so quickly. The afternoon that followed their picnic seemed to stretch to eternity.

The only thing that saved her was remembering Adam's plan to see her tonight. Knowing that when this day ended, and it must end eventually, she would be with Adam.

She counted the moments that stood between them, trying to still her troubled thoughts. Did she have the right to go out with him while she harbored suspicions about Amy's parentage? Didn't she owe it to him to be honest? Maybe she should tell him, she thought, tell him about the horrible crazy feeling that something was terribly, terribly wrong, even though such feelings made no sense. Maybe Adam could do what Stella and Merv had been unable to do; maybe he could put her mind at rest. He might even be able to come up with a plausible explanation.

And if he couldn't, what then? she asked herself. What then? It was a no-win situation. If she told

Adam, he would be hurt and angry and would never want to see her again. Yet, if she said nothing, would she one day regret having held back?

She left work early and drove to the Garden Knolls Cemetery. She parked her car next to a grassy hill that had grown as familiar to her over the years as her own backyard. She walked to a spot beneath a sprawling oak tree to the tiny grave she had faithfully tended for more than ten years. From where she stood, she could see the sparkling ocean in the distance, dotted here and there by sailboats. Farther out, the shadowy outline of an oil tanker hovered between two offshore oil derricks.

Janette turned her attention to the tiny grave at her feet. In the past she'd come to this quiet restful spot whenever she felt sad or lonely. Today, she'd been driven to the grave by a feeling of desperation.

She knelt on the newly mown grass, touching the tiny slab of cold hard marble with her fingertips. It read, Stephanie, My Little Angel.

Next to the stone, the forget-me-nots she had brought the preceding weekend were in full bloom. The tiny blossoms reminded her of the little blue flowers she had embroidered on the baby's nightgown while awaiting her birth. It was this same little nightgown that Stephanie had been wrapped in before being laid to rest. Fighting back tears, Janette stood, dismayed that the peace that usually came to her as she sat by her infant daughter's grave escaped her today.

Seeing Amy again, spending time with her, had only stirred up the torment, making it impossible to think of anything else. Being with Amy made her feel as if a part of her that had been ripped away the day she lost her baby had suddenly been given back to her.

"It's crazy," she said aloud. Crazy! It was a coincidence, all of it. Amy's birth date, the nightmares, both Janette's and Carolyn's. Even sharing the same hospital room was a coincidence. But try as she might, she couldn't still the nagging voice inside that kept asking the same question, over and over. What if Amy really is your child?

Despair filled her as she realized that the thoughts and suspicions were never going to go away. An anguished knot formed inside. She knew that as long as she continued to think she might be Amy's mother, there would always be an invisible block between her and Adam. A block that would keep them from developing any sort of meaningful or long-term relationship. A block that would forever keep her out of his bed. If she wanted any more from Adam than she already had, she had no choice but to be honest with him.

My precious little angel, she whispered. She stared at the place on the stone where a lone tear had fallen. If by some strange miracle Amy really was her child, the baby buried here belonged to someone else: to Adam.

A seagull flew overhead, letting out a lone piercing cry, its wings spread as it followed an air current to the rugged cliffs below. *Caw, caw, caw.* Whose baby? it seemed to ask. Whose baby are you?

CHAPTER SEVEN

JANETTE HEARD Adam's car in front of her house and felt a thrill of anticipation race through her body. A smile on her face, she threw open the door, not wanting to wait until he knocked, not wanting to be away from him a single moment longer than necessary. She was surprised to find him already on the porch, knowing that the only way he could have made it from the curb so quickly was by running. The thought of him wanting to be with her as much as she wanted to be with him filled her with pleasure.

He greeted her with a devastating smile that touched every nerve ending in her body. "For you," he said, thrusting a tiny bouquet of forget-me-nots into her hand.

Startled, she backed away, letting the flowers fall between them, her body turning suddenly to ice. Staring at the flowers at her feet, she struggled for composure, telling herself that he couldn't have known forget-me-nots held a special significance to her, one that she hadn't shared with anyone.

The smile died on his face. He picked up the flowers and followed her into the living room. "So much for trying to be imaginative," he said.

She turned and met his troubled eyes. "I'm sorry, Adam. The flowers. Forget-me-nots reminded me of Stephanie."

"Stephanie?" A look of remorse crossed his face as the name clicked in place. "Your baby." Puzzled, knowing only that he had somehow caused Janette pain, he searched for a place to hide the flowers, finally stuffing them beneath a magazine. "I'm so sorry," he said, cursing the inadequacy of the English language. "I saw this kid standing at a corner not far from here, selling flowers and I couldn't resist."

Janette nodded. She knew the corner he was referring to. It was the same corner and probably the same boy who kept her supplied with forget-me-nots. "His mother grows them in her backyard," she explained.

"That's the one," he said, uncertainty in his voice. "I'm so sorry."

Janette felt any resistance inside melt away. "I thought I had gotten over my loss. I really did think that until . . ."

He took a step closer. "Until . . ."

Panic began to rise inside of her. She knew that sooner or later this moment of truth would have to come. But not yet, not now, not while they were still exploring their feelings; not while love or the beginning of love was still so new to them.

But Adam refused to let it rest. "Last night, something or someone kept you from letting me make love to you," he said softly. "I want to make certain that whatever it was, it never happens again."

"I told you, I've been having these terrible nightmares."

"I know." He watched her lips tremble, noted the haunted look in her eyes. "I think there's more. I felt you holding back even when we kissed." He waited for her response and when none came, he continued. "When I told you about Carolyn, it felt good. I needed to talk about the past, if only to put it to rest." His eyes took on a softness that said more than all the words in the world. "I know it's hard to trust someone enough to reveal painful feelings, but I thought we had made strides in that direction."

"I do trust you!" she insisted.

"Then tell me why I see sadness in your eyes. Tell me why I sense something pulling you away from me. Tell me why my falling in love with you threatens you."

He made it all but impossible for her to deny his request. Beseechingly, he took her hand in his, forcing her to look at him. "Tell me, Janette." She felt trapped; fear coiled in her heart, striking at the small part of her that wanted to believe that nothing she told him would change his mind about her.

"Adam, I don't know how to tell you. Stella thinks I'm crazy. Merv..."

Adam looked confused. "Stella's your roommate? Why does she think you're crazy? And who's Merv? And why are you looking at me with doubt in your eyes? You know how I feel about you. Nothing you say would make me change my mind."

Nothing? She mentally jumped on the word. Nothing? Not even if she told him that Amy might not be his? She pulled her hand free and brushed both hands against the fabric of her skirt. "Do you want a glass of wine or something?" Without waiting for him to reply, she poured herself a glass of rosé from the decanter on the mantel and took a long sip.

Adam watched her with increased anxiety. "None for me...thank you. Janette?" He stepped forward and lay a hand on her shoulder.

"Don't," she whispered, backing away. "Don't touch me because I'll never be able to tell you what I must tell you if you touch me."

Reluctantly, he dropped his hand, the expression on his face telling her how deeply she had wounded him. "What must you tell me?"

She inhaled deeply. "Your wife and I both had our babies at the same hospital."

Adam nodded. "I hadn't thought about it, but I guess you're right. It's a small world, isn't it?" The cause of her distress suddenly dawned on him. "Is that what this is all about?" He gave her an anguished look. "Is it me that is causing you to have these nightmares? Does knowing that I was there in the hospital that day bring back the memories?"

"Oh, God, Adam, how I wish it were as simple as that." She took a moment to compose herself. "The doctors told me that my baby was stillborn. They said something was wrong with her heart."

Adam went to touch her, but when she drew away, he sighed and dropped his hand. "I'm sorry, Janette. I can't tell you how sorry."

She shook her head. She didn't want his sympathy, not that. "I don't believe it. I don't believe my baby died that day, Adam."

Adam's eyes widened in astonishment. "What?"

"I believe a terrible mistake was made." Once she had begun, there was no stopping. Words poured out of her like water from a spigot. Over ten years of bottled-up emotion gushed from the deepest depths of her. She recalled aloud every detail of that long-ago day and when she was finished, she summed it up in one chilling sentence. "I believe that my baby was switched with someone else's baby."

This time Adam ignored the warning look she gave him. He took her by the shoulders and searched her lovely pale face. "This is terrible." His face clouded in a strange combination of sympathy, horror and disbelief. He was surprised by the strong emotions this beautiful woman evoked in him. He was even more surprised by the strong need to right whatever terrible wrongs she'd endured. "Are you sure?"

She pulled away. "Adam," she began with firm, almost frightening conviction, "I think my baby was switched with yours. I think Amy is the baby that I gave birth to that day."

He stared at her in disbelief, so still he could have been frozen in a block of ice. For what seemed like an eternity, they stood facing each other. It wasn't until Adam backed away, his face drained of color, that she was able to find her voice.

"Adam, I'm so sorry," she said. "I didn't want to tell you. Not yet anyway." She moved toward him, but with a thrust of his arm, he warded her off. She felt like her entire world had toppled. "I wasn't going to say anything. Not until I had more to go on. But the forget-me-nots...."

Adam paced back and forth in front of her. He stopped and looked at her with a stranger's eyes. His handsome dark face that had only moments earlier reflected warmth and love, was tight with shock and disbelief.

"I know that losing a baby can do strange things to a woman's mind," he said aghast. "But this!"

"I'm not crazy!" she cried. "I don't want to believe this anymore than you do."

"Amy is my child. Mine and Carolyn's. There was no mistake made at the hospital."

"You can't know that for sure!"

"I know!" he said tersely. "I won't allow you to put this crazy idea into Amy's head!"

His words could have been bullets piercing her heart. "Adam, listen to me. I have no desire to hurt—"

"No!" He whirled about to face her. "You listen to me. I won't have my family threatened by some maternally deprived woman!"

She flinched against the stinging blow of his words. It was the second time that day that she'd been accused of such a thing. "Is that what you think I am? Maternally deprived? Let me tell you something. I've gone through hell these last two weeks. Ever since I first saw Amy. I can't sleep. I can barely think straight."

"You've got that right!" Adam said angrily. Disgust masked his face as he glared at her. "This whole thing was a ploy, wasn't it? Making me think that you were interested in me when the only thing you were interested in was getting close to Amy out of some sick maternal need."

"Oh, God, no." This was the most cruel accusation of all. "Don't think that. You mustn't think that."

His face white with fury, he turned away from her and stormed across the room toward the door.

She ran after him. "Please, Adam. Listen to me."

But he wouldn't listen. He wouldn't look at her. And if he had his way, by God, he wouldn't remember that she was the one woman in all the world who very nearly filled the aching emptiness inside.

ADAM STOOD STARING out the window of his office at the Ashton Tex Corporation. The last two days had been hell. Worse than hell.

Why hadn't he seen the signs? Why had he not suspected that Janette's interest in Amy was in some way abnormal? He had wanted to believe, did believe, dammit, that he had finally found someone to fill the emptiness, someone who would love Amy as much as he did, if that was at all possible, someone who would love him, share his life, his hopes, his dreams. It was frightening to think that wanting something as badly as he wanted this had nearly destroyed his family. He should be happy that Janette had revealed herself to him so early in the game. Instead, he felt cheated, angry and hurt. More than anything, he felt betrayed.

She'd used him in the worst possible way. His only hope was that the woman who had been so easy to fall in love with would be just as easy to forget.

His thoughts were interrupted by Will Hampton, head of communications, who knocked on the door and entered without invitation.

"I just talked to Jack Tanner, the captain of the ship," Will announced in his clipped no-nonsense voice. In his forties, Will's silver hair contrasted sharply with his ebony skin. "I'm afraid the news doesn't look good.

"Give it to me," Adam said brusquely, crossing to his desk. He waited for Will to sit before lowering himself into the leather seat of his swivel chair. Less than two hours earlier, he'd learned that one of their company ships was in trouble off the California coast. Details had been frustratingly slow in coming after the first vague report, but this hadn't kept the media from setting up camp in front of the building.

"The ship is about a mile offshore," Will said, referring to a small notepad. "There's a large hole in the hull and oil is spilling into the water."

"Damn!" Adam shuddered to think what a major oil spill could do to the already ecologically sensitive California coast. "Do you know what happened?"

"The captain says he thinks he hit a rock." Will tugged on his tie. "I don't know. There are no rocks out there."

"Do you suspect alcohol or drugs?"

"Absolutely not. You know as well as I do that Tanner is a family man with an impeccable reputation. In the twenty years he's worked for us, he's not had a single mishap."

Adam did know that. Still, it was his job to consider every possibility, no matter how distasteful. "I think we better let the press know we will be conducting a full-scale investigation. Play up any positive angles. The captain's record, dedication to the company." It was Will's job as communications coordinator to deal with the media.

"I think you'd better talk with the media yourself," Will said. "This could get real sticky."

Adam grimaced. He hated the circus-like atmosphere of press conferences. "Give me some time. As soon as I get more information, I'll prepare a statement."

Will nodded gravely and stood. "Do you think you'll be prepared by late this afternoon?"

Adam swiveled his chair back and forth. Until the investigation was completed, he wouldn't have much information to give the press. Anything he said would be pure speculation, but if he stalled for time, he could well be accused of perpetuating a cover-up. An oil mass heading for shore was bound to bring out environmentalists protesting the transporting of hazardous substances up and down the coast. The company couldn't afford to wait.

"I'll be ready," Adam said. "Tell the captain I want to speak to him personally." He grabbed the phone and began to punch numbers. "And get Cox in here." W. James Cox was the in-house expert on cleanup operations.

His mother-in-law answered the phone on the third ring. "Virginia, I've got a major problem, I probably won't be home until late, if at all."

"Oh, dear. Does it have something to do with that sinking ship?"

Adam groaned. "Don't tell me it's already on the news."

"I just heard it."

"That ship is one of ours. Could you stay with Amy tonight?"

"I'd be happy to," Virginia said.

"Thanks. Tell Amy I'll see her tomorrow." He hung up and stared at the photo of Amy on his desk. How was he going to explain to her that she could never again see Janette Taylor?

How was he going to convince himself that not seeing Janette would only hurt for a little while?

FROM THE MOMENT Adam had stormed out of her house, Janette hadn't slept or eaten. She arrived at the office on that following Monday morning and attacked the coffeepot as if her life depended on it.

Pat shook her head. "That stuff will kill you," she cautioned. "Why not try some herbal tea?"

"Thanks, Pat, but unless that tea of yours is high-octane, I think I'll stick to coffee. Has that Velcro gotten here yet?"

"I'm expecting it at any moment. Lester wants to know when he's going to see *Girl with Gull*. He wants the painters to start on the canvas."

Janette grimaced. Without Amy, there would be no portrayal of her father's portrait. "Tell Lester the painting's been scrapped."

Pat lifted a questioning eyebrow, but didn't pursue the matter. "Shall I call the printers and make the correction on the programs?"

Janette thought for a moment. She'd forgotten that the programs had already been sent to the printers. "Hold off until this afternoon, will you?"

She walked through to her office and collapsed in her chair. What was the matter with her? she thought. There was no way that Adam would allow Amy to model for the pageant. Not now.

She buzzed Pat. The sooner she faced facts, the better. "Go ahead and make the changes on the programs."

"Will do," Pat said. "By the way, Phillips Restoration called. *Girl with Gull* is ready to be picked up."

"Thanks," Janette murmured, wishing with all her heart that her father had finished what he'd set out to do and had destroyed the portrait completely. Maybe then, she would never have met Adam.

After an unsuccessful attempt to work, she drove over to the restoration company, intent upon picking up the portrait and dumping it into the nearest trash receptacle. She didn't want to look at it. All she wanted to do was pay what she owed and get rid of it. But the art restorer was one of those rare people who took exceptional pride in his work. It was obvious that unless she was completely happy with the painting, the poor man would be devastated.

"That painting's worth a lot," he told her. He was a tall skinny man with steel-rimmed glasses that he worked up and down his nose constantly as if he could never quite focus right. He leaned the portrait against the wall behind the counter and stepped back to view it again, adjusting his glasses accordingly. "It doesn't have quite the depth of Cameron Taylor's later works, but it's still magnificent."

Surprised by his assessment, Janette's eyes were drawn to the image of herself as a child. Now that the nose and mouth had been uncovered the portrait didn't just resemble Amy, it was the spitting image of her. She knew at that moment that she could never part with this painting. No matter how much pain it brought her. If Adam refused to allow her to see Amy, this painting would be all that she had left. "You did a magnificent job," she said.

The owner beamed with delight. "That's what we're here for. To make our customers happy."

After paying what she owed, she carried the portrait to her car, an idea forming in her head. They said one picture was worth a thousand words; maybe it was time to test the worth of one portrait.

THE DAY FOLLOWING the tanker mishap, Adam glanced at the latest report handed him by Will. It was frustrating, this trickling in of bits and pieces of information. And the news that was coming in was disastrous. The tanker was completely crippled, and already thousands of gallons of crude oil had been dumped into the ocean. Adam called company headquarters in Anchorage, Alaska, and spoke to Steve Walker, the president of the company.

"Damn!" Steve said, after Adam had given him what few facts he had. "I had hoped it wasn't that bad. What are the chances of cleaning up the oil before it hits the coast?"

Adam glanced out the window. According to the report on his desk, a tropical storm was centered about five hundred miles this side of Hawaii. If the wind picked up, they didn't have a chance in the world of cleaning up in time. "It's hard to say. But I've got my best men on it."

"Do you need more help?"

"I need all the help I can get."

"I'll arrange to have a team of experts on the next flight to Los Angeles. If you need anything else, let me know."

"Thanks, Steve." No sooner had he hung up, when Janette Taylor came barging into his office, his secretary on her heel.

"I'm sorry, Mr. Blake, she insisted upon seeing you."

"That's all right, Miss Steele." He waited until his secretary had left the office, closing the door behind her, then braced himself before turning to Janette, only to find he hadn't braced himself enough. "Damn it, what are you doing here?" *And what right do you have to make me still want you?* "Haven't you done enough damage?"

Ignoring the rage in his voice, she crossed over to his desk and dropped the portrait in front of him.

Adam lowered his eyes to study the portrait, surprised to find his daughter's likeness staring at him. Feeling both anger and fear, he lifted his eyes in astonishment. "I gave no one permission to paint Amy's portrait!" he stormed.

"Nobody's painted her!" Janette said.

"Then how? Where?" He glanced back at the portrait.

"If you would take the time to look at the signature, you'll see that painting was painted by my father, Cameron Taylor, nearly seventeen years ago. That's not Amy in that painting. It's me, painted when I was ten years old."

Adam lifted tortured eyes to meet hers. "All right. Let's say there's a resemblance. What exactly do you think that proves?"

"It doesn't prove anything, but when you add up the rest..."

"What rest?" he demanded. "There is nothing else. What gives you the right to come in here and make rash statements about my daughter?"

"Because, damn it, I think there's a very real possibility that she's *my* daughter."

"I won't listen to any more of this."

"Why not? Are you afraid of what you might hear?"

He looked at her with hard cold eyes. "There's nothing you could say that would ever make me think that Amy is not my daughter."

Fighting to keep a grip on her emotions, she lowered her voice. "Adam, I don't want to make trouble. You've got to believe that. But I have to know the truth."

Adam stood. "The truth is that you lost your baby and you don't want to accept that."

"If you could give me some answers, I promise you I will walk out of this office and never bother you again."

Adam glanced down at the portrait, and then narrowed his gaze back to Janette. Why did she have to look so damned normal and beautiful and so very very convincing?

When he failed to respond, she paced back and forth in front of his desk. "Why did Carolyn suffer from nightmares about giving birth to a baby that didn't cry while all these years I dreamed about a baby who did? What about the fact that our babies were born on the same day?..."

"That proves absolutely nothing," he shouted.

"It was bedlam that day in the hospital," she shouted back. "Over one hundred food poisoning victims were admitted. The hospital was short-staffed. On top of all that Carolyn went into cardiac arrest."

A muscle tightened at his jaw. That day had been a nightmare all right, and the last thing he needed was to be given a blow-by-blow reminder. "I don't have time to listen to your ramblings, Miss Taylor!" He couldn't say her first name, not Janette, for he was still trying to separate the woman in front of him from the woman he had held in his arms.

The look he gave her almost shattered her composure. The formal use of her name nearly provided the last crushing blow. She held on with everything she had. She placed her hands on his desk and leaned toward him. This was no time to back down. At this stage of the game she had absolutely nothing to lose. "I believe that with all the confusion, proper safeguards were neglected and our babies were switched."

Adam stared at Janette, desperate to see some proof of madness or dementia on her part. But all he saw in her face was a conviction so strong that it filled him with cold dread. What Janette suggested was too horrible to contemplate. Amy was his. His and Carolyn's. There was no doubt in his mind, not a one.

"I have to know the truth," Janette said. "And I think you owe it to Amy to help me search out that truth."

"Keep Amy out of this," he warned her, pointing his finger menacingly.

"I wish I could," she whispered. "Oh, God, I wish I could. Adam, please, there's a test."

Adam's eyes sharpened. "Don't even suggest it!"

"Why not? What are you afraid of? If you're right, then the tests will only confirm that. Please, Adam, I beg of you. There's a lab downtown that will do it." She fumbled in her shoulder bag and drew out a yellow piece of paper. "I wrote down the telephone number." She slapped the paper on his desk.

Astonishment crossed his face. "Do you actually think I would expose my daughter to your outrageous theory? If you do, you're crazier than I thought."

She inhaled deeply. There was no reasoning with him. She had no choice but to use her ace card. "I don't want to have to get a court order." She looked at him beseechingly. "Please, Adam, don't make me take legal steps."

Adam glanced at the painting. His mind whirled. A court order? Would she really take legal steps? And if so, how far would she go with this ridiculous notion of hers? He glanced up at her determined face. He swallowed the anger and bitterness that rose up in his throat. This was no time to allow feelings to interfere with his thinking. For the longest while, neither spoke.

"I'll take Amy in for testing," he said finally. It was obvious she wasn't going to back down. "But only to prove how ridiculous this whole damned idea of yours really is. And then, Miss Taylor...if you ever come near me or Amy again, I'll personally haul you into court for harassment."

Janette flinched inwardly at the anger and rage he directed at her. "I hope to God you're right and I'm wrong," she said quietly.

She grabbed her portrait and hastened toward the door. She glanced back at Adam, but the look he gave her forbade any further discussion.

CHAPTER EIGHT

ADAM WORKED until dawn with the top people from every department. The team from Alaska had arrived around midnight, providing information on newly developed techniques for isolating oil spills, none of which had been tested. With the help of maps showing ocean currents and the latest weather report, they devised a plan to divert the oil from washing ashore. Only time would tell whether the plan would work.

The sun was just rising over the mountains to the east when Adam dragged himself home. Amy hadn't yet left for school and he found her in the kitchen, pouring herself a bowl of cornflakes. To his work-weary eyes, Amy looked like a ray of sunshine. She was dressed in a pretty plaid skirt and white blouse, her long blond hair held back with a plaid ribbon.

He measured her appearance, desperate to find tangible proof that she really was his. She was tall like his side of the family. He'd always been puzzled by the green of her eyes. Carolyn's eyes had been hazel and his were blue. Maybe she didn't look much like him or Carolyn; there were a lot of children who didn't look like their parents. But she had her mother's gentle mannerisms; she even smiled like Carolyn, with the right corner of her mouth lifting first before the rest of her mouth curved upward. Then there was the way she turned her head ... Damn!

He couldn't believe what he was doing. She was his, that's all there was to it. His and Carolyn's.

"Grandma still sleeping?" he asked.

Amy looked up from her bowl and nodded. "You look awful. Do you want some coffee? I made a fresh pot."

Adam slumped into a kitchen chair. "I'd love a cup."

Amy poured his coffee and set the steaming cup on the table in front of him. "I saw you on TV last night."

"Oh?" Adam took a sip of the strong hot brew. Amy made great coffee, just like Carolyn. It was a comforting thought, and the fact that he sought reassurance in such things angered him. Damn Janette Taylor for putting him on edge like this. "What did you think of your dad on TV?"

She threw her arms around his neck. "I think you're the best daddy in the world."

Adam grinned, the stiff joints acquired during the intense night at Ashton Tex no longer aching. If only the ache in his heart would stop. "Listen, sport, I need to talk to you." He looked so serious that Amy wrinkled her forehead in a worried frown. "I'm afraid you won't be modeling for the pageant this year."

Amy looked so disappointed he thought she was going to cry. "But why, Daddy? Janette said I was perfect for the part."

Adam rubbed his hand across his whiskered chin. "It's just not going to work out. Okay?" He hated having to pull rank on her and give her one of his because-I-said-so looks. She deserved more than that from him. "The other thing I need to tell you is that I'm going to take you in for testing tomorrow. No big deal," he hurriedly assured her, forcing himself to keep his tone light. "The doctor will take some tissue. It might hurt a bit, but it won't be anything you can't handle. I just wanted you to know."

"Why, Daddy?"

"Don't look so worried, sweetie. It's just a check-up." Hating having to lie to her, he lovingly patted her cheek. "Hadn't you better get going? The school bus will be here any minute."

Amy silently grabbed her backpack, and leaned over to give him a peck on the cheek. Much to her surprise, her father grabbed her and held her so tight it took her breath away. After a moment he released her. She backed away in confusion. The last time her father had held onto her so tight he'd cut off her breathing was the day her mother had died.

All day long Amy worried about the tests. Was that why she couldn't model for Janette, she wondered, because something was seriously wrong with her? She was so worried she could hardly concentrate on her schoolwork; she was too busy counting her heartbeats and poking her stomach with her fingers to write her English composition or to solve her math problems. She'd suffered a stomachache a week earlier that her grandma had said was a touch of flu. But what if it wasn't the flu? What if she had the same heart condition as her mother?

Before lunch, Mrs. White sent her to the nurse, who immediately stuck a thermometer in her mouth, declared her healthy and sent her back to the classroom.

After school, Amy stopped by the Hopkins house on the way home to say hello to Shortstop. But the tiny kitten was no where to be seen. Amy remembered the day she had brought him to live with the Hopkins. He had looked so sad she thought her heart would break.

"Don't worry, Shortstop," she'd told him. "You're still my kitten even if you don't live with me."

Only it didn't feel like Shortstop was her kitten.

Disappointed and feeling close to tears, Amy raced down the block to her house, dropped her school-books on the kitchen table and ran out the back door. She took the path that spiraled downward from her backyard to the private beach behind her house. Slipping off her shoes and socks, she ran barefoot along the sand until she reached a large boulder that jutted out from the towering cliffs. She made a sharp right and, squeezing behind the boulder, she ducked beneath a clump of bushes to her secret cave.

The cave was surprisingly large, as big or bigger than her bedroom at home. To her knowledge no one knew the cave existed, not even her best friend or her father. She'd told Janette Taylor about the cave, but had not revealed its location. That was a secret she would reveal to no one.

Most of their neighbors were elderly, too old or sickly to manage the steep twisting path down to the tiny beach below so Amy practically had the beach to herself. Occasionally, her father would go down to the beach with her and they would run along the sand or try a bit of surf fishing. But she hadn't even shared her cave with her father. He worried too much and she knew he would undoubtedly insist that she stay out in the open where he could see her from the high cliffs above.

Although she felt guilty that she kept this secret from him, she loved her cave. Loved sitting inside all bundled up on a cold foggy day and listening to the pounding surf outside. Sometimes the cave would fill with water and she would have to climb up the rocky walls to the granite shelf overhead.

It was her own private space and it helped her to put her world in order. Today her world had been turned upside down by a frightening thought. She was going to have tests and her father wasn't very happy about it.

She remembered her mother and thought back to the day of her mother's funeral. She had wanted to be brave that day; she was brave. If only she hadn't looked up into her father's eyes and seen the tears. It was then that the full impact hit her; her mother was gone and she was never coming back. Not ever. That's when Amy's own tears began to flow.

She'd never seen her father cry before that day, nor had she seen him cry since. But this morning there was the same look of sadness in his eyes as he held her.

Amy clutched her chest and feeling her heart pound more quickly than usual, she was convinced she was right about inheriting her mother's heart problem. She was almost positive of it.

She was going to die.

POGO GREETED Janette with a low mewling sound, then hopped quickly on his single leg to the food she had tossed on the sand. "How are you doing, little fellow?" she asked, watching the bird peck hungrily at the pieces of fish.

Leaving the gull to enjoy his meal in peace, she continued along the path, slipping her sandals off as she reached the sand. Already the early-morning fog was beginning to lift, revealing patches of deep blue sky.

Cold foaming waves unfurled around Janette's ankles, then receded to the sea. She stopped to pick up a pink shell, but her attention was caught by a black shiny glob of crude that had settled in a nearby tidal pool. Leaning over, Janette got a closer look. She put her hand into the water and touched the glob. Immediately her fingers were coated with the thick black oil. The strong smell of fumes made her eyes water.

Janette straightened and glanced around her. Sickened, she realized that the black ugly sludge threatening her tidal pools was oil from the crippled tanker.

Her thoughts turned to Adam. He must be devastated watching the destruction of the beach he loved so much. If only she could go to him, comfort him, offer him her support. She mustn't think of him, she told herself, but his memory continued to cling to her like the oil clung to the nearby rocks.

She glanced toward the house at the sound of her name, surprised to see Merv. She waved to him.

"I thought I'd find you here," Merv said, joining her. "What are you doing?"

She motioned toward the tidal pools with her blackened hand. "The oil from the tanker washed ashore during the night. I don't know what it's going to do to the wildlife around here."

Merv shook his head. "It's a damned shame. I wish to hell those oil companies would be made responsible for the damage they do to the environment."

Janette felt her irritation rise. Under normal circumstances, she would have let Merv's generalization pass. Today, his comment struck her as unfair criticism. "Most oil companies are working very hard to clean up the environment. From what I understand, this was an unfortunate accident that is costing the company plenty. They are working day and night to remedy the situation." *Adam was working day and night to remedy the situation.*

Merv regarded her with curiosity. Without meaning to, he had somehow managed to touch a nerve. Not wanting to dwell on the matter, he decided to get to the point of his visit, as much as he dreaded it. "I have the test results."

Janette held her breath. She was told it would take days before they learned the results of the tests. Next week at the earliest. "So soon?"

"I was able to talk the lab into giving us top priority. Do you want to sit down?" Merv glanced around for a dry place to sit.

"No. I'm all right. Just tell me." She searched his face, but his sunglasses kept his eyes hidden from view and it was hard to tell anything from his beard-covered chin. For all that his face revealed his head might as well have been in a paper bag. "Forget it. You're going to tell me I'm crazy and—"

"I almost wish you were crazy."

She lifted her eyes and straightened, her mouth suddenly dry. "What did you say?"

"You're right, Janette. Amy is your child."

With a cry of disbelief, Janette sank to her knees. All she could do was stare at Merv, afraid to believe her ears, afraid to believe, period.

"Let's go back to the house," Merv suggested.

Janette reached out and clutched his arm. "Tell me, Merv, is it true, is it really true?"

Merv nodded. "It's true."

"Oh, God." Tears of joy and disbelief ran down her cheeks. She'd known in her heart that Amy was hers, but never did she think she could prove it.

"Let's go back to the house," Merv urged. "We've got a lot to talk about." Dazed, she let Merv lead her across the sand and up the winding path to her back door. He led her to the sink and turned on the water for her, waiting for her to scrub her hands clean, before handing her a towel.

"I don't believe it." She wiped her hands and threw the towel onto the counter. Her thoughts were so disjointed she could hardly make sense of them. Amy, that dear beautiful child was really hers? She had a daughter. "The day I saw her, I knew. The green eyes. My grandmother's voice . . . It's crazy!"

She lowered herself carefully onto a chair while Merv found some brandy and poured her a glass.

"Drink this," he said.

To please him, she forced herself to take a sip, hating the bitterness that filled her mouth. But the brandy did calm her and at last she stopped shaking. Shock left her body and the full impact of Merv's news began to take hold.

She stood, gripping the edge of the table for support. "I can't believe this!" she said. "For over ten years, I've been denied my child! They took my baby away. . . ." Hot tears spilled down her cheeks. She felt, betrayed. Rage replaced the numbed disbelief of moments earlier.

"If it makes you feel any better, rest assured that we will seek restitution."

"Restitution!" she sputtered. They'd taken her child; nothing could make up for that. "Restitution won't bring back those lost years."

"I know that, Janette. But it's all that we have at this point and once you obtain custody . . ."

Janette stared at him, her face drained of all color. The rage that only a moment earlier had threatened to explode inside, deflated with the speed of a burst balloon. "What did you say?" she gasped.

"I said once we obtain custody." He stopped, surprised by the astonished look she gave him. "You do want to try to obtain legal custody of Amy, don't you? I just assumed . . ."

Janette covered her mouth with her hand. Shakily, she sank back onto the chair. It had never occurred to her that she could get custody of Amy. Not once had she considered the possibility of Amy living with her. Of her child . . .

"What . . . what about her father?"

Merv narrowed his eyes. "I take it by her father, you mean Adam Blake."

She sucked in her breath. She couldn't bear to think that Adam wasn't Amy's biological father. "You know I do."

Merv thought a minute. "This Adam Blake has no real legal right to his daughter. He's not her biological father, and as far I can determine, has never legally adopted her."

"But why would he have?" Janette protested. "He honestly thought that Amy was his."

"Maybe, but the point is the child was taken from you through no fault of your own."

Janette felt sickened. There was no question that her heart ached for the daughter she'd been denied. She longed to hold her, tell her all the things that a mother should tell a daughter, longed to do all the things that she'd wished her mother could have done with her. But these thoughts, far from cheering her, only made her worry about Adam. He loved Amy. Knowing that she was not his daughter would destroy him. She couldn't even begin to imagine what losing Amy altogether would do to him.

"Adam has been a great father to Amy. He loves her, Merv. I can't believe the court would take her away from him."

Merv stroked his beard. "I'm not going to kid you about this, Janette. It's going to be tough going. We have a situation where two good people, through no fault of their own, find themselves in an impossible dilemma. I don't envy the judge that's going to have to rule on this one. I think sympathies will lie with you, the natural mother. I don't know. There's no precedent that I know of. In the end, the main deciding factor is going to be what's best for the child. If we can prove that you can give Amy a better home..."

"That's ridiculous!" Janette exclaimed. "How can I prove that? Adam has over ten years of parental experience. I have absolutely none. He's given Amy a wonderful home."

"Great!" Merv said, throwing up his hands. "Next you'll be defending him in court."

"I'm sorry, Merv. I just can't think of the legal ramifications yet. I still can't believe that Amy is my daughter."

"I know this is a shock. Just remember, it's going to be a tough battle, and it's going to attract a lot of media attention, which may or may not work to our advantage."

Janette closed her eyes. She didn't want to think about that. "Does Adam know the results of the tests?"

"If he doesn't yet, he will soon enough."

Oh, God, Adam, she cried in silent anguish, please don't hate me. She opened her eyes. "What should I do? Do I dare put Amy through a custody suit? I'm so afraid, Merv. I mean, me a mother. I don't know anything about being a mother. And what about Amy? Will she end up hating me if I try to take her away from Adam?"

"I can't answer these questions," Merv said slowly, unwrapping a peppermint. "But I can tell you that as her mother, you have the right to play a part in her life."

Janette squeezed her eyes tight. Oh, yes, that's what she wanted more than anything in the world. To be a part of Amy's life. If only there wasn't so much at stake; if only there wasn't a chance that she could lose so much more than she could ever possibly gain.

She looked Merv squarely in the face. "I don't know what to do, Merv. What if I sue for custody and lose? What then? What if the only thing I get out of all this is that Amy comes to hate me for trying to take her away from her father? I don't want to mess up her life." Her thoughts raced. There had to be a way. "Maybe...maybe I should make a deal with Adam. If he lets me be a part of Amy's life, I won't tell her that I'm her real mother. Maybe that will be the best way."

"Does that mean you're not going to file charges against the hospital?"

Janette tightened her hand into a fist. "I've got to, Merv. Someone's got to pay for putting me through this hell."

"As soon as you file charges, everyone is going to know that Amy is your daughter."

Janette felt trapped. "Oh, God, what am I going to do?"

Merv laid a hand on Janette's shoulder. "I don't know the answer to that. But I think you better ask yourself a very important question before you make your decision. Now that you know for sure that Amy is your daughter, can you really walk away from her?"

ADAM CHECKED OVER the list of supplies that had been donated toward the massive cleanup operation by local firms. It was a staggering list. Fifty thousand disposable raincoats had been donated, along with nearly five thousand pairs of boots and over fifteen hundred hard hats and goggles. Just as impressive were the number of rubber gloves, shovels, rakes, waste bags and flashlights that had been sent over by the truckload. Missing from the list were floodlights and cellular phones, but he'd been advised that both were on their way.

Standing, Adam folded the list and slipped it into the pocket of the jeans that had replaced his usual suit and tie attire. He grabbed the red jacket with the logo that identified him as a company employee and walked out of his office, dangling the jacket over one shoulder.

His secretary, Miss Steele, stopped typing and reached for her notes. "Sir, I just got a call from Shell's Catering. They agreed to provide three meals a day for the volunteers for as long as you need them."

Adam let out a low whistle. If any good came out of this whole mess, it was the way the community had so enthusiastically banded together to help out. Hundreds of men and women from every possible walk of life had turned up to assist with the massive cleanup operation. "Do you think you can get them to let up on the caviar and pâté and concentrate more on the coffee and rolls?"

Miss Steele grinned. "I'll see what I can do, sir. But they're used to catering to the rich and famous, not the tired and hungry."

Adam returned her smile. He wished she wouldn't insist upon calling him sir. It made him feel as ancient as when Amy questioned him about the "olden" days. "By the way, get Will working on the cellular phone problem, will you? And—" He hesitated a moment "—if my lawyer shows up, tell him I'm at Tabor's Point."

He walked out to the hall and took the stairs down to the basement parking area. He wished he'd taken the time for another cup of coffee. He'd not slept in over forty-eight hours and hadn't really slept all that much since the tanker had been damaged. Hell, he hadn't slept since Janette had dropped her bombshell.

Actually, he was almost grateful that he had something to occupy his mind, at least during working hours. He only wished this particular something wasn't so potentially dangerous.

As soon as he'd received news of the tanker's problem, he'd acted quickly, following procedures that had been established for such an emergency. Oil skimmers had been dispatched to the tanker to help drain thousands of gallons of oil before it poured into the sea. He'd sent out crews to stretch booms along the bay, hoping to provide protection to the sensitive lowlands. But tropical storms far out in the Pacific had caused rough seas. This along with high tides had pushed the oil slick through the barriers toward shore.

It seemed to take forever to drive the short distance from his office to Tabor's Point. The beach was closed to the public, but this didn't prevent hoards of sightseers from tying up traffic. Gawkers stood along the windy bluffs watching the cleanup through binoculars and posing for pictures. The crippled tanker in the background provided a dramatic setting.

Adam parked next to a van that was used to transport oil-covered birds to a makeshift sanctuary not far from the beach. Nearby, a group of young people were being instructed on how to wash the oil off a stunned grebe. The entire beach was dotted with figures dressed in yellow slickers.

Adam walked up to one of Ashton Tex's mobile units and waited for Will to finish sending instructions through a walkie-talkie. Signing off, Will pushed in the antenna with an open palm.

"How's it going?" Adam asked.

"Terrible. The birds are afraid to land on the beach, because there are too many sightseers. We can't do anything for the birds if they don't come to shore."

"Damn!" Adam considered the problem. "Get on the phone to the mayor and request that all beaches in the area be closed. We've got to have a quiet place for the birds to land."

"Will do." Will pulled out the antenna. "By the way, we did get some good news. The alcohol and drug tests for both Captain Tanner and the skipper were negative."

The news didn't surprise Adam, but it was nonetheless a relief to get official confirmation.

"Adam?"

Adam spun around at the sound of his name and found himself facing his lawyer, Wes Marcus.

"We need to talk," Wes said.

Adam felt a gut-wrenching twist in his middle. Wes was a careful impeccable man who was as precise in manner as he was in dress. Today, Adam couldn't help but notice, Wes looked slightly frayed around the edges. His tie was slightly askew as if he had dressed in a hurry; Wes never dressed in a hurry.

Without a word, Adam led him to a relatively quiet spot next to the picnic grounds. He listened intently to what the older man had to say, hoping for all the world that what he was hearing wasn't true. But he knew. Knew with every breath, every cell, every nerve in his body that Wes was telling the truth.

Without a word, he spun around, walking blindly past cars, mobile units, milling cleanup crews and TV reporters. Wes ran after him and finally, fell in step beside him.

"Damn it, Adam, get hold of yourself."

Adam stopped and turned to his lawyer. "How accurate are these tests?"

"Very accurate."

"How accurate, damn it!"

Wes's jaw tightened. "Nearly a hundred percent accurate."

"I want the tests redone." Adam began walking again. If he walked long enough, fast enough, far enough, maybe he would wake up and this whole nightmare would go away.

"It won't do any good," Wes said, puffing by his side.

Adam stopped, but only because he came to the edge of a bluff and there was nowhere else to go. "Amy is my daughter. No test will ever convince me otherwise!"

"Listen, Adam, this is no time to get overemotional. We've got to sit down and plan our defense."

Adam stared at West. "What defense? You make me sound like I'm on trial here. I love Amy. I don't give a damn about what may or may not have happened over ten years ago. She's my daughter and nothing is going to change that."

"It's my feeling that the mother may go after custody of Amy."

Adam grimaced. It felt as if a stake had been driven into his heart. He glanced out to sea. But the blue-green water only reminded him of certain eyes, and certain eyes reminded him of certain lips...

He shuddered and turned his tortured eyes back to Wes. "Can she take Amy away from me?"

"Honestly? I don't know. What I do know is that you'd better talk to Amy at once. As soon as the papers get hold of this story, there's no telling what's going to happen."

Adam turned back to the ocean. At the bottom of the cliff, giant waves lashed against the rugged coastline. Frothy brown foam replaced the usual white. Blue-green water was beginning to turn black with oil. Adam felt as if everything was closing in on him.

He stooped to pick up a limestone rock and threw it with a powerful thrust of his arm. The rock spun through the air and fell to the rocks below before splintering into a hundred tiny pieces.

Oh, Janette. Her name was an anguished cry, ripping away from some deep private part of him. Wasn't stealing my heart enough for you? Must you also take my daughter?

CHAPTER NINE

AMY LAY FACEDOWN on her bed, her phone pinned to her ear, the cord wrapped around her fingers. She swung her crossed legs back and forth in midair. She'd been talking nonstop to her friend, Tammy, for nearly an hour.

Watching her with a heavy heart, Adam leaned against the doorjamb, his arms folded across his chest. He remembered another time he'd stood in this very doorway faced with the impossible chore of having to tell her that her mother had died. On that long-ago day, he'd thought that nothing could be more difficult than having to explain a mother's death to a child.

He'd been wrong.

Amy glanced over her shoulder. "I've got to go," she said into the mouthpiece, holding the receiver with both hands. "Daddy looks like he's on the warpath." She quickly hung up and rolled over on her back.

"I am not on the warpath," Adam said, walking into her room and checking over the fragile-looking chair by her bed before trusting it to hold his weight.

Amy sat up. She was dressed in an oversized pink T-shirt that reached down to her knees. Her long blond hair, still wet from her shower, hung loosely down her back. She regarded him thoughtfully, eyes dark with worry.

Her father had barely spoken all evening. During dinner, he'd listened attentively as she related what she'd done at school that day, but he'd offered little comment and made no attempt to initiate a discussion of sports or current affairs. She knew her father was concerned about the oil spill. She could see the worry on his face as he watched the channel seven special on the subject. During dinner, the beeper he wore in his pocket had gone off twice, sending him racing to the phone, and coming back looking more worried than before. It wasn't until she had looked up and spotted her father by her door that she suspected there might be another reason for him to look so concerned.

With this scary thought, she picked up one of the stuffed animals from the foot of her bed and hugged it tightly to her chest. It was a honey-colored bear wearing a blue sailor hat.

Watching her, Adam leaned forward, his hands clasped between his knees. Amy had always loved stuffed animals. During her younger years, she had often consoled herself by taking them to bed with her, to school, everywhere that seemed the least bit unfamiliar or frightening. In recent years, the animals were more decorative than useful. Seeing Amy revert to babyish ways disturbed him. Obviously, she sensed something was wrong. Carolyn had always said he did a lousy job of keeping his feelings hidden.

"I have to talk to you about something important," he began. No sooner had he said this when Amy burst into tears.

Alarmed, Adam moved from the chair to the bed and wrapped his arms around her. "Hey, there, sport. What's this?"

Holding her close, he rocked her back and forth until her cries became muffled sobs. "Has someone talked to you?" he asked in sudden alarm. He reached into his pocket for a handkerchief and gently wiped the tears from her cheeks. He fervently hoped it wasn't Janette, although as far as he knew, there was no one else who knew the results of the test, except Wes. Still, he didn't want to believe that Janette would speak to Amy behind his back.

"I'm going to die, aren't I?" Amy sobbed.

Adam's hand froze on her cheek. "What? Where did you get that idea?"

Amy pulled back and buried her face in the furry coat of the stuffed bear she held. "The tests..."

Why hadn't he realized it before? How stupid of him! Carolyn had undergone numerous tests. It would only be natural for Amy to jump to the conclusion that all medical tests related in some way to a serious illness.

He pushed his handkerchief into his pants pocket and pulled his young daughter into his arms. "You're not going to die. There's nothing wrong with you."

She looked at him, her eyes green pools that tugged at his insides. There was so much love and trust in those eyes, and at the moment he felt so undeserving of it. He had to be honest with her. As honest as he could possibly be without revealing how very frightened he was of losing her.

"Those tests had nothing to do with your heart," he continued, hoping, praying that inspiration would strike and he could find the right words for what he must tell her. But as he talked aimlessly about love and how much joy Amy had brought to everyone who knew her, he became increasingly aware that no right words existed.

He cupped her hands in his. "The day you were born, there was a lot of confusion at the hospital. Your mother..." He felt a stabbing pain that nearly cut him in two. Carolyn wasn't Amy's mother!

With great effort he began again. "Do you remember me telling you how your...mother's heart stopped beating after you were born?"

Amy nodded. "You said that the doctors had to work very hard to save her."

"That's right. What I didn't know was that another woman was having her baby at the same time. There was a lot of confusion that day and everything got mixed up..." His voice trailed off. He fought for control. If he could just hang on...

"You're hurting me, Daddy," Amy whispered, frightened by the look on his face.

Blinking, Adam realized how hard he was squeezing the precious small hands. Releasing his hold, he apologized. "I didn't mean to hurt you, baby." God, never that. "As I was saying, everything got mixed up." He paused, then forced himself to continue. "We didn't know this at the time, but the tests that you took last week prove that...that I'm not your real daddy."

Amy struggled to understand everything her father was saying to her. It was so difficult. He kept stopping and starting. But this final statement was the most puzzling of all. How could he not be her real father? Why was he saying these things to her? Did it mean he didn't love her?

She clutched her bear closer, looking at her father through stricken eyes. "Does this mean I can't live with you anymore?"

Adam touched his daughter's flushed cheek. "Oh, sweetie. I am going to try as hard as I can to make certain you always live with me."

Amy studied her father's face. He didn't look angry; he looked sad. "Who is my real daddy?" she asked.

"I don't know, sweetie," he said helplessly, "I don't know."

Amy considered this for a moment. "Didn't Mommy tell you?"

He stared at her in bewilderment for a moment before realizing that she was referring to Carolyn. Oh, God, he hadn't told her everything. "Amy, your mother—she wasn't your real mother..."

Amy's lowered lip quivered and for a moment it looked as if she was going to cry again. She gave him a heart-wrenching look. "Do you know who my real mommy is?"

He nodded. He knew, oh, God, he knew. But it never occurred to him that she would ask for the name. He considered not telling her, but what good would that do? She would know in a day or two anyway, as soon as the story hit the newspaper. "Jan... Miss Taylor is your real mother."

Amy's eyes widened in surprise, her lashes still damp with tears. "Are you... are you sure?"

Adam nodded. "I'm sure."

Janette was her mother! She liked Janette. She was pretty and kind and Amy always felt all happy and giggly inside whenever they were together. But she didn't want to leave her daddy. "Is she going to make me live with her?"

"No!"

The vehemence in his voice surprised them both. Adam leaned his head next to hers and smoothed down her hair with his hand. "No matter what happens, sport, just remember you're always going to be my little girl."

Amy threw her arms around his neck. "Oh, Daddy, I don't want anyone to take me away."

"No one is going to," Adam promised. He couldn't lose her, not his Amy, not his beautiful darling little Amy. He didn't care about test results. Maybe he wasn't her father in the biological sense, but he'd earned the right to be her father by the sheer act of taking care of her minute by minute, hour by hour, day by day since the day she was born. And, by God, he wasn't going to let anyone, not anyone, take her away from him.

THE WIND HAD PICKED UP during the night, carrying with it the sickly-sweet fumes of oil. Volunteers who had worked along the beach all through the long dark night and early-morning hours had complained of headaches and nausea. By the time Adam arrived, the ranks had thinned considerably, many of the workers having been transported to nearby hospitals or sent home. Not only was Adam faced with the need to recruit more workers, he had to find a way to protect the volunteers who remained from the dangerous fumes.

Adam drove back to his office and explained the situation to his secretary. "Do you think you can round up gas masks?" he asked. "We need at least a couple thousand."

Miss Steele never raised as much as an eyebrow. "If you recall, sir, I located fifty thousand raincoats in less than two hours in sunny California. Two thousand gas masks should be a breeze.''

Adam grinned. ''The unsinkable Miss Steele to the rescue,'' he teased. ''By the way, we could use some more shovels. A couple hundred should do it.''

''No problem.'' Miss Steele turned and reached for the phone. Adam hurried to his office to begin calling every service organization listed in the phone book. They needed manpower and they needed it fast! Miss Steele didn't believe in making requests; she issued orders. For that reason, Adam handled the volunteers himself.

In no time at all he had enough workers to see him through the next few crucial days.

Elbows on his desk, he dropped his weary head into his hands. He tried to decide which would benefit him more, a catnap or a strong cup of coffee.

At first he thought he imagined her voice, wafting to him through the fog in his brain. But as soon as he heard his name again, he glanced up and found himself face-to-face with Janette.

In a flash, he forgot about his need for sleep, he forgot his need for coffee. The sun suddenly filled every corner of the room. For a moment he forgot everything that had occurred between them and allowed himself the luxury of enjoying her presence.

Janette was shocked by his appearance. His face was drawn, and dark shadows skirted his weary eyes. She shouldn't have come. He had enough on his mind. ''I'm . . . sorry,'' she stammered. ''Your secretary was away from her desk . . . I can see this isn't a good time to talk.'' Her lawyer had warned her against talking to Adam at all, but she needed so desperately to see him, to make him understand that she wasn't some monster who was trying to make his life hell.

Shocked that he had momentarily dismissed the danger she posed, he glared at her. "What do you want?" he asked sharply.

"Can't we discuss this reasonably?" she asked.

He looked at her in surprise. "What do you expect from me? Not only do you feign romantic interest in me, but you've robbed me of the one link I had to my dead wife. Do you know?" he continued, his voice breaking. "Can you even imagine how it feels knowing that Amy isn't Carolyn's? That was the only thing I had to hold onto after Carolyn died. The fact that I had her daughter to love and to raise, a daughter who carried her genes . . ."

Janette didn't want to hear about Carolyn. It was enough living with her own pain without having to feel guilty for robbing a dead woman. Didn't he know, couldn't he even guess how devastatingly difficult this situation was for her? Did he even care? She turned away, but he was soon at her side. Grabbing her arm, he whirled her around to face him.

Gasping in surprise, she stared into his dark stormy face. "I'll tell you what it's like," he shouted. "It's like losing Carolyn all over again. Worse!"

"And how do you think it feels for me?" she shouted back, refusing to be intimidated. "I've missed over ten years of my daughter's life!" Resenting the look he gave her that said he blamed her for the whole mess, she lashed out blindly. "Do you know what it's like to go home from a hospital with empty arms? To spend every day, every night for over ten years, mourning a child?"

It all came back to her, the Christmases she'd walked past the toy stores, the countless times she'd watched children at play. An unspeakable anger swelled up inside. Not knowing who to blame for the loss of her child, she blamed Adam. Blamed him for not seeing her side. She pounded on his muscular chest with angry fists. A blow for each year that Amy had been denied her.

Adam grabbed her fists and gripped her in his iron-strong arms; he held her close until she slumped against him, her emotions spent.

He was so aware of her nearness, he stopped breathing. His chest filled with a tightness as his air-starved lungs protested. Inhaling, his nostrils filled with the delicate fragrance of her perfume, and his earlier anger faded away like mist. An unspeakable sadness took its place. She spoke of empty arms and he knew about that. She spoke of mourning and he knew about that, too.

She lifted her head and regarded him with tear-filled eyes and his heart nearly stopped. The tears intensified the green and he realized suddenly, why she had always looked vaguely familiar to him. She had Amy's eyes, or rather Amy had hers. To look into her eyes was to acknowledge the honest pain within their depths. He could see she was hurting as much as it was possible to hurt. Hurting every bit as much as he was.

He battled a myriad of emotions. He felt for her and he knew that could be dangerous. She was a threat to his family, to his beloved Amy, to everything he held dear. He released her with a tortured curse. Spinning on his heel, he moved toward the window. He mustn't look at her, mustn't be swayed by her tempting sweet fragrance. . . .

Still reeling from being in his arms, Janette grabbed the back of a chair for support. "I want you to know that I never feigned my feelings for you." The words, torn from a shattered heart, were cushioned in a thick hoarse voice. "I want you to believe that. It's true I had my suspicions about Amy. But it all seemed like an impossible dream. Everyone told me I was crazy and I believed it. I believed it because it was easier than having to face the horror of knowing that my child had been taken from me."

The pain in her voice touched him and he longed to take her in his arms and comfort her. But he couldn't afford to sympathize with her, not when the memory of her kiss was still so fresh in his mind. He couldn't for Amy's sake. He didn't dare.

"Adam, please, I want only what's best for Amy."

Adam whirled around to face her. "I'll tell you what's best for her. To stay with me, the only father she's ever known. To continue living in the house she's lived in all her life. That's what's best!"

"So what do you expect me to do, Adam? Walk away from her? Pretend she doesn't exist? Forget that I gave birth to her?"

He stared at her in uncertainty. "If it's best for her..."

"We don't know that. How do you think she's going to feel when she learns that her own mother turned her back on her and walked away?"

"I'll make her understand that it was the best thing for you to do."

Janette felt stricken. "Is that what you think? That my staying away from her is best for her?"

"Damn it, Janette! Don't put words in my mouth. Three years ago, she lost the only mother she ever knew. Her biggest fear is that she will lose me, too. Can't you understand what this is going to do to her?''

Janette did understand. She also had firsthand knowledge of what it was like to be abandoned. Her mother had walked out of her life when she was a child and had never looked back. And her father... Maybe her father hadn't abandoned her physically but he certainly had emotionally. In some strange way that abandonment hurt more than her mother's desertion. It hurt a lot. It still hurt. "I can't just walk away from her," she whispered. "I can't!''

Feeling more depressed than she had ever felt in her life, she drove home, Adam's hurtful angry words ringing in her ears. How could he ask her to forget Amy? How could he ask the impossible of her?

LATER THAT AFTERNOON, Janette found Stella walking along the beach in the back of the house. Dressed in a gaudy orange-and-purple outfit with Baghdad legs and sheer full sleeves, Stella pointed to a dead halibut that had washed ashore.

Janette examined the halibut. It was hard to tell by appearances why the fish had died, but it wasn't hard to guess the reason. Her nose wrinkled in distaste at the smell of oil fumes that permeated the entire beach area.

Stella tried to pick up a clump of tarry seaweed with a stick. "It's going to take weeks, months maybe to get things back to normal.''

Janette glanced around her. Black globs of oil clung to the outer rocks of the tidal pools, and floated on the surface, the iridescent colors creating a strange shimmering beauty that belied the danger it posed.

Janette shuddered. She wondered if anything would ever be normal again.

VIRGINIA STARED at her son-in-law in stunned disbelief. "What did you say?"

Adam hesitated. He'd dreaded telling Virginia that he was not Amy's father. He'd thought of every possible way of breaking it to her gently, but in the end he thought it best for all concerned if he just said it outright. "Amy is not my daughter."

Virginia's eyes hardened behind a mask of resistance. "I don't believe that for a minute, Adam. Is this your idea of a joke?"

"You know me better than that, Virginia," he said sharply. He immediately regretted losing his temper. This was going to hurt Virginia, too. He softened his voice. "Amy and I were tested genetically. The tests proved that Amy could not be my child."

"I don't believe it," she repeated. Her sharp gray eyes impaled him. "This is insane, Adam. Certainly you don't think that Carolyn was unfaithful to you?"

Adam shook his head in sad resignation. Even that would have been easier to bear. "The child that Carolyn gave birth to was stillborn. Amy was switched with our baby. She's not ours."

"This is ridiculous," Virginia said. "I refuse to believe such poppycock." Anxiously, she searched Adam's face. He looked like hell. He hadn't looked this bad since those first few days following Carolyn's death. "Have you been drinking?"

Adam shook his head. "Don't make this any more difficult than it already is," he pleaded. "There's a good possibility that Amy's real mother will try to obtain custody."

Virginia's mouth dropped open. Adam wasn't kidding. Sickened by the thought of losing Amy, she struggled for control. "Amy's *real* mother?" The question came out in a gasping rasp that hardly sounded human. She felt a sudden rage toward her son-in-law. What was the matter with him? Why was he letting this happen to them? Why wasn't he protecting Carolyn's interest? Amy was her grandchild. Nothing or no one would ever convince her otherwise.

"I guess it's only fair that you know the rest," Adam continued. "Janette Taylor is Amy's real mother."

Virginia stiffened. Just hearing that woman's name made her cringe. She knew from the first moment she met the woman that there was something unnatural in the way she fawned over Amy. Virginia thought it odd from the beginning that a perfect stranger would be so fond of a child she hardly knew. It was a ploy; the whole thing was a ploy. A ploy to get Adam, perhaps? Or was Amy the target? One way or another Virginia intended to find out.

Adam was surprised by Virginia's surprisingly calm reaction to this last piece of information, and more than a bit worried. He had expected a stronger reaction from her. At the very least, he expected one of her emotional outbursts. Even one of her three-day crying jags would have been preferable to the stoic silence that followed his disclosure.

"I know this is a shock, Virginia. It was to me. I still can't believe it."

Virginia gave him a wilted look. If he felt guilty, it was too bad. She remembered the look on his face the night he took that woman, Janette Taylor, to dinner. She remembered and she hated him for it. How dare he allow himself to become hoodwinked by some woman just because he found her attractive? How dare he let some stranger try to fill her dear Carolyn's place?

Carolyn was Amy's mother; nothing or no one was ever going to change that.

AT FIRST Janette didn't recognize the woman on her front porch, who was dressed in a floral print dress, a blue pillbox hat perched precariously upon tightly curled gray hair. Despite the heat the woman wore white gloves. She appeared, Janette thought, to be firmly stuck in some sort of fifties time warp.

"I'm Virginia Spencer," the woman said stiffly. "Amy Blake's grandmother."

"Of course! Won't you come in, Mrs. Spencer?" Janette held the door open for the woman and ushered her into the living room.

"Would you like some lemonade, Mrs. Spencer?"

"No, thank you. What I came to say won't take long. I don't know what your little ploy is, Miss Taylor, but I can assure you it's not going to work."

Janette bit back the harsh words that sprung to her lips. As much as she disliked the woman, she knew that Virginia Spencer had to be hurting, too. "I can assure you this is no ploy."

"Oh, really? You must think I'm awfully stupid. I saw how you tried to worm your way into Amy's good graces. Why? So that you could hook Adam around your little finger?"

"Adam has nothing to do with Amy..."

"He has everything to do with her. He's her father." Virginia peeled off a glove. "I saw how your face lit up when his name was mentioned that day I brought Amy to your office. You may fool Adam, but you don't fool me."

"I have proof that Amy is my child," Janette said.

"I don't need your so-called proof," Virginia snapped, shaking her glove in Janette's face. "I know inside that Amy is my grandchild." Her voice broke and for an instant, her face reflected such despair that Janette forgot her resentment toward the woman.

"You'll always be Amy's grandmother," Janette assured her. "Just as Adam will always be Amy's father." Some things could not be defined by law.

"And you, Miss Taylor, will never be Amy's mother! Not while I have a breath left!"

Upon making her vow, Virginia turned and stormed out the front door. After the woman had driven away, Janette crumpled into a chair. She could hardly blame the woman for being upset. Lord, where would it all end?

"Is the dragon lady gone?" Stella asked, peering into the room. "I couldn't help but overhear."

Janette nodded. "Do you believe her? She accused me of making this whole thing up so that I could hook Adam. Damn it, Stella, I thought Adam and I had something going. We *did* have something going. He actually told me he was falling in love with me." She flinched as a squeezing pain shot through her heart. "If it wasn't for this business with Amy, who knows how far things would have gone?"

"Are you in love with him?" Stella asked.

Janette closed her eyes. "All I know is that it hurts when I look into his eyes and see suspicion and hate." What she didn't say—couldn't say—was that it hurt like hell. It hurt so much that at times she thought she would die. "Oh, Stella, what am I going to do? Merv wants me to file for custody."

"What do you want to do?"

Janette gave a helpless shrug. She didn't know how to answer Stella. All she knew for sure was that now that she had found her little girl, she could never walk away.

CHAPTER TEN

THE LIVING MASTERS PAGEANT opened to a full house, and Janette felt a sense of relief. With so much emptiness in her life, it was gratifying to see the pageant grounds filled to capacity. She only wished so many of the patrons weren't couples who were obviously in love.

Seeing love in bloom only made her own situation that much more difficult to bear. She watched a couple snatch a kiss as they stood in the ticket line and her tightly wound emotions began to unravel. Upon seeing a young man lift his girlfriend off the ground and whirl her around playfully, Janette was forced to rush to her office in tears.

Angry with herself, she walked around her office trying to gain control. Reminding herself that it was opening night and there was no time to brood, she took a deep breath, touched up her makeup and marched out to the amphitheater. She parked herself in her usual spot in the audience and began making notes on a yellow legal pad.

Janette monitored the audience's reaction as one by one each tableau unfolded on stage. For the most part the crowd's response was positive; the audience broke into spontaneous applause following the *Wild Wild West* scene, and laughed uproariously when five-year-old Susie Watkins quickly adjusted her underpants during her performance.

But Janette's father's painting *The Fisherman,* was received poorly, eliciting only polite applause as the curtains closed and the stage grew dark.

The following morning, Janette sat at her desk reading the reviews in various newspapers, and fuming.

"I don't know what you're complaining about," Pat said. "These are great reviews. The best we've ever had. Even the *Reporter's* critic was generous in his adjectives. I mean we're talking about a man who described the *Phantom of the Opera* as a warmed-over soap opera. Come on, the guy's a jerk. But even he knew enough to use words like *insightful* and *tempestuous* in describing our show. Not bad."

Janette was not so easily swayed. "He said my father's painting was a bland combination of sentiment and cheap nostalgia. Listen to this. 'One has to wonder what Cameron Taylor was thinking about when he painted this dull and lifeless painting. It would be more interesting to know why his daughter bothered to stage it.'"

Pat was undaunted. "Considering the source, I'd say that's a great review."

Janette folded the paper. "The truth is the painting does look dull and lifeless. Maybe the lighting is too mute, do you suppose?" She checked the notes she'd made the previous night, but there was no clue why the painting hadn't produced the right effect and it was driving her crazy. She never could understand Cameron Taylor, the father, but she'd always been proud of her aesthetic understanding of Cameron Taylor, the artist. Now it appeared she'd been fooling herself. She didn't even understand Cameron Taylor, the artist.

She was still fuming over the reviews when Merv stopped by. "Do you still want to sue the hospital?" he asked.

She looked at him in surprise. "You know I do."

He drew up a chair and sat down with his open attaché case on his lap. "It could be tricky. I talked with the firm representing the hospital. Needless to say, the hospital has retained some sharp attorneys. They pointed out that your original intent was to put the baby up for adoption."

Janette frowned. "That was my father's intent. I always planned to keep my baby."

"Nevertheless, it's a matter of record that you met with various adoption agencies during the months preceding the birth."

Janette inhaled. "What possible difference does it make whether I planned to keep my baby or not? The hospital neglected to protect my child."

"If they can prove that your intention was to put your child up for adoption, they can claim that you suffered no damages from the mix-up."

Janette's face paled in astonishment. "I don't believe this. Their negligence deprived me of my baby!"

Merv reached over and patted her arm. "I know, Janette. I know."

She jumped to her feet. "Don't patronize me, Merv. What they did was inexcusable."

Merv nodded. "When we spoke last, you were undecided as to whether or not to fight for custody."

She nodded wearily. "I still am. I want my little girl so much it hurts." Hurts, God, that was the least of it. "But...she loves her father so very much. If I take her away from him, she would probably end up hating me. I don't know what to do."

"The point is we may not have a choice."

"What?"

"If you make no effort to obtain custody of Amy, the hospital's defense that you never meant to keep the child could hold up. The court might be persuaded to believe that you had no interest in raising Amy almost eleven years ago, and you have no interest at present. Since Amy is lucky enough to have landed in a good home, the court might decide that no real damage resulted."

"That's the most ridiculous thing I've ever heard!" she stormed. "What you're saying is I can't go after the hospital unless I seek custody."

"I'm just calling it as I see it," Merv said.

"But can't we prove that it's not in Amy's best interest to be uprooted from her home? Merv, I'm telling you there's no better father than Adam. Amy adores him. It would kill her to be taken away from him."

"But what if something happens to her father? What then? Have you thought of that? Who would be responsible for her upbringing?"

Janette sank into her chair. As far as she knew, the only living relative Amy had was her grandmother. The very thought of Virginia Spencer raising Amy made her feel ill. "What you're saying is that it might not be in Amy's best interest for me to leave things as they stand."

"Let's just say that the question might be raised in court."

"So it's not only Amy's welfare that's at issue. You're saying that if I want to go after the hospital, I have to fight for custody."

"I'm sorry, Janette. But I have to be honest with you. There's no sense in going after the hospital if we don't have a chance of winning our case."

She clenched her hands together, her mind a whirlwind. Only one thing was clear. There was no way she could let the hospital off the hook. Not after what they'd done to her. And now that Merv had brought up the question of Amy's care should something happen to Adam, there was yet one more thing to consider. "All right," she said thickly. "Do whatever you think has to be done."

It was a hard decision to make, and the need to see Adam and explain why she had to take him to court was so strong, that she could hardly sleep that night.

She rose at the crack of dawn to the sound of crying seagulls. She dressed in jeans and a sweater, then brushed her hair until it fell in soft waves around her face.

After reinforcing herself with black coffee, she drove to Adam's office only to be told by his secretary that Adam would be spending the day at Tabor's Point.

Janette hesitated only a moment before making her decision. She had to find Adam before he heard of the custody suit from his attorney. Or worse yet, the newspapers.

Tabor Beach was mobbed when she arrived. She asked several officials wearing red jackets emblazoned with Ashton Tex's logo if they had seen Adam. She followed several false leads before she was finally directed toward a canopied area away from the crowd.

She crossed the parking lot, searching for his dark head. As soon as she picked him out, her pulse raced. Her steps faltered. Maybe she had made a mistake in coming. He would never listen to her. Merv was right. This was a job for her lawyer. But something kept her riveted in place, watching him with a heart full of longing and need.

Adam was too busy battling a hysterical pelican to notice her. The pelican, flapping its wings in a tub of water, squawked angrily.

Suddenly realizing the seriousness of Adam's plight, she hurried to his side. Without a moment's hesitation she wrapped her hands around the bird's thrashing body, and spoke to it in a soft lulling voice. Exhausted, the pelican calmed under her soothing touch, its squawks turning into pitiful, heartrending caws.

Surprised by Janette's unexpected arrival, Adam stepped back. But his surprise soon turned to admiration when the bird grew calm and finally downright docile beneath her touch. Janette had a tranquilizing effect on the pelican that couldn't be denied. This struck him as something of a miracle since her effect on him was anything but tranquilizing.

The lovely eyes that briefly met his were more green than usual, and so bright that at first he thought they were filled with tears. But a closer look revealed that there were no tears in her eyes; there was only sadness, a sadness so deep that it reached inside him and wilted his heart. Not the eyes, he thought, his gaze dropping down to encompass her lips, mustn't look at the eyes.

Her lips quivered slightly and parted so invitingly he felt his own lips grow fuller in response. Not the lips, he thought, mustn't look at the lips. Nor the soft round hips or the jean-clad legs. The perfect forehead, yes that was safe. It was shadowed in concentration and traces of windblown hair. If only he didn't remember touching that forehead . . .

Shattered. That's how he felt. Angry for allowing himself to be affected by her, he greeted her brusquely. "What the hell are you doing here?"

She ignored his question, partly because she was afraid if they wasted time arguing, the bird would become agitated again. She could feel the bird trembling beneath her touch. "I'll hold him while you scrub," she offered. Keeping one hand on the bird, she slipped her handbag down her arm, and tucked it beneath the work station. Without fear or hesitation, she wrapped both hands around the frightened bird once again, and spoke to it in a soothing voice.

Much to Adam's astonishment, the bird appeared to be almost asleep. Shaking his head, he picked up a bottle of liquid detergent and poured a portion onto the bird's back. With gentle circular strokes of his fingers, he worked the soap into the blackened feathers.

"You're all right, little fellow," Janette cooed softly to the bird. "Just hold on."

After Adam had worked up a thick lather, she helped him transport the bird to a tub of fresh water. While they worked at rinsing off the soap, a tall teenager with a toothy grin emptied the first soapy tub and refilled it with fresh water.

"How's it going, Sandy?" Adam called.

The boy shrugged. "We've lost seventy-five birds today."

Adam frowned. The twenty-five they had lost the day before had been bad enough. Gritting his teeth, he plunged a plastic cup into the tub and dribbled a cupful of clean rinse water over the bird's back.

After thoroughly rinsing off the soap, he inspected the feathers. Janette watched his firm square hands as he carefully lifted a wing and exposed a pocket of oil. "They tell me it could take as many as fifteen latherings before a bird comes clean," he said grimly.

Janette glanced at his strong firm profile. "I had no idea it was such a job." The bird seemed to have regained its second wind and her arms began to ache from struggling to keep a hold on its beak. The bird showed amazing strength, despite its weakened state. "There, there, now. Calm down. That's a boy."

She held the beak shut while Adam transported the bird to yet another tub of fresh water. His strong arms brushed against hers as they worked side by side, their heads almost touching. Adam began the process all over again, lathering the body with firm but surprisingly gentle hands while she held onto the trembling bird and spoke in a soft soothing voice. She only hoped that Adam would think that the quiver in her voice was due to the strain of holding down the bird, and would never guess how much she was affected by his nearness.

"After we're done here," Adam said, pausing to brush the hair from his forehead with his arm, "the bird will be banded and held for a few days for observation. My guess is that this fellow will be released by the end of the week."

"That's good news." Janette lifted her eyes to meet his and for a moment their gazes held.

Not the eyes, Adam thought letting his gaze settle on a tiny dab of soapsuds that had settled on her nose. Not the nose...

Not the way he kissed her, Janette cautioned herself; she mustn't remember the kisses or the way they danced beneath the moon or the touch of his hands upon her flesh. She dare not remember any of the things they'd shared in the past. She dare not but she did.

The pelican let out a squawk and Adam shifted his gaze to the hapless bird and began the lathering process all over again.

She and Adam worked side by side, as naturally as two dance partners who had practiced synchronizing their body movements for years. He leaned into her; she pressed against him and it seemed the most natural thing in the world to do. Their hands touched, their arms touched and sometimes even their hearts touched.

He looked at her, and feeling her cheeks grow warm she lowered her lids. Regaining control of her senses, she looked back at him and this time he was the one to avert his gaze.

When at last they finished cleaning the pelican, they turned him over to the next station where the bird would be tube-fed a high protein liquid that would clean out any ingested oil.

Adam reached into a box for a seagull. The box was small enough to keep the bird from preening and possibly ingesting more oil. As soon as Adam lifted the bird to the table, it fought a valiant battle and finally surrendered to exhaustion. Thinking the bird had died, Janette cried out.

"It's all right," Adam said soothingly. "He's exhausted and probably in shock."

"Seagulls are my favorite birds," Janette explained, stroking the bird's wet feathers with a finger. The entire side of the bird was covered in oil, along with its feet and beak.

Adam lifted a dark eyebrow, glancing at her askance and feeling his heart leap as flashing blue-green eyes met his. "Most people consider them nothing but scavengers."

"They are scavengers. Without them, our beaches would be a mess." The seagull let out a tiny mew sound, and Janette stroked its head. "Did you know that seagulls recognize people by their faces?"

Adam gave her a doubtful look. "No, I didn't. Are you sure? I didn't think they were that smart."

"You'd be surprised. Recently I read scientists were doing a study on seagulls and were forced to wear Elvis Presley masks so as not to be attacked later."

Adam burst out laughing. "If Elvis Presley really is alive, I hope he has the good sense to stay away from the beach."

Adam's arms brushed against hers, and Janette, momentarily distracted by the feel of him, lost her grip on the seagull. The bird darted its head forward, pecking her on the back of the hand.

"Ouch!" She drew her injured hand back and glanced at the red mark that was already beginning to swell.

Adam passed the bird to Sandy who'd run over when Janette cried out. Adam turned and quickly reached for Janette's hand. "Let me put something on that," he said. Grabbing the first-aid kit, he found a tube of ointment and unscrewed the cap.

"It's all right," Janette said.

Ignoring her protests, he examined the small welt on her hand carefully. "Wild birds can carry all sorts of diseases." He gently smoothed ointment on her skin, looking deep into her eyes as he worked. "That should do it,'' he said softly, holding her hand longer than necessary, holding her gaze far longer than that.

"Special delivery,'' Sandy announced from behind them. The skinny youth placed a cardboard box on their table and stepped away.

Adam opened the box and together they carefully lifted out a seagull that was wrapped in an oil-stained towel. By the way the bird thrashed frantically in the water it was evident that it was in better shape than the other birds had been. It flew up at Adam's shoulder, catching his cheek with the tip of a frantic claw. Adam backed away and the bird flew awkwardly over his head, its oil-soaked wing causing it to land nearby with a dull thud.

Adam cornered the bird, and Janette ran to help him. Together they lifted the bird back to the table. After peering inside the bird's mouth, Adam realized it might be in more danger than he'd first thought. The bird had evidently done a lot of preening and the inside of its mouth was black with oil. "Let me have a Q-Tip,'' he said.

Janette held the bird steady while Adam cleaned out its beak. "How much oil can a bird swallow without harm?''

"Not very much,'' Adam answered. "The gasoline in crude oil can damage the liver and kidneys. The crude oil itself can cause anemia. It's the red blood cells that carry oxygen through the body. For a diving bird, who must hold its breath to feed, damage to these cells can be fatal.''

Janette was impressed with Adam's knowledge of birds. For the rest of the day, she and Adam worked side by side, exchanging information and, to relieve the pressure, making up silly bird jokes. Considering the smoldering emotions that flowed between them, she thought they worked well together. Progress was slow and sometimes their efforts met with disaster. One bird succumbed during its bath, and Janette wanted to cry as the tiny body was reboxed and carried away.

"Poor little guy," she whispered, battling for composure.

"I know how you feel," Adam said, slipping his arm around her shoulder. The tears froze in place and for a moment, so did her entire body. Adam's gaze dropped to her lips and she thought he was going to kiss her. Instead, he released her abruptly and attacked the oil on the next bird with grim determination. Disappointed, she could hardly keep her mind on her job and the bird, a grebe that fortunately only had a spot of oil on the tip of one of its wings, flew out of her hands before it could be banded, and took to the sky.

They lost no more birds, and managed to clean a dozen or so seagulls without further mishap. They were both more than ready to call it a day when two volunteers arrived to take over their station.

Adam led Janette toward the tubs that had been set up for the workers to clean up in. A cold breeze blew off the ocean, cutting through her wet sweater and damp jeans, and whipping her hair around her face. She rubbed her hands and arms with the special soap that had been provided to clean off the black tar stains, and plunged her arms up to their elbows into the hot soapy water. After washing her arms and face, she wiped herself with a clean towel.

"Let's get something to eat," Adam suggested, wiping his neck dry. He nodded toward the catering trucks that were parked fairly close. "The line doesn't look too bad."

"Good idea," she said. "I'm starved." She was also freezing. She'd give anything for a hot bowl of soup or a cup of coffee. She'd give anything to have him wrap her in his arms. No, what she wanted him to do was to complete the kiss that had stretched between them earlier.

Adam, seeing her shiver, grabbed a blanket from one of the empty cots that had been set up for volunteers. "Here," he said, draping the blanket around her shoulders. He studied her pale face and thought how vulnerable she looked. Not the face . . .

She gratefully pulled the blanket around her. "Thanks," she said, forcing a smile, and trying for all the world not to think about how much warmer his arms would feel around her. She mustn't think of his arms . . .

After she and Adam gathered up bowls of steaming hot chili and cornbread, they sat at a picnic bench next to a middle-aged couple, who greeted them with a silent nod. No one felt like talking much. It had been a difficult day, both emotionally and physically.

She and Adam said nothing as they ate. Although she kept her eyes on her bowl, she was aware of his every move.

He steadfastly refused to look at her as he ate, but he was aware of every breath she took, imagined that he could have counted her heartbeats had he tried.

"I really have to go," she said at last, glancing at the sun that hovered above the horizon. She would have to hurry if she was going to shower and change before the night's performance.

He stood. "I'll walk you to your car."

Janette instinctively wanted to protest. The rapport that had flowed between them while they'd worked on the birds had been replaced by detachment. Hands that had readily touched hers earlier now were thrust into the pockets of his jacket as if touching her was to be avoided at all costs. Adam's brusque no-nonsense voice only confirmed her suspicion. Disheartened, she started toward her car, her head down against the wind.

Falling in step by her side, Adam said nothing until they reached the parking lot. "Thanks for your help," he said thickly, resting an elbow on the roof of her car.

"You don't have to thank me." She glanced over his shoulder. "All this, the beach, the sky, the ocean, belongs to us all. It's everyone's responsibility to protect it." She smiled. "Besides, I have a special fondness for birds."

"From what I saw today, I would say the feeling was mutual." He glanced toward the ocean, his eyes riveted on the crippled tanker. Silhouetted by the setting sun, the tanker lay half-hidden behind a golden mist. "You never did tell me why you came looking for me."

Janette swallowed. For a few short hours they had met on neutral ground. She resisted leaving the safe haven that had settled between them. "It's been a hard day. We can talk later..."

"No!" His eyes were daggers pinning her to the side of her car. "I want to know why you came to see me. If it's about Amy, I need to know."

She swallowed wearily, knowing he was not going to settle for any delaying tactics. "My lawyer feels that the only way we can effectively bring suit against the hospital is if I file for custody of Amy."

"Over my dead body!" Adam exploded. He looked at her incredulously. "You can't take a child away from her home."

"I don't want to do anything that's going to hurt Amy!" Janette cried. "But I have no choice."

Adam's face grew dark. "You have a choice. You can drop the lawsuit." He glanced at her in suspicion. "Or is it the money you're after?"

What little hope she'd had that they could reach an amicable agreement died. "Money has nothing to do with it!"

He looked at her sharply. "If it's not money, then what?"

"They took my baby," she whispered hoarsely, astonished that he would have to ask. Angry at him, angry at whoever was responsible for the entire mess, she lashed out. "Someone, somewhere is going to pay for what they did to me."

Unable to bear the rage and bitterness in her face, Adam glanced at the ground. It wasn't hard to imagine how she felt. But dammit, Amy had to come first. He lifted his head. "Janette...I wish I knew what to say to you. I feel for you. I don't know what I would do if the tables were turned. I don't blame you one bit for being angry. But to put a child's life in turmoil because of a need to seek revenge is insane."

He reached out to touch her, but she backed away. She turned and grabbed the handle of the car door. Stopping, she looked back at him. She wondered if he really knew how she felt. "They took your baby, too," she cried. "Yours and Carolyn's."

In a daze, his heart turned to stone, Adam watched her drive off. In the weeks since Janette first told him about her suspicions, he had been so concerned about Amy, he'd never considered anything else. Not once had he thought about the other child. And now that he did, his pain was all that much more difficult to bear.

For the remainder of the night, he stoically supervised the cleanup along the beach, but Janette's last words to him pounded his brain like the oily surf beating on the sand. Her words clamored at him like an overzealous debtor, eating away at his insides, gnawing at each organ in turn until he felt like an empty shell. *They took your baby, too. Yours and Carolyn's.*

CHAPTER ELEVEN

IN THE WEEKS TO FOLLOW, Janette kept up a frantic routine, designed to allow no time for reflection. But somehow the thoughts managed to creep in; the memories clawed at her and nothing she could do would make them go away.

Just thinking of Adam and Amy filled her with such anguish she could hardly hold her head up. She could no longer walk through the lovely pageant grounds without a heavy heart. She even went as far as to avoid the path where she'd first met Amy. She stayed far away from the picnic grounds where the three of them had been a family for one glorious moment in time. But nothing could make her forget, and even if she could, there was the constant smell of oil to keep the memories alive.

The oil spill made an indelible mark on the pageant. During the performances, the sickly fumes floated inland with the ocean breezes, replacing the sweet peppery smell of eucalyptus and cedar, and bringing a grim reality to the fantasy created on stage.

And the fumes triggered further recollections. At times Janette found herself transposing events in her mind until the line between reality and fantasy grew blurred. Time and time again she had to remind herself that the kiss that had seemed so impossibly real the day they'd worked to save birds, had not materialized except in her own imagination. She forced herself to remember that Adam's strong, yet gentle hands had been stroking feathers, not flesh.

And when she wasn't remembering his kisses, real or otherwise, she thought about dancing with him on their own private dance floor, dancing up the walk to her house, seeming to dance even when they were only sitting and gazing at each other.

While concentrating on not remembering, she went through the routine of her day, clipboard in hand, calling meetings, reading the comments she'd written during the previous night's performance. The show must go on, she told herself each morning, dragging herself out of a tangled bed that had offered her no respite or rest.

Despite everything, the show did go on. And no one seemed to guess what it cost her to be there day after day, night after night, working, organizing, directing, smiling—yes, she'd managed that, too—when all the while her heart was shattered.

On the first day of September, she stood in front of Walden's Toy Store staring at an adorable plush brown bear through the window. It was Amy's birthday. Amy's and Stephanie's. And she considered them both her daughters: Amy was her flesh and blood, but Stephanie had been the one she'd buried and grieved for during the last eleven years. If that didn't give her the right to call her daughter, she couldn't imagine what did.

She felt she had less right to call Amy her daughter, and yet the need to do so was overwhelming. Amy was eleven years old that day and Janette had never known the joy of bringing her a gift. She knew that Amy would love the darling little bear that was dressed in a white-and-blue-striped baseball uniform. A jaunty blue baseball cap sat between its ears, a small bat held in its paws.

She was still thinking of the bear later as she walked into the house and kicked off her shoes. She put the kettle on just as the phone rang. It was Merv, sounding pleased with himself.

"We have a court date for the custody hearing."

She was surprised and more than a little apprehensive. If she had to sit across from Adam in a courtroom, there would be no way at all to forget him. "So...so soon?"

"We were lucky. We start the proceedings the twentieth of the month."

She inhaled deeply. It didn't seem real. "Does... does...Adam know?"

"His lawyer got the same information I did." He hesitated a moment. "Can you stop by my office later this week? I want to go over everything with you. We're going to have to prove that Amy would benefit from living with her mother. This means bringing in psychiatrists, the works. But I think we have a good shot at it."

Janette felt her patience snap. "Merv, I told you it won't work. Adam is a wonderful father. He's trying to do everything right. He told me himself his concern at having to explain the facts of life to her."

"When can you come in?" Merv asked, following a long silence.

She could tell by his voice he was annoyed. Well, it couldn't be helped. Merv might view Adam as the enemy, but she certainly didn't. "I'll get back to you tomorrow. I need to check my calendar at work."

She signed off and sat staring at the phone, remembering the bear in the window. Dare she call Amy and wish her happy birthday? She thought of a dozen reasons she shouldn't. But even as she counted them off in her head, she dialed Adam's number.

"I'LL GET IT!" Virginia called. She wiped her hands on her white starched apron and reached over the kitchen counter for the phone. "Hello."

There was a long silence on the line, and then a woman's voice. "Mrs. Spencer? This is Janette Taylor. May I please speak to Adam?"

Gripping the receiver, Virginia glanced out the sliding glass door where Adam was barbecuing steaks on the grill. Amy and her friend Tammy were playing a game of ping-pong nearby on the patio, and their laughter floated through the half-open door.

"What do you want?" she demanded, her voice low so no one could hear. "Haven't you done enough to us? Haven't you caused us enough problems?"

"I don't want to cause any problems for your family. I just want to wish Amy happy birthday."

"You have no right calling this house!" Virginia snarled into the phone. "Don't call again!" She slammed the receiver down and clutched her chest.

"Who was that?" Adam asked from behind her.

Spinning around, she faced her son-in-law. He wore an apron over his slacks and a shirt that declared him Number One Dad, a Father's Day gift from Amy. A matching white hat clung precariously to his head. His almost comical outfit offered a strange contrast to his dark rigid face.

"That woman..."

Adam turned pale. "Janette?"

"She has no right to call here!" Virginia said sharply, annoyed that even now, after Janette had revealed her true nature, he was still obviously smitten with her.

"What did she want?" Adam asked curtly.

"She wanted to wish Amy a happy birthday..."

"Damn!" He pulled off his hat and flung it across the counter. "You should have let me talk to her. It was for me to decide whether or not she could talk to Amy, not you!"

"Amy is my grandchild. I have every right to protect her."

"I'm her father!"

"Not for long," Virginia shouted back. "Not if that woman has her way!"

Not wanting an argument to spoil Amy's birthday, he spun on his heel and stormed outside, only to find the steaks on the grill sizzling under a cloud of black smoke.

Cursing beneath his breath, he grabbed a long-handled fork and, turning his face against the eye-stinging smoke, pushed the steaks to the edge of the grill, away from the fire.

"Is there something wrong?" Amy asked, standing next to him, ping-pong paddle in hand.

"Damn it, Amy, don't bother me now!" As soon as the words had left his mouth, he was filled with unspeakable remorse. Turning, he faced her, the stricken look in her eyes adding to his guilt. "Sweetie, I'm sorry." He flung the fork down and hugged her, holding her tight against him, and wishing with all his heart that he could protect her.

Oh, Janette, Janette! His heart cried her name like a song it couldn't forget. How can the same woman who gave him a touch of paradise lead him to the brink of hell? He smoothed Amy's hair with his hand. "Will you ever forgive your dad?"

Amy nodded against his chest. "You know I do, Daddy." She lifted her head and looked up at him. The eyes looking down at hers weren't smiling, they were sad, almost as sad as they had been on the day of her mother's funeral.

Something terrible was about to happen. She knew it. She could sense it, see it in her grandmother's eyes, hear it in her father's voice, and she was frightened, more frightened than she had ever been in her life.

TWO DAYS AFTER her disastrous call to Adam's house, Janette stumbled through her kitchen door, clutching two bags of groceries in her arms. With a sideward swing of her hip, she managed to shut the door behind her. She had barely taken a step across the kitchen floor when her sandals made a squishing sound that sounded suspiciously like water. She glanced through the leafy stalks of celery at Stella who was pawing through a metal toolbox.

"It's about time you got home," Stella said. Frowning, she examined a wrench and tossed it back into the toolbox. "We've got problems."

Sighing, Janette walked gingerly across the sopping wet floor and unloaded her bags on the counter. "Now what's the problem?"

"A pipe behind the washing machine sprung a leak."

Janette looked down at her feet. The water was at least an inch high. She slipped off her sandals and rolled up the legs of her jeans. "Did you call a plumber?"

"Are you crazy?" Stella asked. "Do you know how much a plumber will cost? I'm fixing it myself. The only problem is I don't have the right-sized wrench." She mumbled to herself as she pawed through the toolbox again. "Maybe Larry will have the size I need."

"Are you sure you don't want me to call the plumber? I'll even pay for it."

"Don't be ridiculous," Stella said, grabbing her car keys and heading out the back door, oblivious to the slurping water beneath her feet. "How hard can it be to fix a simple leak?"

"Probably as hard as it was to put that new sprinkler system in," Janette called after her. She grimaced, remembering the ordeal of digging through hardened clay in the front yard. The grass still hadn't recovered, nor had she. With a resigned sigh, she started on the groceries, putting away the food that needed refrigeration and leaving the rest for later. She then picked her way carefully across the floor to the laundry room and grabbed the mop.

She'd barely begun to mop up the water when the doorbell rang. Glancing upward, she mumbled a prayer. "Please let that be a plumber." She wiped her bare feet on a towel and hurried to the front door.

Her heart stopped at sight of Adam. He was standing on the porch dressed in casual brown slacks and a tan shirt that was open at the neck, allowing a tantalizing glimpse of hair and chest.

She managed to say his name before her brain shut down. After that, all she could do was stare.

He noted her rolled-up jeans and pretty bare feet with their bright red painted toes. Not the toes, he thought reproachfully, forcing his eyes to travel up her trim figure, to her face. "I hope I didn't catch you at a bad time."

"Not at all," she said. She moved aside, gripping the door as if her life depended on it. "Do you happen, by any chance, to know anything about plumbing?"

He looked startled. "Afraid not. But Amy knows how to change a washer."

He noticed the softness in her face at the mention of Amy's name. It was the same softness he had seen on Carolyn's face whenever Amy came into the room. He felt resistance build inside. It was as if someone had invaded a very private part of him. An awkward silence followed. At last he cleared his throat. "I could recommend a plumber."

"Thank you, I—my roommate tends to be allergic to them." She ran her tongue across her lower lip, searching for something to say, something to do. This awkwardness between them was uncomfortable.

"I came to apologize...I..."

She felt a thrill rush through her. He understood why she had to fight for custody.

"Virginia had no right," he continued. "I mean, I'm not sure that it's a good idea for you to talk to Amy. I..." He looked away.

Her heart sank. He didn't understand. "I just wanted to wish her happy birthday."

He raked his fingers through his hair and fell silent. He felt like a heel, the worst possible heel. It seemed so cruel to deny her such a simple request. Yet, he had to think of Amy first and foremost. He'd consulted a child psychiatrist, who told him that before taking the next step, it would be better for Amy to get used to the idea that her mother and father weren't the people she thought them to be. No one, least of all Adam, knew what that next step should be, or when it should be, or even if it should be at all.

"Won't you come in?" she asked, unable to think of anything else to say.

He nodded and stepped inside. He followed her into the living room and stopped in front of the *Girl with Gull* portrait that leaned against the piano. Janette had been unable to decide what to do with her father's painting. Although keeping it only made her feel worse, she couldn't bring herself to part with it.

Adam studied the portrait, noting the all-too familiar green eyes, the gentle upturned nose, the soft curve of the smile. His eyes lingered on the mouth that seventeen years ago had already held the promise of the soft full lips that had since come to haunt him. Stifling the deep longing that welled up from the depths of him, he gazed again at the eyes. Now that he had time to study the portrait closer, he noticed there were subtle differences between Amy and Janette. He had washed Amy's face enough to know every little detail of her dainty features. He had memorized every plane of Janette's lovely face, knew it inch by inch, had run his lips up one side and down another. Had gone over that face in his dreams a million times. Damn! What was he doing? Why did he continue to think of ways to torture himself?

Turning, he looked at Janette. She was sitting on the arm of the sofa, one leg pulled to her chest, watching him. She looked so beguiling with her bare feet and slightly tousled hair. He'd seen her hair in similar disarray once, after he had run his fingers through the silky strands. Quashing the thought, he purposely increased the distance between them.

Feeling her cheeks grow hot beneath his scrutiny, Janette invited him to sit, pointing to an overstuffed chair in the far part of the room. She couldn't bear for him to sit on the sofa next to her.

"The eyes are all wrong," he said suddenly. He opted to stand, feet apart. He didn't trust himself to get too comfortable.

Surprised, her lashes flew up. "I beg your pardon?"

"The eyes." He nodded toward the portrait. "They're all wrong." The artist had captured the thoughtful serious part, but not the lively depths. The serious part is what made Amy's and Janette's eyes so intriguing; the lively part was the magnet that pulled observers in and held them. Held them as her eyes now held his.

Feeling himself drawn to her, wanting her, remembering what he best not remember, he turned abruptly, and faced the fireplace. He grabbed the edge of the mantel, bracing himself. He must remember why he was here. "I'm concerned about Amy." Concern was hardly the word. Out of his mind with worry was more like it. She'd been so insecure lately, barely leaving his side when he was home, calling him two, three, even four times a day at work, waking up at night crying.

Janette dropped her leg to the floor. The sound of desperation in his voice alarmed her. This wasn't the usual parental concern. "Adam, tell me, what's wrong?"

Adam turned. "I'm so afraid of what this case is going to do to her. The publicity is already affecting her. I've had to keep her home from soccer practice because of reporters." This was true, but there was more, much more. He was afraid of losing her.

"Maybe, maybe we can make a deal. Maybe we can make some sort of arrangement where the two of you could meet with a psychologist at first, then later maybe spend time together. I would have no objection to your spending time together on occasion, if it's all right with Amy."

"What you want me to do is drop the custody suit," she said in a flat voice. "If I drop the custody suit, I have no chance of winning the lawsuit against the hospital."

"Nothing is ever going to change what happened. If you get a million dollars or two million from them, will that change anything?"

"I told you, the money has nothing to do with this," Janette said bitterly. How could he even think such a thing? "I have to do this Adam. What they did to me . . . I can't just ignore it. They are going to pay! But there's more. If I drop the custody suit, I have no legal rights to Amy. None. You could move away. Leave the country. Remarry." The word practically choked her, but it was a real possibility. "Another thing," she added hastily. "What would become of Amy if something happens to you? Do you honestly think that your mother-in-law would allow me to see her?"

"I'll talk with Virginia. Make her understand."

"Sorry, Adam. But you're asking me to gamble with my daughter's life and I can't chance it."

"What I'm asking you to do is to drop the damned custody suit! If you really cared for Amy . . ."

His voice trailed off, but the unspoken statement was all too clear to her; what he really meant to say was if she really cared for him.

"What you're asking me to do is to walk away from the fact that Amy is my daughter!" Her eyes flashed angrily. How dare he question her feelings for Amy? How dare he question her feelings period! He couldn't know the anguish she felt.

"Damn it, Janette!" He cleared the distance between them and grabbed her by the shoulders, lifting her to her feet. "Do you think you're the only one who's hurting? Do you know how it feels to find out after almost eleven years that the daughter I love more than life itself is not mine?"

Janette didn't know how to answer him. She didn't even know suddenly, how to breathe. He was so near she could feel the warmth of his body, yet he might as well have been on another planet. The fabric of her T-shirt seemed to melt beneath the firm grip of his hands. Her flesh grew warm. She moved away from him and sucked in a mouthful of air.

"Let me talk to her," she managed. "Please, Adam, let me explain to Amy why I must do this."

Adam hit a flattened palm with a fist, his face darker than a storm cloud. "No!"

She fought back tears. "How can I believe that you will let me see Amy if I drop the suit? You won't even let me try to explain things to her now."

The look he gave her nearly tore her heart out. She saw hate in his eyes, anger. "If you can't trust me on this," he said quietly, "then we have nothing else to say to each other." He stalked across the room, pausing at the doorway as if waiting for her to call to him.

He glanced back over his shoulder, locking her gaze in his. Unable to tell him what he so obviously wanted to hear, she shook her head. "I'm sorry, Adam," she whispered softly. "I'm so sorry."

CHAPTER TWELVE

AFTER ADAM LEFT, slamming the door shut firmly behind him, she was more determined than ever to follow through with the suit against the hospital. Not only had some unknown "they" taken her baby from her, they had deprived her of the man she loved.

Like a woman possessed, she tackled the sopping wet floor with energy lit by fury and despair. She banged the mop down and jerked it up, squeezing the last drop out of the sponge before slamming it down again. Somebody, somewhere was going to pay!

"Hey, watch it," Stella said, guiding a ten foot length of pipe through the kitchen door. "I don't want to have to replace the floor."

Janette swung around, her mouth dropping open. "What in the world are you going to do with that?"

"Larry thought it would be best to replace the whole pipe, rather than patch it up. That way, we can prevent any future trouble." She lay the pipe across the driest part of the floor.

"Do you know how to replace pipe?" Janette asked.

"No, but how hard can it be?"

"That's what you said when you tried to reroof the house," Janette reminded her, squeezing out the mop.

"That wasn't my fault," Stella said, shuddering at the memory. "How did I know that we had dry rot in the attic and that as soon as I added extra weight, the roof would cave in?'' They were still paying for that disaster, which was one of the reasons they couldn't afford to call a plumber. "How about helping me move out the washer and dryer?''

Janette stood the mop on end and sighed in resignation. Every time Stella tried to fix something, it almost always ended with disastrous results. Still, at this point in her life, what was one more catastrophe?

Later that afternoon, Merv stopped by and sat in the living room with Janette. Amid the loud clanking sounds of Stella banging on pipe, he reported on the progress of the lawsuit against the hospital.

"I'd offer you some coffee," Janette said, "but the water's turned off.''

"That's all right." Merv said, glancing at his watch. "I've got some good news. I was able to locate one of the nurses that was on duty the day you had your baby. Name's—" he glanced at the notes he'd spread across her coffee table "—Ginger Baker.''

Janette sat on the arm of a chair, wondering why finding this nurse was so significant. "Really?''

"She's no longer working as a nurse. She quit to become a professional golfer right after the birth of your baby. Doesn't that take the cake? Anyway, she's agreed to testify that she saw the two babies who'd been born that day, side by side outside the delivery room. They were the last two babies she helped deliver. She remembers you.''

"I don't understand. The tests prove that I'm Amy's mother. Isn't that enough? Obviously, a mistake was made at the hospital.''

Merv's face darkened. "This case with the hospital, it's going to be rough. Their defense is going to be that no damages were done to you. Ginger Baker is willing to testify that you were devastated after being told that your baby was dead. With the hospital trying to prove that you planned to give up your baby for adoption, Mrs. Baker's testimony could be vital.''

Janette stood. Between the upcoming custody hearing and the suit against the hospital, she felt as if her life was on hold. She hated knowing that her future was in the hands of the courts.

She couldn't think about the hospital now, not with the custody suit looming ahead. She walked over to the portrait and remembered Adam's strange comment about the eyes. ''What do you think of my father's painting?''

Merv joined her and stared at the painting for several minutes before replying. ''It's okay. It's not your father's best by any means. But it's okay.''

''Why isn't it my father's best work?'' she asked. ''Why could he paint kings and queens, complete strangers, but not me, his daughter?''

''You're asking me, a lawyer? What do I know about art? Maybe an artist needs a certain distance from his subject to capture a person's essence, I don't know. What I do know, is that this painting caused your father quite a lot of grief.''

Janette stared at him in surprise. ''Grief? How do you know that?''

''He talked to me about it. You know he never allowed anyone to see an unfinished painting. This is one time he broke that rule. Late one night, he ushered me into his studio and pulled off the cover. I couldn't believe it when he asked me my opinion. I had to tell him the truth. I said it looks like you physically, but I thought it failed to convey that special part of you that makes you unique. I don't know if that makes any sense, but that's what I told him.''

''What did my father say?''

''That's the strangest part. He didn't say a word. Can you imagine your father accepting criticism without rebuttal? He covered up the painting and that was the end of our discussion.''

''Do you know what happened to the painting after that?'' Janette asked.

''I have no idea. I never saw it again until today.'' Merv studied the painting for a moment before adding, ''To my knowledge it was never exhibited in any of his shows.''

The clanking grew louder, making further conversation difficult. Merv glanced at his watch again. ''I've got to go,'' he said, raising his voice to be heard. ''Margie and I have tickets for the theater tonight. It's our thirty-second anniversary.''

''Congratulations,'' Janette said. She tucked her arm in his and walked him to the door. ''You and Margie give me hope. Maybe one day I'll have what the two of you have.''

Merv hugged her. ''It'll happen. When you least expect it. You wait and see.''

She stepped out onto the porch where it was quieter. ''Merv, do you think that my mother's running away when I was a child had anything to do with the trouble my father had painting my portrait?''

Merv thought for a moment, his eyes focused on another time. ''Most likely. You look very much like your mother. You did then, you do now. Your father never understood your mother's fierce need for independence. He wanted to take care of her, to make everything right. When she got cancer... For some reason she thought it was a battle she had to fight alone.''

Janette stared at Merv. ''Are you saying she knew before she left that she had cancer?''

It was Merv's turn to stare. ''Didn't your father tell you? She left to go to a cancer clinic in Spain that promised her some sort of miracle cure.''

''No, he never told me,'' Janette said flatly. ''I always assumed she took ill after she left.''

''I think your mother viewed the clinic as the last chance to take charge of her life. Your father saw it as rejection of him. He couldn't understand why she had to travel half a world away to die. He didn't understand her and I don't think he ever understood you.''

Maybe not, she thought. Maybe that would explain the trouble he'd had with her portrait. He'd tried to run her life, tried to make her promise to give up her baby. He never understood the concept that love should liberate, not restrict. Had that been why her mother had left all those years ago; not so much to search for a cure but to find freedom? ''Thanks.''

He looked at her puzzled. ''Oh, you mean for my having located Ginger Baker.''

It wasn't Ginger she was thanking him for. It was for telling her the truth about her mother's disappearance. It was for revealing the possibility that her father had ruined the portrait out of artistic frustration and not out of anger at her.

After Merv left, she sat staring at the portrait. Her father was a perfectionist, and she remembered him being ruthlessly hard on himself. He'd once refused a prestigious award because he felt he didn't deserve it. Another time, he'd declined payment for a portrait because he believed it lacked ''magic.''

Memories like these made it easier to believe that maybe she had misjudged her father. Perhaps the need for perfection had blinded him to how his actions might be misconstrued by a sensitive ten-year-old.

Realizing that she may have suffered years of needless pain, she thought of Amy. How does Amy feel, really feel, about the custody suit? she wondered. How much does she really understand about an impossible situation that has everyone involved frightened and confused?

She longed to talk to Amy. She was convinced that she could make Amy understand that it was not her intention to take her from her father. All Janette wanted to do was to be a part of her life, and try to make up for all those lost years.

If only she could talk to Amy. If only she could explain how very much she loved her.

And what if Amy wouldn't accept what she had to offer? For when it came right down to it, Amy was the only one who could accept or reject Janette's right to be her mother. Not the courts, not Adam or Virginia, only Amy. What if Amy turned against her completely?

What then?

"I'M SCARED," Adam confessed to his lawyer. He sat on the couch across from Wes, his hands clasped between his knees. Amy was asleep upstairs, but he didn't want to chance her waking up and overhearing them, so he kept his voice low, barely above a whisper. It was the first time he'd vocalized his feelings, and even whispering the words didn't soften their impact.

Having said what he'd been afraid to say, he stood and paced restlessly around the living room. "I don't know what I would do if I lost her."

"You're not going to lose her," Wes said. "You've been a model father. The best. Besides—" Wes clicked the top of his pen and slipped it into his shirt pocket "—we have a better case than you think."

Adam spun around. "Better? How?"

Wes sat forward, but before he could explain, Amy cried out. Adam cleared the living room with long hurried strides and took the stairs two at a time, rushing anxiously into her room.

"Sweetie, what's wrong?" He flipped on the light and hastened to her side.

Sitting up, Amy blinked against the sudden brightness. "I don't want to die, Daddy. I don't want to die."

"There, there," he said, sitting on her bed and hugging her close. "You're not going to die."

"But what if I have Mommy's heart?" she asked, sobbing.

"That's not possible. Honey, I explained all this. Your mommy...she wasn't your real mommy..." She stiffened in his arms and he cursed himself. He didn't even know what to say to her anymore, how to comfort her. God, sometimes he felt so inept as a parent.

Searching his brain, he tried another tactic. A bit of humor had worked wonders with her in the past. "Your heart is as strong as an old mule's."

She pulled away and looked into his face. "Is my heart strong because Mommy wasn't really my mommy?"

"I don't know, sweetie. Some people have strong hearts and some people don't."

"Does Janette have a strong heart?"

There it was again, the painful tug. "She does," he said in a voice hoarse with emotion. He only hoped it was strong enough, knowing that already Janette's heart was broken in a way that could never be healed. He already knew a lot about broken hearts and now he was learning a lot more.

Amy saw her father flinch as if in pain, and wondered what it meant. Why did he look so sad lately? Sometimes she talked to him and he didn't seem to hear her. At other times, he held her so tight, it was all she could to breathe.

What was it he wouldn't tell her? That he couldn't be her father anymore? The thought brought a shudder to her body and her thin shoulders quivered beneath the thin fabric of her nightgown.

"Get under the covers," her father said. He tucked her in and brushed the hair away from her face. "You okay?"

She nodded, but only because she didn't want to worry him. "When can I go down to the beach?" she asked. She longed to go to her secret cave where she could pretend all the confusion in her life was only something in a movie and she was the star. But because of the fumes from the oil, her father had forbidden her to go anywhere near the beach.

"It's going to be awhile, sweetie. We have to finish cleaning up the public beaches and then we'll get a crew over here." It was difficult. Now that the media had lost interest, so had the public. It was harder to get volunteers, particularly since the local college had begun its fall term.

Disappointed, Amy lowered her chin beneath the covers. "Would you leave the light on?" she asked sleepily.

Adam nodded. "Sure thing, sport."

After he left, Amy pulled the blankets over her head, but she still didn't feel safe. The only place she really felt safe was in her very own cave.

THE NEXT MORNING, Amy's grandmother came over to take Amy shopping for new school clothes. Her father had already left for the office and Amy was still eating her breakfast when Virginia arrived, filled with plans for the day.

"Take your time," Virginia said, helping herself to coffee. "I just thought it best to get to the mall early before it gets crowded."

Amy stared into her cereal bowl. She didn't feel much like eating. She didn't feel much like anything, least of all going to the mall with her grandmother. Her grandmother was so old-fashioned. She had no idea what a sixth grader should wear. Amy was certain that Virginia would insist upon those same little-girl dresses she'd tried to foist on her last year. She would much rather have gone with Tammy's mother. She wished she had a mother. Dreamily, she wondered what it would be like to go shopping with Janette. Instinctively, she knew that Janette would know exactly what a sixth grader should wear.

Feeling guilty for having such thoughts, she pushed them away, along with her cereal bowl. Her father was angry with Janette, and he would be angry with Amy for wanting to go shopping with her.

"Why the long face?" Virginia asked.

Janette regarded her grandmother thoughtfully. "Are you really my grandmother?"

Virginia's eyes snapped. "Of course I'm your grandmother! Who have you been talking to? Not that...that woman, that Janette Taylor. Have you been talking to her?''

Surprised by the sudden sharpness in her grand-mother's voice, Amy shrunk back in her chair. She hadn't meant to make her grandmother angry. Lately, it seemed like she was always making someone angry. ''I haven't talked with her.''

Amy looked so bewildered and upset, Virginia's face softened. ''I'm sorry, Amy. I didn't mean to snap at you. I love you very much. You know that, don't you?''

Amy nodded. She did know that. She also knew that despite her grandmother's old-fashioned ways, she wanted only the best for her. She smiled, determined to make the best of their shopping day. ''I love you, too, Grandma.''

Virginia's face lit up like it always did when Amy told her she loved her. She squeezed Amy's hand and sat on the chair next to her, a cloud of violet perfume settling around her. ''Just remember, I'm your grandmother and your mother might be dead, but she's still very much your mother. Don't you believe one word that horrid woman says.''

Amy's smile froze. ''Do you mean Janette?''

Her grandmother gave her a disapproving glance. ''Where did you learn to call adults by their first names?'' she scolded. ''*Miss Taylor* has no right to try to take you away from your father.''

''Is that what she's trying to do?'' Amy asked, sur-prised. Was that why her father looked so sad lately?

''That's exactly what she's trying to do,'' Virginia said. ''But don't you worry about a thing. We're not going to let her get away with it. Now eat up so we can go.''

Amy glanced at her bowl. "I'm not very hungry."

"Very well. We'll have lunch downtown. Now go get ready while I clean up these dishes." She began clearing the table and Amy went to her room to finish dressing, and to ponder this latest piece of information.

JANETTE STOOD in front of Adam's front door for several minutes before she finally found the nerve to push the doorbell. What if Virginia opened the door, or Adam? The very thought of possibly facing that woman again put her nerves on edge. She didn't even want to think about facing Adam again. Still, she had to take a chance. It was imperative that she talk to Amy; she simply had to try to make her understand that she wasn't going to harm her.

Amy opened the door and it was all Janette could do to keep from throwing her arms around her. It was the first time she'd seen the girl since finding out for certain that she was Amy's mother. Eleven years of deprivation filled her with unspeakable need. How could she ever make up for those years? How many kisses would it take? How many hugs?

Like a starving woman faced with a table full of food, she absorbed every detail of her child. She noticed that Amy's face looked paler than usual, and her eyes, those beautiful green eyes that had captured her heart from the first moment they'd met, blazed with suspicion and fear. They might as well have been daggers pointing straight at Janette. "Amy, I came to talk to you—"

"No!" Amy shouted, her young face twisted with anger and hatred. Her grandmother had said Janette was going to take her away. Feeling guilty for having wished it was Janette who would help her with school clothes instead of her grandmother, she tried to atone for her disloyalty by lashing out. "I hate you! Go away!"

Feeling as if she had been shot through the heart, Janette staggered backward, shocked and confused. She had imagined this meeting with Amy a hundred times. But never had she imagined anything so devastating. Before she had a chance to recover, the door slammed shut. Trying to erase the memory of the hatred in her daughter's face, she raced toward her car blinded by tears.

What had Adam said to Amy to fill her with so much venom? Was that his way of getting back at her? By making Amy hate her? Would Adam really do that? Would he use Amy as a weapon to hurt her? As much as she hated to believe that Adam would do such a thing, it was hard to think otherwise.

Janette did not remember the drive home, and when she pulled up in front of her house she stared in shock at the number of cars and people that blocked her driveway. Thinking something terrible had happened to Stella, she left her car double-parked and ran across the front lawn. She was immediately swallowed up by a crowd of people, jostling one another, shoving her, all talking at once. It wasn't until someone stuck a microphone in her face that she realized that these were reporters, firing questions at her like bullets at a target.

"How does it feel to be in a custody battle with a man you hardly know?"

"Do you plan to raise the child yourself?"

"Don't you feel guilty for taking a child away from her home?"

Pushing her way through the crowd, she tried to hide her face from the flashing cameras. "Please, just go away!" she cried. "Leave me alone."

"Is there any truth that you tried to abort your child?"

Shocked by the question, Janette turned a stunned face toward the man who'd asked it. It was a mistake because it allowed the photographers a clear shot of her face. Blinded by bright flashing lights, she stumbled up the porch steps, the reporters crushing in behind her.

The door opened and Stella beckoned wildly. "Hurry."

Slipping through the door, Janette helped Stella push it shut and turned the bolt. "They're like a bunch of hungry wolves," Stella grumbled. She peered through the lace curtains and pulled down the shades.

"What are they doing here?" Janette asked in bewilderment. She felt as if she had fought a war single-handedly—and lost.

"What do you think? This is the biggest story that has hit this town since the mayor's wife posed for that men's magazine."

Janette groaned. Merv had warned her, but she never thought it would be as bad as this.

"Come on," Stella said, leading her away from the door. "How about a glass of sherry?"

Janette shook her head. "Maybe a cup of coffee..."

Stella shrugged. "Sorry. We don't have any water."

"Stella, damn it, please, please call a plumber." She felt her control slipping away. Hot tears began to roll down her cheeks.

"Don't cry," Stella pleaded. "I—" She stopped as a tall burly man walked into the room. Acting more flustered than usual, Stella introduced the man as the owner of Hodges Hardware store. "Larry agreed to come over and help me replace the pipe."

Noting Stella's red cheeks, Janette studied Larry Hodges with more than fleeting interest, guessing him to be in his early forties. He had a pleasant round face, tawny-colored eyes as soft and appealing as a cocker spaniel's, and brown thinning hair. "Pipe's all fixed, ladies," he said, his gaze lingering on Stella. "You did a great job. You just used the wrong-sized washer, that's all. That's why it still leaked." He glanced at Janette. "No call to cry, ma'am." He nodded his head toward the front door. "I'll get rid of those pests."

Stella glanced anxiously at Janette. "That might not be a bad idea. I don't care if they are from the media. They don't have the right to trespass on people's property."

"Thanks, Larry," Janette said, wiping away her tears. "But maybe we should call the police. They're pretty vicious out there."

"Now don't you worry about a thing." He patted Janette on the shoulder with a strong firm hand. "I'll get rid of them."

Larry disappeared out the front door, his voice booming. "Get out of here, you hear me? This is private property!"

Janette and Stella held their breath and listened. The noise of the crowd subsided and soon they could hear car doors slam shut.

Stella lifted a shade and peered through the window. "What did I tell you?" she said, beaming. "Larry's the greatest!"

Janette smiled. Thanks to Larry, she was already beginning to feel better. "What you told me was that Larry had the best tools in town."

With a wicked smile on her face, Stella glanced at Janette. "Oh, yes, that too."

Janette studied Stella thoughtfully. "Why do I get the feeling, suddenly, that you don't just mean hammers and saws?"

Stella shrugged, her face masked with feigned innocence. "Why, Janette Taylor, shame on you!"

JANETTE'S FACE was plastered on the front page of the newspaper. Staring at it, Adam sat forward, surprised by how her picture affected him. She looked scared and vulnerable. He felt a sudden rage. What had they said to her to make her look so afraid?

Feeling a protectiveness surge inside, he read the accompanying story, his chest tight with anger as he ripped the paper apart searching for the page where the article continued. The paper made her sound like a monster, a home breaker who had no regard for anyone or anything. His face twisted in disgust, he finished the biased account and threw the paper down.

The reporter had even presumed to refer to Amy as a poor frightened little girl. How dare anyone describe his daughter that way? Amy was going through a difficult, confusing time; they all were. But to refer to her as a poor frightened little girl did her an injustice.

He had been described as a man at the end of his rope. That part was true, at least. All he wanted was to be left alone, to be left in peace to raise his daughter without being hounded by reporters, lawyers and the plaguing memories of kissing Janette and holding her in his arms.

CHAPTER THIRTEEN

THE BAILIFF ROSE. "Family court case number 2124 is now in session, the Honorable Judge Charles Wendall presiding. Please remain seated."

"I thought you had to stand when the judge was announced," Stella whispered in Janette's ears from the row behind where she was sitting beside some of Janette's colleagues who had come to offer their support.

"Shh." Janette glanced nervously at Merv who was thumbing through a stack of papers. She looked straight ahead, repressing the urge to seek out Adam who sat on the far side of the room, next to his lawyer. She studied the judge, guessing that he was in his early sixties. He had an abundance of gray hair, and a wide, almost jovial-looking face. She wouldn't be surprised to learn that at Christmastime the man donned a beard and played Santa Claus. It was hard to believe that this kindly grandfatherly man had the power to change her entire life.

She glanced down at her hands. She didn't want to be caught staring. More important, she didn't want to chance turning her head toward Adam. Even without seeing him, she could feel his strong presence and that was difficult enough.

Earlier, she had walked into the courtroom next to Stella, who had taken the day off work to be with her.

Janette had picked out Adam's dark head immediately and for a moment she felt as if her heart had stopped beating. He had been bent over the table in conversation with a man she guessed was his lawyer. As if some silent signal had passed between them, he'd lifted his head, his eyes meeting hers.

For a moment they'd stood staring at each other. He looked tired, she'd thought during those electric moments when no one else in the courtroom seemed to exist. She longed to go to him and smooth the lines from his forehead. She wondered if her touching his cheek would relax the tenseness at his jaw. She might have done just that had Stella not grabbed her by the arm and led her to the front of the courtroom where Merv waited for her.

The first witness to take the stand was a Dr. Wong from the Swift-Langley Laboratories, who testified about the results of the genetic tests.

Merv stood in front of the witness. "Could you describe the tests, Doctor?"

Janette listened, mesmerized as the doctor explained the results of each of the twenty-six tests he'd personally supervised.

"In your professional opinion, Doctor, what is the conclusion of these tests?"

"My conclusion is that Adam Blake could not have fathered Amy. The tests also indicate a strong possibility that Janette Taylor is the girl's natural mother."

Merv stroked his beard. "A strong possibility. How strong?"

Dr. Wong didn't even blink. "The test showed a 99.9 percent probability that Janette Taylor is Amy Blake's natural mother."

Janette covered her mouth with her hand. 99.9 percent. She'd had no idea the evidence was that strong.

"Thank you, Doctor. That will be all." Merv turned and took his place next to Janette.

Since Adam's lawyer had no further questions of the witness, Merv called his next witness. "Mrs. Ginger Baker."

Mrs. Baker was a tall thin woman with cropped brown hair and glasses. She had been on duty the day that Janette had had her baby. The woman provided a detailed account of that long-ago day, filling in the holes that Janette had been unable to fill.

Janette glanced over at Adam. His profile was so rigid it could have been chiseled from stone. That day held as many painful memories for him as it did for her.

"Did you see Miss Taylor following her delivery?"

"Yes, she had been moved out of the room to make room for Mrs. Blake. I passed her bed in the corridor on my way to Mrs. Blake's room."

"When did Mrs. Blake go into cardiac arrest?"

"A short time after delivery. The doctor who delivered her baby had left in a hurry to attend to an emergency and we assumed this was why she was so agitated. Her regular doctor didn't arrive until some time later. By then, Mrs. Blake was resting comfortably."

Janette could almost guess what was going through Adam's mind at that very moment. There was a strong possibility that the reason Carolyn had been agitated was that she knew something was wrong with her baby.

"What about the babies, Mrs. Baker. Did you see either baby?"

"Only one. I remember one of the doctors asking why the body of the one baby had not yet been taken to the lab."

"And where was this baby in relationship to Janette Taylor?"

"Right next to her bed," Mrs. Baker replied. "All the nurses were busy. I called the lab myself and told them to send someone at once. I assumed since the dead baby was next to her, it was her child. I don't know what happened after that."

Shuddering, Janette searched behind the closed doors of her mind trying to remember what she had tried so hard through the years to forget. But all she could remember was shadows and the murmur of voices. It wasn't until much later that she'd been told about her baby. Why hadn't she followed her instincts and gone to the nursery? Checked for herself? Would seeing the babies have made a difference? Would she have known that Amy was her baby?

"What was Miss Taylor's state of mind following her delivery?"

Mrs. Baker hesitated. "She was extremely agitated. She kept screaming out that her baby had cried. We finally had to tranquilize her."

"Were you there when the doctor told her that her baby had died?"

"I was."

"What was her reaction?"

"She didn't believe it."

"Would you say that Janette Taylor was devastated by the loss of her baby?"

"Objection!" Adam's lawyer was on his feet. "Your Honor, Mr. Davidson is leading the witness."

Merv spun around to face the judge. "I'm asking for a professional opinion. At the time in question, Mrs. Baker was a well-respected registered nurse. As such, it was her job to attend to her patients' emotional as well as physical needs."

"Your point is well taken," the judge said. "But please rephrase the question and allow Mrs. Baker to answer the question in her own words."

Merv turned back to his witness. "What would you say was Miss Taylor's state of mind upon learning that her baby was dead?"

"She was devastated."

"Thank you, Mrs. Baker. No further questions."

He turned to Wes. "Your witness."

Following a lunch break, Janette was called to the stand. Shakily, she stood, feeling everyone's eyes on her, feeling most of all Adam's. She prayed her legs wouldn't buckle under her as she walked the distance to the witness stand and took the oath.

She forced herself to concentrate on Merv. She wouldn't look at Adam, she mustn't. She couldn't bear to see the hatred that must surely be in his eyes. He hated her for being the mother of the child he wanted so much to believe was his own.

For the most part, Merv asked all the same questions that he told her he was going to ask. As clearly and quickly as possible she told the court everything she could remember about the day she gave birth to Stephanie. Remembering that it was Amy not Stephanie she'd given birth to, she could no longer hold back the tears. Through the long years of grief, she'd loved Stephanie, had spent hours by her grave. Stephanie was a part of her in a way that Amy never could be. She wasn't ready to give her up, not yet. Maybe never. She took a moment to collect herself.

Merv reached over and patted her arm. "I'm sorry, Janette, I know this is difficult for you." He backed away and waited until she showed him with a slight lift of her chin that she was ready to proceed.

"What kind of father would you say Adam Blake is?"

The question surprised her. They had not rehearsed this one. She glanced over at Adam, but his feelings were held behind a rigid mask that gave nothing away. She thought about the many times she'd seen him with Amy. He'd always been so loving toward her. And until she had seen the loathing in Amy's eyes, she'd never thought he lacked parental skills. Would he really try to turn Amy against her? She hadn't thought so in the past, and she was having a difficult time thinking so now. "I . . . I think he's an excellent father."

"Would you agree that it's difficult raising a child alone?"

She nodded. "I would."

"Would you agree that a single parent, especially a father of a soon to be teenaged girl, would have an especially difficult time?"

She nodded again. "Yes, I would."

"Isn't it true that Adam Blake confided his feelings of inadequacy at raising a preteen girl, particularly in dealing with things of a sensitive nature. Sex, for instance?"

Janette couldn't believe the question. She glanced at Adam, who sat staring at her, his face etched with disbelief and shock. Too astonished to speak, she wondered if she could ever convince him that she'd never meant for something he had shared privately with her to be used against him in court. Helplessly, she watched the surprise on his face turn to hurt and finally, anger.

"Answer the question, Miss Taylor," the judge ordered.

She turned back to Merv, glaring at him. "I...I..."

"Shall I repeat the question?"

"No." She swallowed hard. For a moment it seemed to her that no one else existed in the courtroom but Adam.

"Please answer the question, Miss Taylor," the judge prodded. "Did Adam Blake confide that he was having difficulties talking to his daughter about sex?"

Adam looked like a man who had found his wife in another man's bed. She was cornered. "Yes," she said shakily. And with that one word she felt a final door between them slam shut.

OH, GOD, he thought, watching her, how could you do this to me? He had trusted her, trusted her with his heart, his soul even. Would have trusted her with his life had she let him. But never again.

He should be grateful, he thought as he stormed out of the courtroom later that day, refusing to talk to his lawyer or even his mother-in-law. He should be grateful that she had killed everything inside him. Maybe it was only a matter of time before the pain would go away.

JANETTE WOULD HAVE followed Adam out of the courtroom had she thought she could catch up to him. Instead, she remained in her seat, waited until she and Merv were the only ones left before she allowed her full rage to explode.

"How dare you use that information in court!" Never in her life had she been so furious.

Merv slammed his folder on the table between them. "Damn it, Janette, if you can think of another way to establish the fact that Amy would be better off living with her mother during her adolescence, I would very much like to hear it."

Janette inhaled deeply. "Adam told me his concern about fathering during a very private conversation. I only told you because I wanted you to know how much he loves and cares for Amy. You had no right to take what I told you and twist it like that. We're not fighting a war, Merv, we're trying to decide a child's future."

Merv grabbed the handle of his attaché case. "After Adam Blake's attorney gets through with you tomorrow, you tell me whether or not we're fighting a war. Now I suggest we go back to my office and get ready because it's going to be rough, I guarantee it." He walked past her and through the open doors where Stella stood waiting.

Janette felt a sinking feeling in the pit of her stomach. It might be rough, but nothing that happened tomorrow could possibly be any worse than what she'd been through today. Nothing could ever be worse than watching any hope that Adam still had any feeling for her die.

SHE HARDLY SLEPT that night and was up at dawn. Dressed in a blue sweat suit, she fed Pogo, who grabbed the food from her fingers before hopping away.

She began jogging along the beach in an attempt to calm her churning insides. The steel-gray sky provided the perfect complement to her mood. The ocean mist that wet her cheeks could just as easily have been her own tears.

She stopped to examine a fresh glob of oil that clung to the outer edges of a teeming tidal pool. According to the media, it was going to take months before the cleanup was complete and some environmentalists predicted the beaches would never be the same again.

She cut short her jog; she had no heart to continue. Turning back toward the house, she wondered if anything would ever be the same again.

Stella had already made the coffee by the time she returned. "Want something to eat?" she asked, handing Janette a steaming mug.

"I think not." Janette wrapped her cold hands around the hot mug before taking a sip.

"I told Merv I want to testify," Stella said.

Janette glanced up. "Really? Why?"

Stella ran her fingers through her mussed orange curls. "Maybe, just maybe I might have something of value to say. I've known you a long time. I knew you before you had a baby. So I told Merv if he needs a reliable character witness, he's got one."

Janette smiled. "Thanks, Stella. You're a good friend." She watched a cloud of smoke shoot up from the toaster that Stella had spent the better part of the previous evening repairing. "Be sure to mention how very understanding I am."

Stella dashed across the kitchen and pulled the plug from the electrical outlet. She hopped back and forth in front of the toaster, waving her hands through the air until the smoke dissipated. "You weren't very understanding when the roof caved in."

"Everyone's entitled to a lapse now and then," Janette said, flinging open a window.

The phone rang and Janette jumped. Stella reached out and squeezed her arm. "I'll get it."

There was no one on the line and after a moment, Stella hung up in disgust. "Probably some cub reporter lost his nerve when he actually heard a voice."

"I think I'll take a shower." Janette glanced at the phone. If only she had the nerve to call Adam and explain that she'd never meant for Merv to use that information against him. She had begun to dial his number from her bedroom phone the night before, but she had slammed down the receiver before she got to the last digit. Although she was no closer to getting up the nerve this morning, she sat on the bed and stared at the phone as soon as she reached her bedroom. She lay her hand on the receiver, but couldn't bring herself to pick it up.

ADAM SAT with his hand on the receiver. It had taken him all night to get up the nerve to make that call. But hearing a voice other than Janette's had thrown him off guard. He'd tried to say Janette's name, but the name stuck in his throat. He hated hanging up without a word, but there was nothing else he could do.

He stood up and jammed his hands into the pockets of his robe. Why, Janette? Why did you betray me in court? It wasn't what she'd said, exactly. He did find it difficult talking to Amy about certain subjects. Didn't every parent have the same problem on occasion? Hell, he knew nuclear physicists who turned pale at the thought of explaining sex to their children.

No, it wasn't what she'd said that was so damaging, it was that she had betrayed a trust. She took a special night they'd shared and used it against him. He thought that night had meant something to her. He'd believed her when she'd said she hadn't gone out with him because of Amy. He'd believed her when she'd told him her feelings for him had been real. He'd believed her because he had to believe. His heart wouldn't let him do otherwise.

Until yesterday...

JANETTE SAT in the witness stand facing Wes Marcus, and restated her name and occupation, spelling her name carefully for the court reporter. Simple questions requiring simple answers. But Adam's attorney had no intention of keeping it simple.

"Miss Taylor, would you please tell the court how old you were at the time of your baby's birth?"

"Seventeen."

"I assume you were not married."

Janette inhaled. "That's right."

"Do you know the name of the baby's father?"

She glared at the attorney. "Of course I do."

"Is it safe to state that the man in question had no desire to marry you?"

Janette swallowed. "We were young..."

"Seventeen," Wes said dramatically. "Unmarried, afraid." He leaned toward her. "How did you plan to raise your child?"

"I'd planned on getting a job."

"A job, Miss Taylor? What about your education?"

"I was going to go to night school."

"Let me see if I have this straight. You planned to work all day and go to school at night. Who was going to take care of your baby?"

Janette felt trapped, confused. What difference did it make? That was then and this is now. In her confusion, she let her eyes meet Adam's. His eyes were dark and impenetrable.

The stern unyielding look he gave her ignited something deep inside. Instead of pain, anger sprang up. She could almost hate him. How dare he sit behind his rigid mask and pass judgment on her? What gave him the right? He couldn't know that being alone when you were carrying a child was far worse than any other form of loneliness. He couldn't know the depth of fear she'd felt at the time.

With new resolve she faced his attorney. "I would have taken care of my baby if I had been given the chance."

Wes grabbed hold of the witness stand. "Isn't it true, Miss Taylor, that you planned to give your baby up for adoption?"

"Your Honor," Merv said, rising, his voice thin with exasperation, "I see no relevance here. Miss Taylor is no longer a seventeen-year-old without an education. She is a mature woman with a responsible position."

"On the contrary, Your Honor," Wes argued. "I think whether or not Miss Taylor ever intended to raise her child *is* the issue."

The judge hesitated. "Very well, I'll permit this line of questioning."

"Thank you, Your Honor." Adam's attorney turned to Janette. "Again, Miss Taylor, did you plan to put your child up for adoption?"

"No."

"Isn't it true, Miss Taylor, that you even considered abortion?"

Janette stiffened. "No! I never did!"

Wes turned and grabbed a paper from his notes. "Isn't it true that a certain Nancy MacIntroy came to your house to discuss the possibility of abortion?"

Janette wavered. She never knew the woman's name, never cared to. It was her father who had arranged the meeting. Her father who had insisted on her listening to what the woman had to say. "No!"

Wes stepped back in surprise. "No, Miss Taylor? The woman never came to your house?"

Janette leaned forward. "No, I never considered abortion."

Wes wasn't about to allow this one to stand. "Never considered it. According to a signed statement from Mrs. MacIntroy—" he handed a copy each to the judge and Merv Davidson before continuing "—she said you were very interested."

"That's not true," she gasped. She had never considered such a thing. She had wanted that baby, wanted it more than life itself. The need for someone to love who would love her back had been so strong she had been determined to raise that child despite her youth and lack of education. She and her father had fought bitterly over this issue. He had been so furious upon learning her decision, he had bombarded her with information on adoptions and abortions, but she had resisted it all the way.

How he'd hated her stubbornness, her independence. He'd hated it so much that he'd refused to escort her to the hospital. After she lost the baby, he insisted it was for the best. She never believed that, not for a moment. Losing a child could never be for the best.

But the questions continued, despite Merv's objections, despite the dazed and sometimes even contradictory answers she gave.

"Isn't it true that you never meant to keep your baby?"

Her head ached, the room seemed to spin. "Don't..." she pleaded. Desperately, she chanced a glance at Adam and realized too late her mistake. Instead of the earlier unfeeling look on his face that had infuriated her and strengthened her resolve, his eyes were filled with sympathy. A moment of recognition passed between them before the brutal reality of the proceedings intervened. But it was a moment that cost her plenty in terms of emotional stability. His anger had made her fighting mad, but his affinity tore away her defenses. Compassion could be a powerful weapon and Adam used it well.

Interpreting her silence to mean she refused to answer the question, Adam's lawyer grew more insistent. Leaning over the witness stand, he again hammered out the question. "Isn't it true that you never meant to keep your baby?"

ADAM WATCHED HER FACE, stunned by the sorrow he saw mirrored there. He'd understood how she'd felt from the moment she first told him about the baby. And now this. This was beyond human endurance. He had the greatest urge to go to her and wrap her in his arms, to wipe away her tears, to make those blue-green eyes laugh again. He wanted to lash out at everyone and everything that had ever hurt her. His hands curled into tight angry fists.

Adam willed her to look at him and she did. Hold on, his eyes told her.

Help me, she answered back.

With her plea to him came the realization of his helplessness. Then came the rage, so strong he felt he would explode. He wanted to explode, he did explode, shooting to his feet. "That's enough!"

A stunned silence filled the courtroom. One by one, all eyes turned to Adam.

It took Janette a moment to realize that the attorney had backed away. Slowly, she fought her way out of the confused fog. It was then that she saw Adam on his feet. There was anger in his face, raw anger, and it was directed toward Wes Marcus.

"That's enough," Adam repeated. This time, the eyes that moments ago had been filled with compassion now bore into his attorney with cold contempt.

"Mr. Marcus," the judge said in irritation, "would you please instruct your client to control himself?"

"I apologize, Your Honor, on behalf of my client." Wes walked over and after a whispered conference with Adam, turned to the judge. His face was livid but his voice remained calm as he requested a recess.

The judge glanced at Janette. "This has been a difficult day, Miss Taylor. We'll adjourn until tomorrow morning."

Shaken, Janette stumbled from the witness stand and clung to Stella's arm.

"Let's get the hell out of here," Stella said.

WES FOLLOWED ADAM into a deserted conference room across from the courtroom. He threw his attaché case on the table and spun around to face Adam.

"What the hell are you trying to do?" he demanded. "Do you want to keep Amy or don't you?"

Adam was so angry he could barely contain his voice. "You know very well I want to keep Amy. But what you were doing in there was inexcusable."

Wes swore beneath his breath. "I've got to prove that she had no intention of keeping her baby."

"Damn it! What difference does it make? She was only seventeen!"

"It makes all the difference in the world. If I can prove that she never meant to keep her baby, I might also be able to convince the court that she has no interest in Amy now. Her only reason for seeking custody is to paint this tragic picture of a loving mother denied her baby for her upcoming suit against the hospital."

"I don't believe that!" Adam protested.

"We're talking millions of dollars. There's no telling what a person's likely to do for that kind of money."

"I don't care how much we're talking about. Janette cares about Amy." Adam closed his eyes, trying to shut out the memory of her face while she was on the witness stand. The pain had been real. He would bet his life on it. "You'll have to find another way for me to keep custody of Amy!"

"What do you think I am? A miracle man? Come on, Adam. The only way we have a shot at this is to prove that Janette Taylor is either a woman of poor moral character or that she's out for monetary gain. Take your pick."

Adam's face grew hard. "I won't sit back and let you destroy Amy's mother!"

"Damn it, Adam, you're asking for the impossible. The court always sympathizes with the mother. Do you know what makes this case so damned difficult? If you're right about Janette Taylor, and I'm not convinced that you are, then neither one of you deserves to be in this situation. But the plain fact is that you are and if you want to keep Amy, you'd better give it all you've got, because, damn it, you don't have much.''

Adam slumped down on a chair. For eleven years he'd loved Amy, walked the floor with her, dried her tears, held her, worried over her, gave parenting his all. How could eleven years of caring for a child count for so little? ''Isn't there some other way?''

''I'm afraid not. Either you destroy Janette Taylor or—'' he grabbed his attaché case ''—you lose Amy.''

ADAM SLEPT LITTLE that night. Mostly he paced the floor or stood outside Amy's room. He was tempted to wake her, to hug her and hold her like he'd never held her before. But afraid of frightening her, he resisted the urge. Instead, he stumbled through the dark to the kitchen, switching on the light and heating up the leftover coffee. Pouring himself a cup, he slumped down in a chair at the kitchen table and rested his head in his hands.

Every time he thought of losing his beloved daughter, he strengthened his resolve to keep her whatever it took. With this thought came the memory of Janette on the stand as she told the story of being seventeen, alone, afraid—and pregnant.

He remembered her trembling lips as she testified. If this wasn't difficult enough, he also remembered how they were the same lips that had once trembled against his. He was tortured with the memory of her eyes brimming with grief as she talked about wanting to keep her baby. Torture turned to anguish as he remembered they were the same eyes that had once looked at him with the sweet promise of love. Damn! What a mess.

What was Janette's real motive for pursuing custody of Amy? Was it love or was it revenge? Was she really the conniving person his lawyer made her out to be? Oh, God, what if Wes was right? What if she was putting him through this hell for the sole purpose of monetary gain?

Someone's going to pay for what they did to me! she'd said. He remembered all too well the look on her face when she'd flung those words out, and even now those words made him shiver.

You're asking me to walk away from my daughter! She'd said that, too. Only that time there had been no anger or revenge on her face, only pain.

Which one? Which one could he believe?

"Daddy."

Adam's eyes flew open. It took him a minute to get his bearings. He was sitting at the kitchen table and the blinding light was the sun streaming through the sliding glass door. He drew his hands across his face. He must have fallen asleep right there at the table.

Amy drew nearer. "Are you all right, Daddy?"

"I'm fine," he said. He picked up his coffee cup and stared at the mudlike coffee at the bottom that had long grown cold. He grimaced.

"Aren't you going to work?" Amy asked.

Adam shook his head. "I've got to be in court."

Watching her father with concern, Amy grabbed the carton of orange juice out of the refrigerator and poured two glasses. Carrying the glasses to the table, she dropped one. It shattered and Adam jumped to his feet. "Damn it, Amy! Can't you be more careful?"

Amy burst into tears and ran upstairs to her room, slamming the bedroom door shut behind her.

Cursing himself for his foul temper, Adam ran after her. "Amy, I'm sorry," he called through her door. "May I come in?"

The door opened and Amy stood looking at him sadly. A knife twisted inside him. "I'm sorry, sport." It seemed all he ever did anymore was apologize to her. "What do you say we go to La Fiesta tonight and order a plate of enchiladas as big as all get..." He stopped himself in time. What was the matter with him? He couldn't even open his mouth without Janette's words coming out. "As big as all Montana," he finished lamely. It was a weak attempt to bribe a smile out of her. Lately, he was beginning to wonder if he had any business being a father.

Amy bit her lip. "I'm sorry about the orange juice."

Adam wrapped his arms around her. "I don't care about the orange juice," he said. "I only care about you."

Amy pressed her head against his chest, her eyes filling with tears, as she slipped her arms around his waist. "I hate her, I hate her!"

Stunned, Adam lifted her head and held her face between his hands. "Who do you hate?"

"Janette!" she sobbed. "Grandma says she was never my friend. She only pretended to be my friend so she could take me away!"

Damn Virginia, he thought, drawing Amy into his arms again. With fresh anguish, he remembered Janette's silent plea from the witness stand. *Help me!*

"Do you believe that?"

Amy stopped crying and drew away from him. "No, but Grandma said—"

"Hush, now." He wiped away her tears with his fingers. "Janette is your real mother and she loves you very much. Just as I do, just as your grandmother does."

"But grandma says that Janette is trying to take me away."

"She's not trying to take you away," Adam said. "She just wants you to live with her instead of me. That's not the same as taking you away, because no one could ever do that. No matter what happens you're always going to be my girl, and I'm always going to be your daddy. Do you understand?"

Amy wasn't sure if she understood or not. But she nodded anyway because she knew it was important to him.

"Good." He straightened. "What do you say you get ready for school while I fix you one of my kitchen-sink omelets?"

Amy smiled. Adam hugged her again, and hastened downstairs.

AMY CLOSED her bedroom door and pressed her forehead against the cool hard wood. Her father had said that no matter what happened he would always be her daddy. With this warm thought tucked safely inside, she finished dressing for school.

On the way to the bus stop later that morning, Amy walked passed the Hopkins's place and peered through the border of hollyhocks. She caught a glimpse of Shortstop chasing the fall leaves that were blowing around the yard. A grin on her face, Amy walked around the fence to get a better view.

"Here, Shortstop, come here. I have something for you." She reached into her pocket for the dry cat food she'd brought with her and held her hand through the gate.

At the sound of Amy's voice, the kitten stood still and stared at her. "Come on, Shortstop. The bus will be here any minute. Hurry!"

The kitten dashed away from her as fast as his little legs would carry him; he ran up to the front door and frantically pawed the screen. The door opened and the kitten dashed inside.

Heartbroken, Amy straightened. Shortstop had forgotten her.

Don't worry, Shortstop, she'd said that day she had brought the tiny kitten to live with the Hopkinses. You're still my kitten even if you don't live with me anymore. And with this memory came another:

You'll always be my girl.

Panic filled her.

You'll always be my girl.

Her heart thudded.

You'll always be my girl.

Hot tears ran down her cheeks. What if she had to live with Janette? What then? How long would it take until her daddy forgot her just as Shortstop had?

How long would it be before she was no longer her daddy's little girl?

CHAPTER FOURTEEN

THE LIVING NIGHTMARE continued. Janette's third day on the stand was every bit as difficult as the first and the second. Her whole life, it seemed, was being subjected to cruel scrutiny. Why did you do this? Why did you do that? When did you do it? How? And when she thought there was nothing left for Adam's attorney to ask her, he speared her with perhaps the most difficult question of all.

"When did you first think that Amy was yours?"

She closed her eyes, remembering. "From the moment I first saw her," she whispered. The day when Amy had visited the Living Masters Pageant with her class. That was the day it had all begun.

A murmur snapped through the courtroom like a lazily cracked whip. She kept her eyes averted from Adam.

"How is this possible, Miss Taylor? How could you have been so sure that Amy was your child on the basis of a single meeting?"

"It was a feeling I had inside. I can't explain it. All I know is that from that first day I couldn't stop thinking of her."

"Are we to understand that you went out with Amy's father knowing that you were the child's mother?"

Janette turned to look at Adam. "I went out with Adam Blake because I thought he was the most attractive man I had ever met." Suddenly she was oblivious to everything around her. All she could think of, all she could see, was Adam as he had looked on the night he'd told her he was falling in love with her. "Amy had nothing to do with why I went out with you." Her voice was strong again, confident. There was no uncertainty about which words to choose. Only the simplest words would do, spoken from the heart.

Something changed in Adam's expression. The rigid lines of his face softened. She couldn't tell by his expression whether or not he believed her, but she could tell he wanted to, and for now that was enough.

"Miss Taylor!" Wes roared. "If you don't mind! Would you please address your comments to the court!" He waited until he was certain he had her attention before he continued. "You expect us to believe that you knew from the start that Amy was yours and yet you claim that dating the defendant had nothing to do with Amy. I find that hard to believe."

"I didn't trust my feelings. I kept telling myself I was crazy. I kept going to the cemetery, telling myself that Stephanie was my little girl, not Amy." Something made her stop. Her gaze swung toward Adam. He sat rigid, staring at her as if he'd seen a ghost.

To her horror she remembered all too late that he didn't know about the grave.

THE GRAVE! He hadn't been able to think of anything else since hearing Janette's testimony. He hadn't known about the grave.

Adam paced around his living room trying to forget the events of the day as he waited for Amy to come home. She had called and told him she was at Tammy's house and would be home by six. It was a quarter of. He had fifteen minutes in which to calm down. All these weeks since this nightmare had begun, he'd been too concerned about Amy to think much beyond that. But a grave. A grave! That made the other baby seem real in a way she had never been before. His baby and Carolyn's.

With this realization came the feeling of being cheated. He and Carolyn had never been allowed to bury their baby, to grieve for her. They'd not even been allowed to name her. Anger rose inside, aimed at some nameless "they" who had denied him his right as a parent.

Stephanie. He rolled the name slowly in his mouth, said it aloud. He liked the name. He wondered if the name held some special meaning for Janette. He still remembered how her eyes had softened each time she'd mentioned Stephanie. Even on the witness stand there had been a catch to her voice when she said the child's name as if she was reluctant to let go of her or to share her with anyone else.

He grabbed a bottle of mineral water from the refrigerator and unscrewed the cap.

"Knock, knock. Anyone home?"

Adam turned and saw his mother-in-law on the patio waving to him though the sliding glass door.

He set his drink on the table and let her in. "What are you doing back here?"

Virginia studied his face. "I rang the doorbell but no one answered. Your car's in the driveway so I knew you had to be home. Are you all right? Wes said you had a tough day in court."

"You talked to Wes?" he asked in surprise. After the first day, Virginia had decided to stay away from the hearing. Actually, Adam had insisted she stay home when he saw how a single day in court had affected her.

"I just wanted to know what was going on," she said defensively. "Amy's my grandchild!"

"Speaking of Amy, I'm disturbed by something she told me. She said that you told her Janette was trying to take her away from me."

Virginia's eyes clouded in confusion. "Well? Isn't she?"

"That's not the point. The point is I don't want Amy bearing ill feelings toward her mother. Toward either one of us."

"Carolyn is Amy's mother!"

Adam rubbed his hand across his chin. "I think Amy will always think of Carolyn as her mother. One of her mothers. She certainly had a great influence in making Amy the person she is today."

Virginia heaved angrily. "Carolyn raised Amy from birth."

"Believe me, Virginia, I'm not likely to forget that."

"It seems to me there's a lot you're forgetting lately. Since that Taylor woman has walked into your life you've not only forgotten your poor wife, but it seems that you've forgotten that Amy is your daughter!"

"I haven't forgotten anything!" Adam replied stiffly. "Amy will always be my daughter, no matter what the outcome of the hearing."

Virginia's eyes grew round. "Do you think...I mean is there a chance we'll lose her?"

"We'll never lose her!" he said stubbornly. Then in a deep low voice he added, "She may have to live with Janette."

"I won't have it!" Virginia shouted. "She's my grandchild."

Adam lifted weary eyes toward Virginia. He couldn't bring himself to remind her that she was not Amy's grandmother, not legally. Just as he wasn't Amy's father. "I know that Amy means a lot to you," he said.

"She's my life!"

"Maybe that's a mistake," he began tactfully. "Maybe it's time you develop some other interests, meet other people." Virginia had centered her life on her daughter. He supposed it was only natural she would transfer her attention to Amy now that Carolyn was gone.

"I'm not interested in meeting people," Virginia said. "I'm interested in Amy."

"That's my point. Amy is growing up. She needs room to grow. She needs us to support her, not smother her." Alarmed by the look on her face, he tried another approach. "You're still a fairly young woman." He didn't know much about women's clothes or makeup, but he suspected that if she updated hers, or at least got rid of the dreadful blue eye shadow, she would look much younger than her fifty-eight years. "I just think it would be a good idea if you got out more. Take classes at the college maybe, or do volunteer work."

"What you're saying is that we're going to lose Amy, isn't it?" Her eyes filled with tears. "This is your way of preparing me, isn't it?"

"Damn it, Virginia, what I'm trying to say is that it's time for you to make a life of your own."

"I have a life. Amy is my life. And I'm not going to let anyone take her away from me!"

Adam grimaced. He hadn't wanted to get into an argument with Virginia. He combed his fingers through his hair. "We're both upset. Maybe it's better if we talk about this another time."

Virginia nodded. "I wanted to take Amy out for dinner. I won't keep her out late. If you want, you can join us."

Adam shook his head. "I need to talk to her privately tonight. I want to explain to her that she's got to testify in court."

Virginia's eyes narrowed spitefully. "Good! I hope she tells the court what that horrible woman has done to this family!"

AMY FROZE outside the kitchen door, surprised to hear her grandma's voice sound so hateful. Terror filled her. She heard her father say she had to testify. She knew what it was like to testify. It was awful. She'd seen enough court cases on TV to know that you had to tell the truth when you were on the stand or you would go to prison. But what if they asked her if she hated Janette? She couldn't lie about that, could she? But if she told them how much she liked Janette, she might have to live with her and then her father would forget her like Shortstop had forgotten her and that would be awful and . . .

Panic filled her. She backed away from the kitchen door. Every corner of the room seemed to hold a hidden danger. Shadows loomed like arms waiting to grab her. Running blindly away from the angry voices of her father and grandmother, she tore out the front door and dashed into the cold dark night.

WHERE IS SHE? Adam asked himself for at least the tenth time in that many minutes. It was after six-thirty. It wasn't like Amy to be late without calling him. She knew how much he worried whenever she was the slightest bit late.

He thumbed through his phone book, looking for Amy's best friend Tammy's number. He wondered vaguely if he wasn't every bit the overprotective parent he'd accused Virginia of being. Still, it was dark outside and they did live in a relatively isolated neighborhood. He punched out the number and held his breath. Tammy's mother answered on the third ring.

"Mrs. Parker? Adam Blake here. Is Amy still there?"

"No, I dropped her off at home about forty minutes ago." Mrs. Parker sounded surprised and a bit guarded. "Is everything all right?"

"I'm sure it is," Adam said, trying to sound more confident than he felt. "She might have gone to the store or something," he finished weakly, although he doubted it. She wouldn't go to the store without telling him. She wouldn't go anywhere without telling him, would she? Feeling foolish, Adam thanked her and hung up. Maybe she was in her bedroom. He never thought to check. Feeling a sense of relief, he walked through the living room, noticing for the first time that the lamp had been turned on.

"Amy!" He took the stairs two at a time. "Where are you?" He opened up the door to her bedroom. It was dark. "Amy?"

He turned on the light. Her schoolbooks were heaped unceremoniously on the bed. She had been home then, but when? And why hadn't she announced her arrival? A cold chill shimmered up his spine in answer. Had she heard him arguing with her grandmother?

He hurried from her room, dashed downstairs and out the front door, calling her name. His voice cut through the damp darkness and was answered only by silence and the distant roar of the ocean. He turned back to the house and checked every room one by one. After he finished downstairs, he started on the upstairs.

More worried than ever, he returned to the kitchen and grabbed the wall phone. Cradling the receiver between his ear and shoulder, he thumbed through his address book and began punching out numbers. He called everyone he could think of. He called her teacher, her softball coach, her friends, her classmates. He even called Mrs. Tumble, their hard-of-hearing neighbor down the street and, after a frustrating conversation, was convinced that she had not seen Amy, either.

Coming to the end of his address book, he stood with his hand on the receiver, thinking, trying to recall every detail of their last conversation. Maybe she'd spotted her grandmother and gone home with her. Of course. Why hadn't he thought of that earlier? Virginia was pretty upset when she left. Maybe Amy had decided she needed company. Maybe she'd even tried to call him, but the line had been busy. Feeling a sense of relief he punched out Virginia's number.

"Virginia. May I speak to Amy?" He could tell by the silence that followed that Amy wasn't there, hadn't been there.

"What makes you think she's here?" Virginia asked, her voice shrill with alarm.

"I can't find her anywhere. She was due home—" he glanced at his watch "—over an hour ago. It's not like her to be out this late."

"Do you suppose that she...that woman?..."

"What are you talking about?" His mind reeled in confusion. "What woman?"

"Janette Taylor. Do you suppose she kidnapped her or something?"

"Don't be ridiculous," Adam stammered, numbed by the thought, stunned that a part of him hoped that Amy was with Janette. At least with Janette, she would be safe.

"I'm telling you, Adam, that woman has something to do with this. I feel it in my bones. I'm calling the police!"

"That's a good idea. Meanwhile, I'm going to drive around and see if I can find her." He hung up. It was crazy, impossible. Janette wouldn't do such a thing, would she? He snatched the receiver again and began dialing. Janette's line was busy. He slammed the receiver down with a curse and raced out to his car.

CHAPTER FIFTEEN

JANETTE LAY stretched out on the floor directing the beam of a flashlight to the open vent beneath the furnace, while Stella read off the model and serial number into the phone to Larry.

Janette felt tired and depressed. During the last week she'd gone through extensive court-ordered psychological testing. The worst test had been the symptom checklist, which asked such questions as, if a child cries in the middle of the night would it bother you "not at all, a little, a lot, or extremely." How were you supposed to answer a question like that? she wondered. Was a sane person bothered or not bothered by a crying child? She didn't know; all she knew was every time she heard a child cry in her dreams, it nearly tore her heart in two.

"I think the next number's a zero," Stella said into the phone, then contradicted herself immediately. "Make that an eight." Years of damp ocean air had rusted the metal plate beneath the furnace, making it all but impossible to read its model number.

"You know," she said with a sideways glance at Janette, "it could just as easily be a three." She held the receiver away from her ear and shrugged. "I think Larry needs a vacation. He's getting grouchy. Yes, Larry, I'm here. I'll give it to you again. The number is five. The next number is either a three or an eight. Then there's a..."

Janette shifted her legs. The wood floor was hard. It was also damp and cold. The weather had suddenly grown chilly and that morning Stella had decided to light the pilot of the furnace. The furnace had made a loud clanking sound, which Stella insisted was nothing to worry about. The noise was followed by fumes that filled the house and made their eyes smart. Stella opened windows and doors, letting in more cold air and assuring Janette that everything was under control. "It's just dust burning off inside," she'd insisted.

Not until black smoke began to snake out of the heat vents did Stella finally concede that they might possibly have something to worry about.

"It's either a five or a six," Stella continued. "I think the next number's a nine."

Janette shifted the flashlight. Her arm ached from holding it up so long. The doorbell rang, followed by a loud knock. Grateful for the interruption, she handed Stella the flashlight and stood.

She opened the door and froze. Not waiting for an invitation, Adam pushed pass her. He glanced around, noting Stella on the floor in the hall off the living room, before turning and facing Janette.

"Where is she?" he demanded. "Where's my daughter?"

Janette's mouth fell open in surprise. "Amy?" she stammered in confusion. "Why would you think she was here?"

Adam could see the surprise on her face was genuine. He regretted letting Virginia sway his thinking. Aware of how appealing she looked in blue jeans, a soft blue-green sweater that matched the color of her eyes,

her blond-red hair seductively tousled, he was sorry
he'd come. Sheepishly, he turned away. "Amy's missing."

Janette gasped. "Oh, no!" Then with a quickening
pain, she added, "You thought that I . . ."

He glanced up. "I'm sorry, Janette. I didn't known
what to think."

Stunned, she fought the bitter anger that assailed
her. How could he?

Seeing the look on her face nearly crushed him, but
he couldn't think of that now. Not with Amy God only
knew where. "I've got to go."

"I'm going with you."

"No."

The look on her face was as if a bullet had pierced
her heart. Adam felt worse than he had ever felt in his
life. He was scared, so scared, for Amy. Scared of losing her, scared that someone would harm her. But he
was also scared for this woman, who looked every bit
as vulnerable tonight as she had looked on that damned
witness stand. He reached out and touched her arm,
feeling the soft sweater give way beneath his fingers,
and the arm that had seemed to grow so thin during the
last few weeks shiver beneath his touch.

"There's nothing you can do," he said gently. "Virginia's called the police. I was just going to drive up
and down the streets." It seemed foolish, but he had to
do something. He couldn't just sit around and wait.
"Maybe I'll spot her somewhere, I don't know."

"I'm going with you," she said again, this time more
firmly. She stepped back, away from him, but her arm
still burned from the memory of his touch. Whirling
around, she reached into the hall closet for her jacket
and grabbed her shoulder bag from the end table. She

waved to Stella who was still doing battle with the furnace, and walked out the door ahead of Adam.

For a while neither spoke. She sat pressed against the passenger door, worriedly scanning the dark streets and deserted sidewalks as Adam drove slowly up one street and down the next. He slowed down in front of an ice cream parlor, but the place, normally filled with families and teens during the hot summer months, stood deserted on this cold autumn night.

"Do you think Amy ran away because of the custody suit?" Janette asked, breaking the silence. The question hung between them like an ugly open wound. It was a stupid question, she thought. Why else would an otherwise happy and well-adjusted child run away from home? When he didn't answer she said, "I never meant for this to happen."

He glanced at her, grateful for the darkness that kept her face in shadow. "Did you honestly think that Amy could come through a custody suit unscathed? No matter what the outcome, she will always feel a sense of guilt."

"Why guilt?" Janette asked, feeling a twist inside. "None of this is her fault." She let her eyes scan the empty sidewalks, the dark streets, the deserted alleys and vacant lots.

"No, it's not," he said. "But being blameless doesn't always remove the guilt." He was speaking from experience. Hadn't he harbored and nurtured guilt when he'd sat in that courtroom so long ago and said he wanted to live with his father? Even then, at that young age, he'd sensed that his father was far weaker than his mother. He'd wanted to stay with his father not because he would be the better parent—far from that—but because he thought he could protect his father and maybe help him stop drinking. As long as he lived, he would never forget the look on his mother's face after he'd told that lie on the stand. His mother never forgave him; his father never stopped drinking and he never stopped feeling guilty.

Janette kept her eyes on the road ahead as the silence stretched between them. It was too dark to see much beyond the headlights. Too dark to know what lay ahead. "I never thought you'd turn Amy against me."

He glanced at her sharply, noting how pale her face looked as they passed beneath a streetlight. "I didn't. I would never do that, Janette. Never. She's confused. Frightened."

Janette clung to his words, wanting to believe him, needing to. But Amy hadn't seemed the least bit confused that day. She had said exactly what she thought. Janette closed her eyes against the memory of Amy's young face twisted in hatred.

"When I was six," she began slowly, "my mother left my father and me. I didn't know until recently why she left and the truth is I don't know if it would have made any difference had I known then. I don't think I'll ever get over the feeling of being abandoned. A parent can offer all sorts of excuses for leaving, but I don't think the reasons matter to a child. That's why I can't walk away from Amy." Silence fell between them as they continued their search.

Suddenly Janette leaned forward. "Over there," she cried, pointing out the window. "I thought I saw someone behind that rock."

Adam slammed on the brake and jumped out of the car. They were in front of a picnic area on a cliff overlooking the ocean. Janette ran after him, her tennis shoes sinking into the sand. It was freezing cold on the bluff; the wind tore through her jacket like icy knives, biting into her flesh. Her hair whipped across her face and she fought to keep it out of her eyes.

Adam disappeared for a moment before she spotted him again in the beam of the headlights, talking to a young couple who glanced over at her as he spoke. It was obvious that the couple hadn't seen Amy, and Janette felt herself crumbling inside as Adam started toward her looking dejected.

"I'm afraid I startled two lovebirds," he explained. He draped an arm around her shoulder. "You're freezing. Let's get back to the car."

Grateful for the warmth he offered her, she leaned against him. It took sheer physical effort to pull away from the shelter of his arms and slip into the car.

"Maybe we should check the house," Adam said once they were on the road again. "Maybe she came back home and is looking for me."

As soon as they drove into the driveway, Janette felt certain that the house was deserted. She scanned the second story, wondering which of the dark rooms was Amy's. The fact that she didn't know reminded her how very little she knew about her daughter, and the old rage began to rise inside.

She sensed by the way Adam got out of the car that she was right about the house being empty. Still, he went through the motions, calling Amy's name as he unlocked the front door, listening for the voice they both knew he wouldn't hear. Silently, she followed Adam from room to room, and waited at the bottom of the stairs while he checked the second floor.

She watched him descend the stairs, the lines in his face deepening as his eyes met hers. "She's not been home." The hollow ring of his voice hit her like well-aimed blows to the heart. She felt so helpless. Unable to speak, she followed him silently into the kitchen.

Adam called Virginia while Janette made a pot of coffee. After a short conversation, he hung up and slumped onto a kitchen chair. "Nothing," he said, holding his head with both hands. "Virginia talked to the police. They've put out an all points bulletin."

Janette poured him a cup of coffee and placed it on the table in front of him. She stood holding her hand in midair, inches away from his shoulder, unsure if he would let her comfort him, not knowing if she could. Unable to stop herself, she let her hand drop to his shoulder, bracing herself for the rejection she was sure would come.

Instead, he surprised her by grabbing her hand and holding on to it as if he would never let it go. "I've got to find her," he said in a tortured voice.

"Oh, Adam." His name fell from her lips in a sob, ripped from the inner depths of pain, pain for him, pain for herself, pain for the child they both loved. She dropped to her knees by his side and gazed into his face. "We'll find her," she whispered earnestly. She pushed aside the lock of hair that had fallen across his forehead, pressed her fingers against the shadow that had gathered at his forehead. "I promise you we'll find her." She wrapped both arms around him and lay her head against his chest; it felt so right, so perfectly right, to hold him, for him to hold her back.

For several blissful moments, they clung to each other. At last, Adam cupped both her hands in his, and gazed into the face that had haunted him since the first day they'd met. He studied the soft mouth that he had come to know by heart, the blue-green eyes that held such sadness. Even now, in the fog of his despair, he could feel her utter sorrow.

"When I first learned that you were Amy's mother, all I could think about was that I had lost a part of Carolyn that I thought I could never lose," he said.

"Oh, Adam, I don't want you to lose any part of Carolyn. She was Amy's mother for seven years. Nothing can change that. A part of her will always be with Amy."

He squeezed her soft hands and drew them to his chest. "Thank you for saying that."

"It's true," she whispered. It hurt to think that Carolyn was the only mother Amy had ever known. Maybe the only mother Amy would ever know. It hurt, but she would do everything in her power to preserve what Carolyn and Amy had shared. She wanted to be a part of Amy's future, but she knew she could never be a part of Amy's past.

Adam saw a tight look in the depths of her eyes, a look that told him that somewhere inside a knife had twisted. "I never resented that you were her mother. I was never angry at you, Janette, I want you to believe that. The fact that I wasn't her father—" his voice grew thick "—that's what I'm finding so hard to live with. Knowing that I'm not her father."

Janette's eyes widened. "But you *are* her father," she protested. She'd never thought otherwise. "You're the only father she's ever known. You'll always be her father, Adam. Why, she's like you in so many ways."

"Maybe," he said, but there was a lot of Janette in Amy, too. In fact, the look of concern on Janette's face at that very moment was the same one he had seen countless times on Amy's face.

He slipped his hands around Janette's small waist. It felt like the most natural thing in the world to hold her, to feel her soft sweet breath mingling with his. He knew that if he turned her head toward him, he would find refuge in the soft sweet lips that were murmuring words of comfort in his ear.

Refuge. It was almost enough to sell his soul for; it was not enough to still the part inside of him that cautioned him to stay away from her or the voice deep inside that kept saying, she's the enemy...she's trying to take Amy away from you.

Sensing him suddenly grow tense, she backed away. "Do you want some more coffee?" she asked, searching his face for a clue to his sudden withdrawal. For a moment their eyes held, questioned and, finally, each pair sought a safer focal point. He gazed at the cup in front of him; she turned to the wall over the stove.

"No, no thank you." He lifted his cup and emptied it.

Janette stared at the kitchen clock, watching the second hand sweep around its face. It was nearly ten.

"Where is she?" Adam asked. "God, I've got to think. There's got to be someone I haven't called..."

Janette felt so helpless. She didn't even know the names of Amy's friends.

As if trying to guess her thoughts, Adam studied her face. "I called everyone I could think of. Maybe we should check the streets again."

We. He'd said we. She closed her eyes. "She's not going to be walking the streets." How she knew this, she couldn't say. She just did. Oh, Amy, where are you? She tried to think where an eleven-year-old would go. Some place safe or at least a place that felt safe to her. But where? Janette thought back to when she was that age. Her safe place had been the attic. She would go up there to think and . . .

Her eyes flew open. "What about the cave?"

Adam looked blank. "Cave? What cave?"

"I . . . I'm not sure. But Amy told me once that she had this secret cave that she liked to go to."

"She must mean the cave down on the private beach below." He narrowed his eyes in thought. He remembered vaguely coming across the cave a few years back. He didn't even know that Amy knew about it. "I doubt she would be there. She never goes down to the beach at night. In any case, I told her not to go there because of the oil spill."

"I think we should check it out, Adam," she said, her excitement growing. "There's no telling what a child would do if she's afraid enough."

"I suppose we could check." If nothing else, it gave him something to do. "You sure you want to come? It's a pretty steep climb down that bluff."

She nodded. There was no way that she was going to stay behind. She waited for him to get a flashlight, then followed him out the back door. The wind hurled against them, carrying with it bits of sand and salt air. Heads down against the wind, they cut through the yard and out through a gate in back.

Adam reached for her hand. "Be careful," he shouted above the howling of the wind and the roar of the ocean waves pounding against the rocks below. Slowly they began to make their way down the steep path. Her foot slipped on a rock and Adam's hand tightened its grip, his other hand reaching around to grab her other arm.

"You all right?" he shouted.

"Yes," she shouted back.

Finally they made it to the narrow strip of beach.

"High tide," he said grimly. Her heart froze in fear. But there was no time to dwell on the possibility that Amy might be trapped. A wave of cold water washed over them, catching them by surprise and drenching them. Janette reached out blindly and was suddenly in Adam's arms.

Clinging to him, she began to sob. "Hold on," he said. "We're almost there."

Carefully they inched their way along a rocky ledge. Janette tried not to think of Amy, of the sea that was moving in with thunderous force or the wind that battered them. She tried only to think of Adam's strong arm around her.

They practically crawled through a narrow opening in the rocks. Protected from the wind, Janette allowed herself to breath. It was a mistake. Instead of fresh air, she took in a lung full of oily fumes, and coughed.

"Breathe through your mouth," Adam shouted in her ear. He patted her on the back. It was too dark to see his face, but she could feel his eyes on her.

It took a moment for her to catch her breath. But breathing through her mouth, she gradually felt her head begin to clear. The rocky chamber sheltered them from the wind and the crashing waves, but she felt a fine spray wash over her each time a breaker hit the outer wall.

"Stay here," Adam said, releasing her. He disappeared and she clung to the jagged rock wall behind her, afraid to move. Cold icy water lapped around her ankles. She shivered, wondering vaguely why suddenly she could see flickering shadows ahead.

With each passing moment, she grew more anxious. "Adam?" She moved along the ledge, surprised to see a lantern on the ledge directly across from her, its light casting ghostly shadows along the rugged walls of the cave. It was then that she saw Amy wrapped in her father's arms.

Tears of relief and joy sprang to Janette's eyes. A prayer of thanksgiving fell from her lips. She had never seen a more beautiful, wondrous sight in all her life.

"I'm sorry, Daddy," Amy sobbed as she clung to her father. "I was so afraid. I don't want to testify, Daddy."

"We'll talk about this later, sport. Right now we have to get you home and into some dry clothes. You're freezing."

Janette watched father and daughter and felt like an intruder. Anger reared its ugly head as she remembered the circumstances that had cut her out of her daughter's life, perhaps forever.

Adam lifted Amy in his arms and headed in Janette's direction. He stopped in front of Janette and she lifted her hand to touch her daughter on the arm.

Amy swung her head around. Her eyes rounded in surprise, then a look of uncertainty clouded her already pale face. Adam felt his daughter stiffen in his arms. "It's all right," he said softly. "Janette helped me find you. If she hadn't mentioned the cave, I might never have found you."

Amy never took her eyes off Janette while her father explained all this. But there was still suspicion in the dark green eyes, and fear. Janette thought her heart would break.

Janette bit her lip. "I'm not going to take you away," she whispered. "I'm not going to take you away from your father."

Amy's face softened, and radiated a quiet happiness that filled Janette with joy. There was no malice there, no hatred.

"We better get back." Adam said.

Janette nodded, then followed Adam and Amy back into the dark brutal night.

BACK AT THE HOUSE, Adam showed Janette where the downstairs bathroom was, and then left to run Amy's bath. Freezing, Janette pulled off her wet clothes and stepped into the shower. She stood beneath the stream of hot water until the warmth finally seeped into her bones and she stopped shaking. After toweling off, she donned the blue robe Adam had loaned her, burying herself in the yards of soft velvety velour that was steeped in Adam's wonderfully masculine smell.

She walked into the kitchen and after tossing her clothes into the dryer, she thought about making hot chocolate but, unable to find cocoa in the cupboards, she decided to make tea, instead. After putting the kettle on to boil, she slumped onto a kitchen chair, exhausted and emotionally drained. Folding her arms across the table, she laid her head down, too tired to think, but more than anything too tired to feel.

ADAM TUCKED the blankets around Amy. "You okay, sport?" He brushed her damp blond hair back from her face, his chest feeling as if it were about to burst with gratitude for her safety.

Amy snuggled beneath the bedclothes. "I'm sorry, Daddy. I didn't mean to scare you."

He ran a knuckle across her pale cheek. "Just don't do it again, you hear? I don't think this old heart could take another scare like that." He was joking, but the look of horror on her face made him want to rip out his tongue. "Nothing's going to happen to me," he added quickly. "I was only kidding." He leaned over and kissed her forehead until the shadow of worry disappeared from her face.

She lifted her eyes. "This morning I went to see Shortstop and he didn't recognize me. I thought he would always remember me. I thought it would make no difference where he lived."

Adam groaned inwardly. He knew what she was really saying, could see it in her eyes, in her face, in the small hands that curled tightly around the top of her blankets.

"I'm not going to forget you, Amy. I don't care if you move to the North Pole. You're always going to be here in my heart. People don't forget those they love." There were times he wished he could forget. Would give his soul to forget. "Shortstop... well, he's just an animal. You're always going to be my girl. You got that?"

A soft smile touched her mouth. "I got it."

He nodded. "Good."

"Daddy? When are they going to clean my cave? It's awful. It's all covered with oil. The walls, everything and—"

He touched a finger to her lips. "I know, sweetie. I don't want you down there. Those fumes can be dangerous. Just as soon as we finish with the public beaches, I'll see what I can do." He didn't want to tell her it could still be weeks or even months before they got around to cleaning her cave.

"You go to sleep now, okay?" He didn't have to ask her twice: the words were barely out of his mouth when her eyes flickered shut and her deep even breathing told him she was asleep. He watched her for a few minutes, saying a silent prayer of thanks for her safety. God, if anything had happened to her...if he ever lost her. With this thought came thoughts of Janette. He reached up and turned off the lamp by her bed and tiptoed from the room.

CHAPTER SIXTEEN

THE WATER IN THE KETTLE was boiling furiously as he entered the kitchen; huge puffs of steam floated in the air. He hastened to the stove to shut off the flame and, pulling a potholder off the wall, he picked up the tea-kettle and moved it to a back burner. Then he tossed the potholder aside.

Janette was asleep at the table, and his heart nearly stopped as his eyes came to rest upon her tousled head. She looked so beautiful wrapped in his robe, her hair still damp from her shower. He could hardly take his eyes off her, and it was only out of a strong sense of duty that he forced himself to call Virginia and give her a full report on Amy. He was careful not to mention Janette's name, careful, while he was talking, not to even look at her for fear that Virginia would detect something in his voice.

"Would you call the police and let them know Amy's home?"

"Of course. Adam—" Virginia hesitated "—do you think I should come over there?"

Adam glanced at Janette. "Absolutely not. Amy's asleep and she's going to be fine. I'll have her call you tomorrow. Good night, Virginia."

He hung up and turned toward Janette. She looked so soft, so vulnerable to him, fragile in a way that a flower was fragile, able to withstand rain and yet likely to wilt beneath a too-harsh sun. The thick fringe of her eyelashes fanned upon cheeks that were still flushed from the shower. He'd never noticed before how long her lashes were. He realized as he moved closer that it was because they were part red and part gold, like her hair when it was dry. It was damp now, and the dampness made it mahogany in color. He drew in a breath and let his eyes travel along the length of her. The small frame of her body was literally buried in his robe. Even so, he could make out the gentle roundness of her breasts, the narrowing of her waist beneath the belted robe, the soft curve of her hips.

Something tugged inside his chest. The paternal part of him wanted to protect her, much like he would a child. But there was nothing paternal about the ache in his loins as he took in the soft rise of her breasts.

He visually traced the curve of her mouth, remembering how that very mouth had come alive beneath his probing lips. Had come alive and merged with his, had become ingrained so permanently in his memory, that her lips seemed more a part of him than of her. Even now, he could feel his own mouth tremble with the sweet memory of her kisses.

With a deep groan that rumbled in his chest, he stooped down and swooped her into his arms. A soft sigh escaped her parted lips as she settled her head against his shoulder. The fresh smell of soap mingled with her feminine scent, rendered him nearly helpless. Afraid to breath, afraid to give into his feelings, afraid, afraid, afraid, he carried her up the stairs to his bedroom and lay her tenderly upon the bed. He meant to leave her there, let her sleep, meant to walk out of the room and never look back. He tried, how he tried to walk away from her, but he couldn't. Nor would she let him.

For her hand had reached up to touch his cheek. Touch him, hell, her hand seemed to stroke the very essence of his being, of his soul. He grabbed her hand to stop her, only to find that he couldn't. Instead, he pressed her hand harder against him. He looked deep into her eyes as he worked her hand from his cheek to his mouth and pressed his needy lips onto each delicate finger of her dainty hand. The shadows of the unbelievably long night still hovered over them. She looked at him with eyes misted with worry. "Amy?" she whispered.

"Amy's safe," he assured her. And with those two words, the demons of the night were put to rest.

Groaning, he lifted his legs onto the bed, and stretched alongside her until his head was only inches from hers. He lowered his head until their lips met.

Closing his eyes, he feathered her mouth with gentle kisses, savoring the sweet taste on her lips. Not her lips, he'd cautioned himself countless times in the past; mustn't remember her lips. But tonight, he not only wanted to remember her lips, he wanted to possess them.

It was wrong, he told himself, wrong to hold her even though his heart would let him do nothing else; wrong to kiss her even though he couldn't seem to help himself. Wrong didn't even begin to describe his wanting to bury his body into hers, to merge and become one with her. But after the harrowing night they'd spent together, he simply didn't have enough resources left to fight her alluring warm softness.

She sighed deeply; her lips parted enticingly. Unable, suddenly, to remember the reasons why he mustn't kiss her, he pressed his mouth hard against hers and pushed his tongue through her velvet-soft lips into the sweet cavern of her mouth.

Fully awake now, Janette clung to him, his hot kisses searing her soul; his lips demanding and giving, seeking and accepting. She wanted him, how she wanted him. Wanted everything he could give her, wanted to give him everything back. She arched her body next to his and thrilled at the manly hardness that molded against her feminine curves.

He reached down to her waist and tugged at the tie. The robe fell open, exposing her lovely nakedness. Gasping with pleasure, he lowered his head to capture an enticing pink nipple between his teeth. He moved his hand up to take the other breast, marveling at how it filled his hands with its warm tempting loveliness. At that moment he felt that surely he was the first man to have ever touched a woman so.

Moaning, she writhed beneath him. His name falling from her lips sounded like music to his ears. Could have been music for all he knew.

He lovingly caressed the soft rise of her breasts, and ran his fingers along her smooth flat stomach and curving thighs. Her gentle gasp when he touched the dark softness between her legs filled him with such pleasure his whole body seemed electrified. He could have lain next to her forever, touching every part of her, the folds, the curves, the smooth skin that seemed too perfect to be real. But when she worked her way beneath his shirt, pressing her fingers into his chest, touching was no longer enough. He needed more, much more. He needed to merge with her, to become a part of her, to claim her in the deepest, most meaningful sense.

Reaching to his waist, he unbuckled his belt. Unwilling to move away from her, he managed to undress as they kissed. She was so beautiful, opening to him like a flower opens to the sun. He lowered himself on her until every part of him was as deep within her as possible. He shuddered as her body rose up to meet his, then closed around him in a velvety warmth that nearly drove him out of his mind.

Adam felt his entire being drain into her and something wonderful take its place. It was as if the essence of her had replaced his pumping blood. As if by giving so completely to her, he'd succeeded in embracing everything about her he loved.

In the afterglow of their lovemaking, they clung to each other as completely as two people could. For Janette, there was no other world but the one created in his arms. For Adam, everything outside his arms had ceased to exist. There was only one world and only two people.

SOMEWHERE IN THE DISTANCE, a telephone rang. Adam broke through the surface of his sweet warm dreams to grope sleepily for the phone on his nightstand. He managed to grab the receiver and pull it to his ear without opening his eyes. Somehow he sensed that he must avoid opening his eyes at all costs. "This better be important," he growled into the receiver.

"Adam, dammit, what the hell is going on?"

At the sound of his attorney's voice, Adam's eyes flew open. Reality struck with the force of a bowling ball as he glanced at his clock. It was ten after seven. "What are you talking about?"

"I'm talking about Amy running away from home. Tomorrow a child psychologist takes the stand to testify that Amy is a happy well-adjusted child. Hell, who's going to believe that after reading the morning papers?''

Adam grimaced as the memories of the night came tumbling on top of him. ''Amy didn't run away from home. In any case, how did the papers get the story?''

''Probably because some jerk called the police.''

Adam's temper flared. ''What did you expect, Wes? Amy was missing.''

''The least you could have done is call me. Everything you do could have an effect on how this case turns out.''

''The only thing I cared about last night was Amy's safety. I wasn't thinking about the case.'' During the latter part of the night, he hadn't even been thinking of Amy. He felt a surge of guilt for putting his own feelings before Amy's. For the last three years since Carolyn's death, he'd been a father first and foremost. Everything he did was weighed by how it would affect his daughter. Until last night. Last night his needs as a man had taken priority, along with an obsessive desire to fulfill Janette's needs as a woman. His role as parent had not played a part and for this he felt an overwhelming guilt.

''Are you there, Adam?''

''Yeah, I'm here.''

A sweet soft feminine fragrance rose from the empty pillow next to him. He stifled a groan. Had it been a dream? He glanced over to the other side of the bed. She was gone and it was as if she'd taken the bed with her, and the room, and even the oxygen from the air. More than anything he felt an essential part of himself missing, a gaping hole centered in his chest. Had she taken his heart, as well?

"Do you understand what I said?" Wes continued. "Everything you do has a bearing."

"Dammit, Wes, when it comes to Amy's welfare, I will act in her best interests. Even if it means calling the police."

"All I'm saying is that the next time call me. And whatever you do, stay away from Janette Taylor."

Adam stiffened. "Janette?"

"According to the papers, a couple claim they saw you on Pioneer Bluff with a woman who fits Janette's description. You're somewhat of a celebrity. Your picture's been on the newspapers and TV—it's only natural that you'd be recognized."

Adam winced. "All right, Wes, you've made your point." He hung up, feeling more miserable than he had ever felt in his life.

Despite last night, the battle lines still stood rigidly in place. Nothing had changed. There was still one child and two people who loved her. There was still the ugly shadow of suspicion that tiptoed around the edges of his mind, waiting for the least thing to consume him. The suspicion that Janette may have feigned interest in him only because of Amy. And with this came another more chilling thought. She had used something against him in court that he'd told her in confidence; would she hesitate to tell the court about the night they'd spent together?

He moaned aloud. Dear God, don't let losing Amy be the price he must pay for making love to her mother!

JANETTE WATCHED AMY stab the last piece of pancake with her fork and mop up the syrup on her plate. "More pancakes?"

"No thanks," Amy said. "That was great. We usually have cold cereal in the morning. Except on Sundays. Then Daddy fixes French toast or his kitchen-sink omelets."

Janette laughed. "Kitchen sink? Is that before or after he does his rendition of the giraffe who swallowed a tuba?"

Amy's eyes twinkled. "After."

Janette watched Amy finish her orange juice, and felt a warm glow. Somehow it seemed so right, her fixing breakfast for Amy; Adam upstairs in bed where she had left him and where she could, hopefully, rejoin him later.

Amy coughed and Janette anxiously studied Amy's face. Amy looked pale and her eyes seemed over-bright. Still, there was nothing wrong with her appetite. Rolling up the sleeves of Adam's robe, she sat opposite Amy. "Amy, I hope you're not mad at me for telling your father about the cave. I know you said it was a secret, but I was so worried about you."

"I'm not mad," Amy said. She reached over and rested her hand on Janette's arm. "I'm glad you and Daddy found me. I was going to come home but when the cave filled with water, I was scared. I'd never been to the cave in the dark before." Amy coughed again, covering her mouth with her hand.

Janette lifted her hand to Amy's forehead. Amy felt cool to the touch. Too cool, perhaps? She couldn't be sure. "Maybe you should stay home..."

"I can't. I have a test. Besides, it's just a cough. I don't have a fever or anything. My teacher says that if you don't have a fever, you're not sick."

"Well..." Janette drew her hand away. Did a parent always know whether or not a child should stay home from school? Was a fever really the only indication of illness? Feeling inadequate, she reached for Amy's math book. "Here's your homework," she said, grateful that at least she was knowledgeable in sixth grade math. "I think you should recheck the last problem. Seven times eight . . ."

Amy grinned. "Is fifty-six." Usually she didn't make careless errors, but she'd done her homework in a hurry that morning, in between getting dressed and making her bed. She reached into her backpack for a pencil and set to work erasing her answer and writing in the right one. She then pushed her schoolbooks into her backpack and slipped the straps up her shoulders. She stood facing Janette, uncertainty on her face. "Janette, will you be angry with me if I don't live with you?"

For a moment Janette couldn't move. She had told herself these past few weeks that if she failed to gain custody, it would not be the end of the world. Amy would still have a wonderful home. Janette's life would continue as before, sadder perhaps, lonelier, but otherwise much the same. At least this is what she'd told the court-appointed psychiatrist during a recent session.

But that was before she had fixed Amy's breakfast, and checked over her homework, before she had brushed Amy's hair and tied it back with a bright red ribbon. Before Janette had known what it was like to share the minute-by-minute details that normally filled a mother's day. Now that she'd experienced the special wonderful ways a child enhanced one's life, Janette knew that life without Amy would be only half a life. She didn't even want to consider what life without Adam would be like.

"Angry?" she said, fighting for control. "No, not angry." Sad, heartbroken, in fact, but not angry.

Amy bit her lower lip. "I hope you don't forget me, Janette."

Janette was shocked that Amy would think such a thing. "I could never do that, Amy."

"Shortstop forgot me. I went to see him yesterday and he ran away."

Amy sounded so forlorn that Janette wanted to cry. She felt so helpless. "We have all sorts of ways to protect ourselves from pain and injury," she began, framing Amy's face with her hands. "If a light is too bright, we close our eyes. If there's too much noise, we cover our ears. I believe that one of the ways we keep from hurting too much inside is to shut our hearts and pretend to forget."

Amy tilted her head, her green eyes searching Janette's face hopefully. "Do you think Shortstop is trying to forget me because it hurts for him to remember?"

"I think it's a possibility," she said softly. Something, a feeling, perhaps, or a sound too soft to register made her glance up, and into Adam's dark questioning eyes. At the sight of him, her heart quickened and she released Amy.

Adam walked over to Amy and tugged her hair. "Hey, sport. Feeling better today?"

Amy teasingly wrinkled her nose at her father, then glanced back at Janette. "A lot better." She turned toward the kitchen clock. "I've got to go." She gave him a hug and waved to Janette before dashing toward the back door.

"Mind your p's and q's," Janette called.

Amy hesitated by the door. "Doesn't the rest of the alphabet count?"

Janette laughed. "It has nothing to do with the alphabet. That's what my grandmother used to say to me. It means watch your manners."

Amy grinned. "You mind your p's and q's, too," she said and dashed out the door.

As soon as she was gone, Adam turned his attention to Janette; the heavy heart that he'd carried downstairs suddenly grew wings. She looked like an angel dressed in blue velour. His heart took flight as he remembered the lovely firm body that lay hidden beneath the folds of the robe. Now that he knew her body intimately, she was more beautiful to him than ever. And with this thought came the wretched knowledge that she would be that much more difficult to forget.

"Good morning," she said, surprised to find herself suddenly feeling shy beneath his penetrating gaze. Her cheeks colored and she glanced toward the coffeepot. "I...I got up before Amy awoke. I didn't think it was a good idea...I mean she might not understand. She thinks I slept on the couch."

He cringed inwardly. All night long he'd held this woman in his arms, and never once had he considered how Amy would react upon finding her in his bed. He hadn't considered the morning at all, hadn't wanted to. He had blocked out the morning, blocked out all reality that would in any way spoil what they'd shared.

"Thank you," he said. He met her gaze. "I overheard what you said about a person pretending to forget in order to ease the pain. I... Thank you for finding a way to explain Shortstop's behavior that Amy could accept." It was difficult to show his gratitude because to acknowledge that she was better than he was at finding the right words to say to Amy, meant he also had to acknowledge his failure as a parent. And with this thought came the fear that maybe he had no right to fight for custody, that Amy really might be better off living with her mother.

Besides, what he really wanted to thank her for was last night. But, because last night could never happen again, he dared not say what was in his heart. He shouldn't even be thinking it. He hoped the time they'd spent together would not come back to haunt him, but more than anything he prayed that the beautiful wonderful moments in her arms wouldn't be used against him in court.

Basking in the warmth of his compliment, she poured a cup of coffee and handed it to him. He took it from her. She noticed he was careful to avoid touching her hand.

"Would you like some pancakes?" she asked, sensing his withdrawal. She shoved her hands into the deep pockets of the robe. "I made some for Amy."

Adam shook his head. "How did she seem to you?"

"I think she might be coming down with a cold. She had a bit of a cough, but she insisted upon going to school. I suppose it's not surprising that she caught a cold. It was freezing last night."

There was something else she wanted to tell him. "Adam? I . . . I apologize for yesterday in court. I forgot that you didn't know about Stephanie's grave. I should have had Merv talk to your lawyer ahead of time to prepare you."

"It's all right," he said curtly.

He inhaled, hating what he had to do. But he was Amy's father, first and foremost. He might have pushed his parental responsibilities aside last night, but he would not make that same mistake again. "You said that you weren't going to take Amy away from me."

Feeling a sudden chill, she clutched at the collar of the robe. She'd hoped after what they'd been through, things would change between them. Maybe they could reach some sort of understanding away from the public glare. Obviously, that wasn't to be the case. "I meant it, Adam."

"Does that mean that you're going to drop the custody suit?"

The chill turned to an arctic wind. "You know I can't. I can't walk away from her. She's my child...my flesh and blood." Never had she believed that as strongly as she did now. She may have told herself that the only reason she'd filed for custody was that winning her legal battle with the hospital would be jeopardized if she didn't, but, after this morning, she could no longer deny that the real reason was that she wanted to be Amy's mother in every sense of the word.

Adam lifted his tortured eyes toward her. "I'm not asking you to walk away from her. All I'm asking is that you let things stand as they are. You can be a part of her life on an informal basis."

"No!"

She saw the withdrawal on his face, the hardening of his jaw, but she couldn't help saying what she had to say. "I want...I need to have a mother/daughter relationship with Amy. As long as you agree to let me see her whenever I want, I'll let Amy live with you even if I get legal custody."

"That makes no sense!" he stormed. "I've offered to let you see Amy."

"But without custody, I have no proof that you'll keep your word. You may decide to move. I'm sorry,

Adam. But custody is the only insurance I have that I can see Amy. It's the best I can do."

"Not acceptable!"

She was stunned. Why did he find her proposal so objectionable? "Why not?" she stammered.

He looked at her incredulously. "What happens if you're not around and she needs emergency surgery or something? With your having legal custody, my hands would be tied. Legally I'd have no say in how I raise my daughter!"

"Adam, please try to understand. If something happens to you, I'd have no rights whatsoever."

"What about my rights? What about me?"

"I told you last night that in my mind you are Amy's father. I meant that. And I will do everything within my power to preserve that. But I won't walk away. I can't."

"I'm not asking you to walk away." He drew in a breath. "I'll have Wes draw up papers that say in the event that something happens to me, Amy will live with you."

"It won't work. Virginia would fight me every step of the way and you know it. I don't want to spend the rest of my life in court."

"You're not going to change your mind on this, are you?" he asked. Maybe it didn't matter; Amy had been taken away from him in a way that had nothing to do with legal custody. Knowing that he wasn't her real father had been a tremendous blow. He didn't love her any less; in some strange way, he loved her even more. But it was a stunning blow, and he wasn't sure he would ever recover from the shock.

Janette didn't answer him, but the look on her face was so sad, he felt compelled to add quietly, "I don't blame you for wanting legal custody of Amy."

She felt her spirits suddenly soar. But it was only a moment of reprieve, for his next words brought her crashing down to earth.

"But I'll never forgive you."

A pall hung over them as he drove her home. Feeling numb, she staggered out of the car. Eyes blurred with tears, she watched him drive away and tried with all her might not to think of the night she'd spent in his arms.

THE FOLLOWING FRIDAY in court was the most difficult day that Janette had ever endured. She listened with a heavy heart as various pediatricians, teachers and psychologists testified that Amy was a well-adjusted child who would benefit from both a mother and a father's love.

I'll never forgive you.

The words seemed to take on a life of their own, overshadowing everything else that was said that day in her presence. "Do you think that Adam Blake is a good father?" Wes Marcus asked Dr. Wayne E. Bennelton, the psychologist who had put Amy, Adam and Janette through a battery of tests.

"I do."

I'll never forgive you.

"Do you think that Janette Taylor could make a good home for Amy?" Wes asked the same man.

"Yes."

I'll never forgive you...

She tried not to look at Adam. But once he took the stand, the difficult became impossible. The eyes meeting hers were cold and remote. His last words to her hung between them like a crumbling bridge that must forever be crossed.

I'll never forgive you.

And during the long nights to follow, the question she had to ask was if she could ever forgive herself.

TOWARD THE THIRD WEEK of proceedings, Amy, dressed in a plaid jumper, took the witness stand. Janette's heart went out to her as Amy bravely raised her right hand and took the oath. She looked so grown-up, poised beyond her years, and yet there was a vulnerability about her that nearly broke her mother's heart.

Amy felt anything but poised; she felt sick to her stomach. She glanced nervously at her father, who winked at her, and she forced herself to smile for his benefit. Behind him, her grandmother sat looking as if she was about to cry. Amy hoped she wouldn't. She hated it when her grandmother cried. Amy's gaze slid sideways and met Janette's. Janette smiled at her and some of the butterflies went away.

Janette's attorney questioned her first. He began by asking her various questions about school and friends. Soon, she forgot about the butterflies inside and was actually beginning to enjoy herself. She loved talking about her school and friends, liked talking about sports even more.

"I understand your mother died four years ago," he asked abruptly, cutting her off in midsentence. "I bet you still miss her."

The change of subject surprised her. For some reason the butterflies returned. "She wasn't my real mother, but I miss her very much anyway."

"How do you feel about your real mother?"

Amy answered slowly. She didn't want to make a mistake or say the wrong thing. "Janette's really neat. She said she wouldn't be angry if I don't live with her."

"Would you be angry if you had to live with her?"

Amy wiggled in her seat. "I wouldn't be angry no matter who I lived with."

Not wanting to look at Janette or her grandmother, or even at her father, she glanced at the judge, who sat back in his chair, stroking his chin thoughtfully as he watched her.

"Which would make you feel sadder? If you lived with your father or if you lived with your mother?"

"I would feel sad no matter who I lived with," Amy answered truthfully. "I know that both my daddy and Janette would feel sad if I didn't live with them. So that would make me feel sad."

The attorney nodded and patted her on the arm. "You're an intelligent young lady. I have no more questions."

The court was adjourned for the remainder of the day. Janette longed to hug Amy and tell her what a super job she'd done on the stand. Instead, feeling very much alone, Janette was forced to watch as Amy rushed into her father's arms and was hurried out of the courtroom. Adam's last words continued to ring in Janette's ears. *I'll never forgive you.*

ADAM WHISKED AMY through the crowd, refusing to let her talk to reporters, and led her to the car. Virginia practically had to run to keep up with them. Once the three of them were safely in the car, Amy looked at her father, her eyes filled with worry. "He never asked me who I would *rather* live with," she complained.

"Don't you worry about a thing," Virginia said from the back seat. She patted Amy on the shoulder. "You still have a chance to tell the court how you feel when Wes questions you."

"I was going to tell him that I wanted to live with you, Daddy." Amy watched her father's profile.

A lump rose to Adam's throat as he pulled away from the courthouse. His heart swelled with the love he felt for this lovely child who had found her way into his life quite by accident. Although he was deeply touched by her answer, he had strictly forbidden Wes to ask the question. Some questions should not be asked. He'd come to learn that the hard way. A child should never be asked to choose between parents; a man should never be asked to forget the woman he loves.

THE NEXT WEEK, it appeared that the tide had turned permanently in Adam's favor. Then Stella took the stand and read a letter that Janette had written shortly after the birth of her child. " 'Today, a part of me has died, I may live to be a hundred, but my arms will always ache for the baby I can never hold...' "

Janette had forgotten about the letter. But how like Stella to keep it all these years. She could tell that Merv was pleased by the impact the letter had on the court. It would be hard for anyone to deny the sincerity of that letter or to question that the woman who'd written it had had every intention of keeping her baby.

The letter provided a poignant ending to the weeks of harrowing testimony. It was up to the judge to decide the outcome of Amy's future. There was nothing to do but wait.

While leaving the courtroom that day, Janette practically bumped into Adam. It was obvious he wanted to talk to her. For a moment, she could only gaze into his eyes, sensing a battle raging within him.

"Janette . . . I . . ."

A reporter stepped between them. "Miss Taylor, do you remember when you wrote that letter?"

With a disgusted glance at the reporter, Adam turned on his heel and disappeared into the crowd.

DURING THE DAYS that followed, Janette tried not to think of Adam, of Amy, of the judge who was sifting through the facts trying to make a sane and fair decision out of a situation that was anything but sane and fair.

Throwing herself into her work, Janette spent hours going through museums, looking through art books and visiting private collections, searching for paintings, tapestries or sculptures that demanded to be recreated on stage.

On a dull rainy Saturday, she stood for hours in the attic in front of her father's paintings, wondering why she couldn't successfully recreate his work. The inability to do his work justice gnawed at her. She had the feeling that she was missing some vital element, something that prevented her from getting to the heart of his work. She had never understood the man, but she was determined, somehow, to understand his work. Perhaps the two were linked: the man and his work. Perhaps she must first learn to know the one before she could know the other.

She checked each canvas, looking desperately for the right one. Her eyes were drawn to the gloomy painting called *Fog Bank*. She stared at it, remembering that the day he'd begun to paint it, was the day her mother had walked out of their lives, never to return. Not that one, she thought, flipping through to the next canvas.

Nightwatch. She'd been pregnant when he'd worked on this picture of a policeman quietly walking the street. He'd been obsessed with paintings of policemen during this period. What was it he'd been trying to say? That law and order must prevail at all costs? That she had been bad because she'd gotten pregnant? Not *Nightwatch.*

She was still thinking of her father's paintings when she walked into her office the following Monday morning.

Pat greeted her with a smile. "Wait until you see these great photos." Pat followed Janette to her desk, her high heels clicking across the linoleum floor. "Here's the picture of the Mandarin plate you wanted. Aren't the colors exquisite?"

Forcing herself to concentrate on the photos, Janette studied the colorful details of the Manchu court, a meeting place of scholars and princesses.

Janette held the photos up one by one, calculating costs and production problems. Living Masters had never recreated a china plate on stage. It would be the sort of challenge she enjoyed. It would also offer a nice contrast to the predominance of Western art that seemed to be shaping up for next year, and to her father's painting if and when she could make up her mind which one that would be.

"What do you think about this one?" Pat asked. "I love Norman Rockwell, and his paintings are always so popular with the crowd. This one is called *Welcoming The New Baby.*"

Janette glanced at the photo in her hand and felt her heart twist in a knot. The tiny baby lay in a bassinet, surrounded by the entire family from great-grandparents to the dog. "Not that one!" Janette said too harshly, then grabbed the next photo in Pat's hand.

"I'm sorry," Pat stammered. "I wasn't thinking."

Janette waved her concern aside. She would have to get used to seeing babies and bassinets. There was a lot she would have to get used to. The next picture was a Currier Ives winter scene. Janette had nearly decided to add it to the list of possibilities when she noticed the long blond hair on one of the ice skaters. Hair like Amy's.

She stacked the photos neatly and returned them to Pat. "I'm sorry, Pat. I'm not up to this today."

"No problem. We still have three weeks before we have to present them to the board. Are you okay?"

"I'm okay," she said.

I'm not okay, she told herself later, much later. I'm never going to be okay again.

OKAY, ADAM THOUGHT, where are you? He'd walked up and down the hill twice already, and he had not yet found the grave. The caretaker had told him it was on the crest of the hill beneath the sprawling oak tree. Only there were lots of hills; the entire cemetery was spread up and down velvety grass-covered hills. There were also lots of oak trees, all of which could be described as sprawling.

He spotted the flowers first, tiny blue forget-me-nots, a hundred little blossoms spread beneath the sun. His legs practically turned to rubber as he walked toward the grave and read the name: *Stephanie* . . .

A cry tore from some deep hurt inside and fell from his lips. Sinking down on his knees, he let the baby roses he carried in his arms fall to the grass.

Forget-me-nots.

He'd given forget-me-nots to Janette the day that his nightmare began. He'd never forget her face when he'd handed them to her. Nor would he forget the sorrow he'd seen in her eyes. He hadn't understood it at the time, but now as he stared down at the tiny flowers adorning his baby's grave, he understood it all too well. She had confided that she had embroidered forget-me-nots on her baby's nightgown. What she had failed to say, and what he hadn't suspected until this moment, was that Stephanie had been buried in that nightgown.

He placed his hand on the stone that was still damp from the recent rain, and traced his daughter's name with his fingers. He wondered how many times through the years Janette had sat in this exact spot, tracing these same letters. He wondered how it must feel to give birth to a child and have only a tiny grave left.

He felt like an intruder. He knew so little about the child buried there. Didn't even know the color of her eyes. Were they hazel like Carolyn's or blue like his? And what about her birth weight? Such little things and yet suddenly so important. How must Janette feel not knowing these same things about Amy? She didn't know when Amy cut her first tooth or took her first step. She had no way of knowing that Amy's first word was not mama or dada as expected, but pony. He blinked back the burning sensation in his eyes. What a mess, what an absolute mess.

Would Janette ever come to this grave again now that she knew the baby buried here was not hers? Would she ever again feel the need to trace the letters of Stephanie's name? Would she feel like an intruder, too?

With these dark thoughts, Adam walked away from the tiny grave, cursing himself for coming and knowing now that he'd come, he could never stay away.

HER FINGER BURNED as she traced the letter *S*. Pulling her hand away, she stared at the tiny grave. She had the strangest feeling since coming here. Even before she had climbed the hill she felt something.... Even before she spotted the pink baby roses.

She decided that the roses were a mistake. Someone had laid them on the grave in error. Of course that was it, and yet...

She touched a finger to a soft pink petal. A half-forgotten memory came to mind. *I hope you don't think me unimaginative.* A warm shiver washed over her. Adam?

She reached out once again to trace the letters of Stephanie's name. Again, the strange feeling that the rough ridges of the etching had been altered in some way, although she was positive they hadn't been. Confused, she drew her hand back.

She saw the caretaker at the bottom of the hill and she stood and waved her hand. He waited for her, his face anchored by a great big grin.

"Good afternoon, Miss Taylor. You're looking might' pretty today."

Janette smiled. "Thank you, Mr. Roberts. Did you see anyone over by Stephanie's grave today?"

Mr. Roberts pushed back his old felt hat and gazed at the ocean that was but a silvery strip in the distance. "Seems to me there was someone. A man. Tall. Dark hair."

Biting her lower lip, Janette murmured her thanks and stumbled past the caretaker. "There's nothing wrong, is there?" he called after her.

"No, no," she flung back at him. "There's nothing wrong." Nothing, she said, half walking, half running to her car. Only that she no longer had a claim to the little grave that had been the center of her life for so many years. Only that she had nothing left in the world to call her own. Only that Adam Blake had claim to both her daughters and all of her heart.

CHAPTER SEVENTEEN

THE COURTROOM WAS PACKED that Wednesday morning by the time Janette arrived with Stella. From the moment they stepped from their car, their every move was recorded with the relentless flashing lights of dozens of cameras.

"Do you believe this?" Stella mumbled, barging her way through the crowd like a bulldozer, her arms folded in front of her, her elbows shoulder high.

"You do that well," Janette said, glancing around the courtroom as soon as they were inside. She smiled at Pat and nodded toward Sally, grateful for the support of her friends throughout this entire ordeal.

Kevin, from the Fur and Feathers Pet Hospital, walked over to her and wished her luck. "I heard on the news that the judge had made his decision," he explained. "Thought you could use a cheering section."

"Thanks, Kevin," she said, squeezing his arm. On the outside she looked perfectly confident and collected. On the inside, thousands of nerve endings screamed out the very thing she was trying to ignore: Adam hadn't arrived yet.

"There's the dragon lady herself," Stella said, nodding toward Adam's mother-in-law who had just entered the courtroom.

Janette turned and watched as Virginia, looking harried and distressed, adjusted her hat and sat down.

"I'll be back," she said, weaving her way across the crowded courtroom.

"Excuse me, Mrs. Spencer," she said, stepping in front of the woman. "Do you know where Adam is?"

Virginia lifted bright blue lids to give Janette a look of disdain. "Adam stayed home to take care of Amy," she said, her voice as hard and cold as her face.

Janette's entire body froze in alarm. "There's something wrong with Amy?"

"Amy has a respiratory infection. Probably because of the cold she caught on the night she was in the cave." There was no question that she personally blamed Janette for that night. Blamed Janette for the whole mess.

"I'm so sorry," Janette whispered.

"We don't want your apologies," Virginia snapped. "What we want is for you to get out of our lives."

Janette turned. There was nothing more to say. Judge Wendall made his entrance and a hushed silence settled over the spectators. Janette sat next to Merv, feeling as if she were facing a firing squad.

The judge cleared his throat. "I've spent a great deal of time going through every piece of information pertaining to this case," he began. "As you are well aware, we have a tragic situation. A terrible mistake occurred eleven years ago, and because of this a mother was mistakenly told that her baby had died." The judge took a sip of water before continuing. Janette didn't realize how much she was shaking until Merv took her hand and squeezed it.

Clearing his throat again, Judge Wendall continued, "Unfortunately, Janette Taylor is not the only one to have suffered a great tragedy. Adam Blake has also suffered greatly."

Janette listened while the judge outlined the full extent of Adam's tragedy. Finding out that the child he thought he'd fathered wasn't his. Learning that his own daughter had died years ago.

"Believe me, I feel for the parties involved in this tragic case. This brings us to the most important consideration of all. Amy. I thought her a remarkable and intelligent child who is understandably confused and frightened by these events. This has been an extremely difficult case, made more difficult because there are no precedents. My main concern, as it must be in such cases, is for Amy's welfare."

He glanced at his notes. "I considered the possibility of joint custody. There are many pros and cons to joint custody, but the most important ingredient in making such an arrangement work is for the participants to work together. Since Mr. Blake and Miss Taylor only recently met, it's hard to determine whether or not such an agreement would work in their case. For that reason, I ruled out the possibility of joint custody. It seems to me that the better choice would be to give one parent legal custody while providing liberal visitation rights to the other. Taking the child's age into consideration and her obvious fondness for both parents, I have decided to award custody of Amy to her legal mother."

Janette couldn't believe her ears. She was mistaken, she must be. She never thought a judge would rule against Adam. She glanced at Merv, who confirmed what she'd heard with a thumbs-up sign.

An anguished cry cut through Janette's numb brain. She groped through the fog. It wasn't until she spun her head around that she realized the cry came from Virginia.

"Amy is my grandchild," Virginia sobbed. "I won't let anyone take her away!"

Adam's lawyer was trying his best to console Virginia. Wrapping his arms around her, he finally led her out of the courtroom, but her pitiful sobs could still be heard.

Not waiting to hear the details of the custody agreement, Janette grabbed her purse and left the courtroom, dodging the reporters and spectators who had gathered outside the doors. She flew down the steps of the courthouse and ran outside to her car.

No sooner had she pulled up in front of Adam's house, than the door flew open and Adam, looking grim, walked outside to greet her.

Standing by her car, she met his eyes and for a torturous moment they gazed at each other.

Amy, dressed in a bathrobe, appeared at the front door. Her cheeks flushed with fever, she clung to her father's side and watched Janette with wary eyes.

Janette felt a knife twist inside. She suddenly realized that no matter what the judge had ruled, no matter what the state of California deemed to be true, Amy would never be her daughter. Not in the sense that mattered.

"I'm sorry, Adam...I..." She looked away because she couldn't bear to look at him. It hurt too much. "The judge ruled...for me. All these weeks, I never believed this could happen." She'd hoped, how she'd hoped...

"No!" Amy cried. "Oh, Daddy, I don't want to leave you." Amy wrapped her arms around him. "It's because I didn't tell them on the stand that I wanted to live with you. It's all my fault, I know it is."

"Listen to me, sport," Adam said, shaking her gently by the shoulders. "Nothing is your fault."

"Your father's right," Janette said. She walked up to Amy and placed her hand on Amy's feverish cheek. Amy looked up at her and pulled away. The physical rejection was hurtful, but nothing could be more painful than the look Amy gave her, a look that said all too clearly that Amy would never forgive her for taking her from her father. A look that said there was not a chance in the world they could ever really be mother and daughter.

"Please, Janette," Amy sobbed. "Please let me stay with my daddy."

Janette felt faint. She was prepared to give Amy anything—anything, the moon, the stars, her very life if necessary—anything at all that might possibly begin to make up for the years they'd been separated. But this ... It had been so easy to promise to let Amy live with Adam when she thought she didn't have a chance of gaining custody. Oh, my dear precious daughter, she thought, why must you ask of me the one thing that's so terribly, terribly difficult to give, and maybe not even possible to give?

"Amy, I told you that I wasn't going to take you away from your father and I meant it. This is your home." She looked up at Adam. "Amy..." She bit back the pain and began again. "Amy belongs with you."

Amy's body shuddered in a contained sob. With a cry of joy, she flung her arms around her father's neck. "Oh, Daddy, I get to stay here. I really get to stay here!"

Adam hugged Amy. "I told you things were going to work out." His eyes held Janette's and she hated the unspoken questions she could see in their depths, the doubt so clearly written on his face.

Don't do this, he seemed to say as he watched her. Don't say anything that you don't mean. Don't lift our hopes only to disappoint us later. Don't make me believe you....

Feeling the last threads of her control begin to slip away, Janette turned and rushed to her car. Adam called to her but she didn't stop; she didn't dare.

ADAM HAD MANAGED to get Amy calmed down and back into bed by the time Wes arrived with Virginia.

Virginia looked pale and exhausted. She pulled off her hat and tossed it on the couch. Sinking into the cushions, she held her head. "Have you heard?"

Adam glanced over at Wes, surprised to find his attorney watching his mother-in-law with concern. It was totally out of character for Wes to hover over anyone.

"I heard," Adam said grimly.

As if he suddenly remembered his responsibility to his client, Wes straightened and turned to Adam. "The judge is being extremely lenient about visitation rights. Two weekends a month, plus a month in the summer, and you get her every other holiday. Considering the circumstances, this is a victory."

Adam lifted his hand. "Janette told me that she's not going to make Amy live with her. Amy can continue to live here."

Wes frowned. "You've talked to Janette?"

Adam nodded. "She was here a few minutes ago."

"How dare she..." Virginia began, but Wes pressed her shoulder with his hand and she fell silent.

Watching his mother-in-law thoughtfully, Adam rubbed his chin. It wasn't like Virginia to be restrained so easily.

"Do you think she means it?" Wes asked.

Adam remembered the tortured look on Janette's face. That had to be sincere. Didn't it? "I don't know," he said. "Can a woman really walk away from her child?" Even as he asked the question, he knew the answer. Janette could never walk away from Amy, not emotionally. And probably not even physically.

Wes scratched his head. "I know that you're not going to want to hear this, but she must know that she'll be in contempt of court if she refuses legal custody of Amy."

"She said that Amy can stay with me!" Adam snapped. "I believe she meant it."

The silence that followed Adam's outburst was punctuated with the sound of Amy's coughing in the distance. Adam frowned. Maybe he should give the doctor another call.

Virginia stood. "I better check on Amy."

Adam waited until Virginia had left the room before turning back to Wes. "So what do we do now?"

"There's nothing you can do. The judge ruled that Amy must live with Janette. Unless of course she agrees to give you power of attorney...."

"You mean she can do that? Give me power of attorney?"

"She can, but I wouldn't get my hopes high. Don't forget that lawsuit against the hospital is still pending. Not taking custody of Amy could put her suit in jeopardy. I doubt that her attorney would let her do that."

Adam winced. What Wes said made sense. Merv would be a fool to let his client do something so foolish as to jeopardize a multimillion dollar lawsuit. Janette had to know that. Was her promise to let Amy stay with him a promise she had no intention of keeping?

"I'll talk to her lawyer," Wes said. "I'll ask for a power of attorney."

"No!"

"Dammit, Adam, why not?"

"I can't ask her to sign away rights to her child. Wes, what if she really is sincere? What if her motives for letting Amy live with me are purely out of love?"

"What if they're not?" Wes shot back. "I think she went after Amy to strengthen her suit against the hospital, and for no other reason."

"She wouldn't play games with Amy's life."

"I don't think that was her intention. I don't think she thought she would win. I saw her in court when the judge ruled. Believe me, she was one shocked lady. I think she wanted to make it look as if she wanted custody to try to disprove the hospital's contention that she had no intention of raising her child. I think her plan backfired."

Adam didn't want to believe a word Wes said. Wes made Janette sound cold and calculating.

But Wes's argument made some sort of crazy sense. Could he be right? Adam had to know; he had to know for sure if he should believe his lawyer—or his heart.

"YOU DID WHAT?" Merv practically choked on his peppermint. Clearing his throat, he stared at Janette in disbelief.

"You heard me, Merv. I told Adam that Amy can stay with him."

"You can't just make a decision like that. The judge ruled that Amy was to live with you. You're required by law to fulfill the court's decision."

"Then figure out a way around it!" She felt her temper rising. The last thing she needed was for Merv to get difficult. "Dammit, Merv, when are we going to get a court date for the hospital suit?" Maybe if she concentrated her efforts on the upcoming lawsuit, she could put the rest behind her.

Merv watched her as she paced back and forth in front of him. "Your suit against the hospital is going to be tough. There's a lot at stake. And now that you're giving up custody of Amy, I'm not sure at this point if we can even come out victorious. In any case, Janette, are you sure you're up to another legal battle?"

She didn't know how to answer him. Without Amy, there was nothing left. Not even the will to fight. Without Adam, there wasn't even the will to breathe. "I don't know anymore what I'm sure of," she said. It was so much simpler when she was filled with anger and rage toward the hospital. But her grief over Adam and Amy left no room for any other emotion.

After Merv left, Janette sat at her desk going over the dozens of photos that Pat had picked out. Next week she would have to come up with a proposed list of artworks that would make up next year's pageant. She had finally decided to include her father's painting entitled *Day in the Park*. The painting held no special meaning to her. She couldn't even imagine when he'd painted it. She could only guess that he'd painted it during one of the few happy times in his life.

The door flung open and without looking up, she called to Pat. "What do you think about this painting...?"

She glanced up and froze. *Adam*. He slammed the door shut and stood facing her.

The room suddenly seemed to shrink. Her every sense, every cell, every nerve was focused on him. A single voice inside called his name.

"What kind of game are you playing with me?" he asked in a ragged voice that nearly tore her in two. There was suspicion in his eyes, but something else, as well. Don't let it be hatred, she thought. She dropped her hands onto her lap and pressed them together, hoping to conceal how much they shook. She had to be strong, stronger than she'd ever been in her entire life. For Amy's sake. For her own sake, as well.

Damn, why had he come? She almost thought she might get through the day without resorting to tears. "I'm not playing games," she said. She worked so hard to keep her voice steady it sounded harsh even to her own ears.

Surprised by her coldness, he wondered if Wes had been right all along. "I think you are." He moved toward her desk, searching her face for a sign that she felt every bit as wretched as he felt. Much to his dismay, she looked beautiful. No shadows, nothing. Just clear blue eyes, minus the green, cold and businesslike eyes that were but a shadow of the eyes that had burned with fire and passion the night they'd made love.

She wished he hadn't moved so close. It was hard enough when he stood across the room. She only hoped that he couldn't detect how much makeup she was wearing to cover up the shadows and the paleness. She shrank back against her chair, drawing upon some inner strength to keep her resolve. She couldn't allow even the slightest vulnerability to show.

"You know very well that now that you have custody, you're required to take Amy. You'd be in contempt of court if you didn't. Was that your plan?" he asked bitterly. "To make us think that you were willing to let Amy live with me when in reality you knew that to be impossible."

"I'll give you power of attorney," she said.

He looked at her in surprise. "You'll sign—"

"Yes, Adam." She looked at him with hard cold eyes, praying for all the world that she could keep up the pretense. "I want this over with so that I can get on with my life."

For a moment he stared at her, dumbfounded. "So easily?" he asked. "You'll give her up so easily."

Hold on, she told herself. You're not going to cry. You're not to cry, and you're not to let him know how much you hurt, and you're not going to let him know that nothing would ever be easy again. "As easily as that," she managed. "Now, if you'll excuse me, I have work to do." She glanced down at her desk, willing him to go quickly and knowing that it could never be quickly enough.

Adam stumbled out of her office in a daze. He hadn't known what to expect when he'd gone charging down to her office. To find her devastated? Wracked with pain? He didn't know. What he did know was that he hadn't expected her to look so cool and controlled. He hadn't expected her to look at him with eyes as hard as stone. He hadn't expected to find that Wes had been right all along; he'd been played for an utter fool!

Damn her for putting him through hell. Damn her for touching his every emotion, the very core of him. Damn her for making him believe her.

MERV STOPPED by her house the following Monday morning, armed with legal documents for her to sign. Looking grim and disapproving, he tried to explain all the legal mumbo jumbo that came down to one basic truth; once she signed the power of attorney, Amy would continue to live with Adam.

"Just tell me where to sign," she said. She had to do this without thought. Because with thought came emotion, and with emotion came pain.

"I want you to be sure you know what you're doing," he argued.

Please, Janette, please let me stay with my daddy. "I know what I'm doing," she snapped. "Just give me that damn paper!"

Merv shrugged. "You're every bit as stubborn as your father." He pulled a blue-backed document from his attaché case, laid it on the table and handed her a pen.

She hesitated a second, then took the pen and scribbled her name. With that she rose, and walked out the back door.

It was drizzling outside. Pogo was waiting for her at the edge of the ice plant, and after she'd tossed him his morning allotment of fish, she started jogging. Lifting her face toward the gray skies she let the cool mist fall upon her fevered forehead.

She had no idea how far she'd jogged. Miles. When at last her legs refused to run any farther, she collapsed on the beach, falling to her knees and resting her head on a boulder. Gasping for breath, she closed her eyes. She mustn't feel. She mustn't think. If she could avoid those two things, she could hold on.

She had no idea how long she sat there in the soft drizzle of the cool gray morning. She might have sat there for an eternity had it not been for a sudden fluttering sound by her ear, a brush of her shoulder. Startled, she looked up to see a seagull land at her feet. Noticing the aluminum band wrapped around one leg, she wondered if it was one of the seagulls that she and Adam had washed that day. There it was again, the thinking, the feeling.

Talking in a soft soothing voice, Janette crept slowly toward the bird. She dug out the plastic container and scraped out a bit of fish left over from Pogo's breakfast. She held out her hand and the bird moved closer, taking the tiny scrap of fish from the tip of her finger.

Janette had spent enough time studying seagulls to know they didn't eat out of someone's hand this easily. This bird recognized her. That's why it had brushed her shoulders. She sat up and regarded the gull more closely, looking to see if there was the least residue of oil among its pearly-white-and-gray feathers.

Spreading its wings wide, the bird took flight. He sailed over the rocky cliffs that guarded both ends of her beach like bookends and disappeared from view, its cry settling in her heart. The bird had lived, she thought. A bird she and Adam had fought to save had lived. With this thought came the tears.

CHAPTER EIGHTEEN

RAIN FELL like teardrops on Adam's windshield as he pulled into Ashton Tex's parking lot. Ducking his head, he hurried to his office.

The official report on the tanker accident and oil spill was on his desk, waiting for his approval before it would be forwarded to company headquarters in Anchorage. The Federal National Oceanic and Atmospheric Administration had ordered new soundings to be taken at the accident site, and the preliminary results showed that the water was nearly six feet shallower than indicated on current navigational charts. As a result, the tanker had run over its own anchor as it had tried to moor.

The good news was that the captain and his crew were absolved from responsibility for the accident. The bad news was that despite weeks of cleanup, there were still stretches of beach covered in oil. It would be weeks, maybe months before Adam could file a final report. Meanwhile, he continued to list the damaged areas in order of importance. Amy's cave was on the bottom of that list.

Wes called at eleven that morning. "I have some good news," he said without preamble. "I've just spoken to Merv. Janette gave you full power of attorney."

Adam felt a sense of relief at this news, but strangely enough, little joy. "Thanks, Wes."

"Don't thank me. Thank Janette Taylor."

Adam's mouth went dry. Thank her, he thought. For what? For turning his life upside down? For playing havoc with his heart? He dropped the receiver in its cradle and told himself he had everything he wanted in life.

Everything, he reminded himself whenever thoughts of Janette intruded on his day. Everything, he affirmed later as he stopped at Virginia's house to tell her the news. "You don't have to worry, Virginia. Amy is ours."

"You can't know how very relieved I am to hear this."

"I know." He studied his mother-in-law. There was something different about her. He couldn't quite put his finger on what it was, but something. "I thought you'd be jumping up and down with joy."

"I am, Adam, believe me. You'll never know how relieved I am. But I can't forget the day I heard the judge give Amy to Janette. Something happened inside of me that day. It was like losing Carolyn..."

"I know..." He'd thought he'd never feel the same again after losing Carolyn. Thought he'd never again know such devastation. And until he met Janette he never had.

"I realized something that day," Virginia continued. "I realized what a mistake it is to live your life for only one person. When I thought I'd lost Amy, I realized I had nothing left."

"That's how I felt," Adam said, not wanting to remember.

"But it was different with you," Virginia said quietly. "You have your work."

He did have his work and he was grateful for that. "Speaking of work, I may have to work this weekend. I lost a lot of time during the hearing and there's still a lot of cleanup left to do."

Virginia studied him thoughtfully. "Adam, what I've been trying to tell you is that I think it's time I made a few changes."

Adam stared at Virginia in surprise. "Changes? You?"

"Yes, me." She patted her hair. "I thought I would start with my appearance. Get my hair restyled. Change my makeup. Amy says that blue eyeshadow is old-fashioned. Can you imagine an eleven-year-old being an expert on makeup?"

Adam gave his daughter a mental pat on the back. "She's probably right. She's always reading those glamour magazines."

"I know. By the way, I won't be able to watch Amy this weekend. I have a date."

"A date?" Adam stared at her in astonishment. "You?"

Virginia scowled at him. "Don't look so surprised. Besides, it's only Wes. He asked me to go sailing with him."

Adam noted the color that suddenly crept into Virginia's cheeks. "Good for you," he said. Virginia and Wes? He couldn't believe it. "And don't worry about Amy. I think anyone who's an expert on eyeshadow is probably old enough to stay by herself."

Virginia looked worried at the thought of Amy staying by herself. But the look soon passed. "Maybe you're right."

Adam frowned in uncertainty. "Do you think so? She's only eleven."

Virginia laughed, tugging his tie playfully. "And you accuse me of being overprotective." Virginia hesitated. "Adam, about Janette..."

"I don't want to talk about her."

"I just wanted to say it was a generous thing she did. It couldn't have been easy, giving up her child. I feel terrible for being so...rude to her."

Adam tried to remember how cold and distant Janette appeared the last time they'd met. But the vision kept fading. Instead, he remembered her in the moonlight, dancing in his arms, rolling on the grass. Somehow he had to forget the dream and learn to accept the reality. "Don't worry about it," he said with stoic heart. "She probably came out of this better than the rest of us."

JANETTE WALKED into the kitchen and found Stella on hands and knees trailing a tape measure behind her. "Grab that end, will you?" Stella asked, pointing to the end.

"What are we measuring?" Janette grabbed the steel ribbon and pulled it toward the baseboard, dropping down on hands and knees.

"The floor. The water from the burst pipe crept under this old linoleum. See how it's curling at the edges?"

"I hate to ask this question, but have you ever replaced a floor before?" Janette glanced at Stella. "Don't tell me, I know. Larry is going to help you."

"You don't give me any credit. I fixed the furnace, didn't I?"

"Stella, you didn't fix the furnace. We put in a new one."

"That's beside the point," Stella sniffed. "Anyway, I want to redo the floor before..."

There was something odd in the way Stella seemed to be avoiding her eyes. Janette sat up on her knees. "Before what? Stella?"

"I guess I'd better tell you." Stella stood and wound up the tape measure. "I wasn't going to tell you so soon. I mean you've got enough on your mind without worrying about losing a roommate."

Janette stared at her in dismay. "I'm losing a roommate?"

"Either that or you're going to gain one. I mean Larry could move in here, I suppose."

"Stella, would you please tell me what's going on? Why would Larry move in here other than the fact that we owe him so much money he probably owns the place by now?"

"He proposed to me."

"What?"

"Don't look so astonished. Some men get turned on by orange hair."

"I didn't mean to imply... What I meant was that I didn't know things were that serious." Janette blinked. "He asked you to marry him?"

"Not in those exact words. What he said was that he wanted to give me a lifetime supply of wrenches. What could I say? How often do you get an offer like that?"

Janette laughed. "Congratulations, I guess."

"As soon as I replace the kitchen floor, I'd like to invite him over for dinner. I'll let you regale him with one of your pasta creations. What do you say?"

"Well . . ." She glanced at the linoleum. "You don't suppose the floor is going to cave in or anything, do you?"

Stella made a face at her. "Don't worry about the floor. I guarantee that anyone can lay a new floor."

Not wanting to argue the matter further, Janette got Pogo's dinner from the refrigerator and started out the back door.

The sky was streaked in yellow clouds as she made her way along the winding path. Pogo usually waited for her where the path gave way to the beach, but today there was no sign of the little seagull.

Starting across the beach, she called his name. "Hey, there, Pogo, where are you?" An unspeakable panic surged inside; she dropped the plastic bowl and ran toward the ocean. She felt as if she was losing everything. First Adam, and then Amy. God, Amy. Stella was getting married and Stephanie, her dear sweet Stephanie was no longer hers to love. Now Pogo.

Where was he?

She tightened the grip on her emotions. It was only a seagull. A *seagull,* for God's sake. Dragging her feet across the sand, she tried to convince herself that she was happy for Stella. Stella deserved love and happiness. Still, Janette couldn't help but feel that in some strange way, she was about to be abandoned once again. Anything and everything that meant something to her invariably slipped through her fingers.

"Pogo!"

She found him floating in a tidal pool. He lay on one side. His eyes blinked as she lifted him from the water, his breathing alarmingly labored. Holding him close to her, she examined the feathers that were mired together with crude oil.

Quickly, she carried him back to the house. "Hurry, Stella, help me!" she shouted as she rushed into the kitchen. "Call Kevin at the pet hospital. Tell him that I have a seagull covered in oil and I need something to clean out its intestines."

While Stella ran to the phone, Janette laid Pogo on a towel next to the sink. He looked so fragile, so trusting lying there. Fighting back tears, she placed the plug at the bottom of the sink and ran the warm water.

"Kevin will be here as soon as possible," Stella reported.

"Let's hope he gets here in time. I'll hold him while you work the lather into his feathers."

Stella hesitated. "You want me to give a seagull a bath?"

Janette glanced up at her in surprise. Could the woman who thought nothing of taking on the endless repairs of a deteriorating Victorian house be afraid of one frightened seagull? "For goodness' sake, Stella, this isn't the time to go chicken on me. This bird is in bad shape. Believe me, he's not going to bite you. He's too weak."

Gingerly, Stella lowered her hands into the water. "I'll hold you to that."

While Janette cooed softly to the seagull, Stella worked the liquid soap into its feathers. Several lathers and rinses later, they lifted the shivering body onto a towel.

Janette checked beneath the wings. "I think we got all the oil out."

Kevin arrived, black bag in hand, and the three of them force-fed the bird a special liquid to clean out any ingested oil.

But it was too late. No sooner had Kevin left when Pogo died in Janette's arms, wrapped in a warm Turkish towel.

"I'm sorry," Stella said. "We did everything we could."

"I know," Janette said. Deep in her heart she knew that was true. But why wasn't it enough? She wrapped Pogo's wet little body in a clean towel. "I'm going outside to bury him."

"Do you want me to come with you?" Stella asked.

Janette shook her head. There were things that you had to do by yourself. Grieving was one of them.

In the dim light of dusk, she buried Pogo next to the ice plant where he'd waited for her each morning for months. Tearfully, she stood over the tiny grave feeling as if yet another "baby" had been cruelly snatched away.

She needed to do something, anything, and because there was nothing else for her to do, she ran, ran harder than she'd ever run in her life. Somewhere in the confusion of her mind, she believed that if she ran far enough and long enough, she would leave it all behind. Adam, Amy, baby Stephanie whom she no longer had the right to call hers, Pogo, the oil that kept creeping into her life destroying the very sand beneath her feet.

The oil.

She slowed her pace, Her feet dragging now along the sand. She remembered Amy's cave. The one safe place that Amy could go had been ruined by oil.

Maybe there was something she could do. Maybe there was a way to tell Amy that she had never meant to hurt her; she only wanted to love her, be her mother, make up for all those lost years. Maybe there was a way to make the pain go away.

EARLY THE FOLLOWING morning, Janette maneuvered herself along the rocky cliff leading to the cave, armed with a bucket filled with scrub brushes and other cleaning supplies. The smell got stronger as she ducked beneath the overgrown branches and worked her bucket through the ragged opening.

She was in luck. The tide was low and the water had receded from the cave. She set the bucket on a ledge and walked around the edge of the cave, examining the oil-blackened walls. Water, also black with oil, oozed from the tarry sand beneath her feet. It was going to take much more work than she had anticipated.

Undaunted, she spent the rest of the day shoveling up the sand and scooping it into the green plastic trash bags she had brought for the purpose. After laboring all day Saturday and Sunday and barely making any headway, she decided to take a short leave of absence from work. Just for a week or two, she explained to Pat.

"I'll be back by the time the board has approved the proposal for next year's pageant."

Pat nodded. "After what you've been through, a vacation would do you the world of good."

Not a vacation. She didn't want a vacation. A vacation allowed time to think and she didn't want to do that. What she wanted was to fill every moment of every day so that there was no time to think.

To this end, she arose at dawn each day, and drove over to a point where she could reach the private beach without being seen from Adam's house. She worked harder than she had ever worked in her life. Digging, shoveling, raking, hauling. When at last every bit of oily sand had been removed and carted up the hill to her car—she planned to call the city later to find out how to dispose of the toxic material—she returned to the cave and began scrubbing. She scrubbed every rock, every shell, every rugged square inch of the walls.

Day after day, she scrubbed. Her hands grew red from the exposure to cold saltwater and detergent; the knuckles grew bloody.

And still she scrubbed.

Her knees were so raw that the saltwater stung her skin, making her eyes tear; her back ached, her head grew dizzy.

And still she scrubbed.

Somewhere in the recesses of her mind was the thought that if she scrubbed hard enough, long enough, fast enough, the hard knot of pain inside would disappear along with the oil.

Eventually the pain didn't matter. What did matter was that Amy would have her cave back.

ADAM ROSE at dawn that Saturday morning to work in the yard. The grass had been sorely neglected in recent weeks.

By noon, the sun beat against his head and feeling hot, he pulled off his shirt. He wiped his forehead with the back of his hand and leaned on the rake trying to decide if he should cut back the overgrown geraniums or pull them out altogether. Lately, the simplest decision put him in a quandary.

Something touched his shoulder. Startled, he spun around. A seagull flew overhead, letting out a loud cry, then circled and landed on the roof of the garage. Shrugging, Adam carried the rake into the workshed, but as soon as he emerged again, the seagull buzzed him. Adam managed to duck in the nick of time.

Puzzled, Adam straightened and watched as the bird circled overhead, then settled on top of a nearby fence post. Never had he seen a seagull so aggressive. Strangely enough, he had the feeling that the bird didn't mean to hurt him, only get his attention. Suddenly, Adam remembered something Janette had said about seagulls recognizing people by their faces. He stiffened. Could it be that this was one of the seagulls that he and Janette had saved?

He didn't know why the thought made his heart pound faster. He couldn't imagine why suddenly he had the need to reach out and stroke the feathers. He didn't know why he felt a deep and abiding sadness when the bird took flight and disappeared over the rocky cliffs.

He had to find out for certain. He let himself through the gate and followed the winding path down to the beach. He spotted the seagull on the rocks below. Cautiously, Adam moved toward the bird, talking in a smooth gentle voice. The bird watched him, but didn't move. Finally, Adam was near enough to pick out the aluminum band on one leg that confirmed his suspicions.

For the longest while, man and bird eyed each other. At last, the seagull took flight, spreading its wings as it soared. With a piercing cry, the bird circled Adam three times and disappeared somewhere among the cliffs overhead.

Feeling depressed, Adam started up the path again, but then remembered that he had promised Amy he'd take another look at her cave. It seemed as good a time as any. If things continued to go as well as they had during the last week or so, he could order cleanup crews to start on this beach by the end of the month. They would then work on Amy's cave.

He tried not to remember the last time he'd taken this path. The night that he and Janette had searched desperately for Amy seemed like a lifetime ago. So much had happened since. How could he have guessed that the concern and love he'd seen on her face that night had been an act? How could he have known that beneath that warmth was a heart as cold as ice?

Pushing the memories away, he quickly crossed the sand and climbed up the rocks. Following the narrow ledge, he ducked beneath the growth of bushes and followed the chamber to the cave.

A movement at the back of the cave caught his eye. Startled, he froze. He hadn't expected anyone to be inside the cave. Allowing his eyes to adjust to the dim cave, he stayed hidden and peered cautiously through the rocks that jutted out from the sides.

It was then that he saw her. *Janette*. His heart practically jumped out of his chest at the sight of her. Flattening himself against the wall behind him he forced himself to regain control of his senses. What was she doing here?

Peering around the rocks again, he watched as she picked up a scrub brush and tackled the back wall of the cave. His mouth fell open. He couldn't believe his eyes. She was cleaning the cave, Amy's cave. Cleaning hardly seemed the right word; she was scrubbing it as if her life depended on it.

Stepping out of his hiding place, he watched her work. He couldn't see her face, only her back. But he could feel her anguish, and he knew that it was real.

As he watched her scrub the oil from the wall, the recent weeks seemed to dissolve, as well. He remembered something she'd said to Amy about a person pretending to forget sometimes, in order to ease the pain.

Is that what she had done? Is that why she had been so cold to him that day in her office? Had her coldness been her way of trying to make the pain go away? Suddenly, it seemed so clear to him; his heart had been right all along. The Janette he had first come to love was the right one after all.

He moved soundlessly toward her. "Janette," he whispered, feeling her name fill his mouth with sweetness. "Janette."

I'm hearing things, she thought, drawing the scrub brush out of the bucket of cold water. Deep bitter anger filled her; it wasn't fair. She'd always loved nature, but suddenly it seemed that even nature conspired against her. Every sound had taken on his voice. Even the ocean sounded like him, and the seagulls. And the wind blowing through the eaves at night. There were times she even imagined the twinkling stars were sending his name back to her in some sort of coded signal.

Biting back her tears, she pressed harder. No longer did her fingers feel sore. They were too numb to feel anything. At least part of her plan had worked. She only wished she knew how long it would be before the rest of her grew numb, as well.

"Janette."

There it was again, his voice. Only this time, she turned and glanced over her shoulder. That's when she saw him, standing directly behind her, looking more handsome, more wonderful, more dear than she had ever seen him look, his bare chest glistening in the dim light of the cave.

"Dear God, no!" she cried out. It had taken her weeks, weeks to try to forget him. But any progress she might have made toward this end had been wiped out in a single moment, and she suddenly realized what a waste of time it had all been. She was never going to forget; not a single kiss, not a single moment. Not a single thing!

"Why are you here?" she demanded, angry now. "Wasn't it enough that I've signed over Amy? What more do you want from me?" What more was there to give?

"I..." The words caught in his throat. Catching his breath, he started again. "I came to check on the cave for Amy. I promised to clean it up for her..."

Janette felt her anger desert her, and this was almost her undoing. Without the anger there was so little left to hold onto. "It's...it's almost done."

His eyes traveled down the length of her. Her legs were raw, her hands red. She looked so thin, so fragile. "What you did..." He glanced around, amazed that even the sand at his feet was clean. A pure white seashell lay half-hidden in the sand. He glanced up again, taking in her pale face, and her soft trembling lips.

When she'd signed over custody of Amy, he thought that at long last he would be free of her. But that was never the case. He knew that now. She was as much a part of him as the very heart that was racing in his chest.

Her name falling from his lips, he moved toward her. "Janette, what you did here...I can't thank you enough." It was an act of love, pure and simple, even

Wes would have to admit that. Her feeling for Amy had nothing to do with money, or revenge. How could he have ever thought otherwise?

He reached out, cupping the side of her face with one hand. "Janette, I once told you that I was falling in love with you. But I don't think I could love you more than I love you at this moment."

Astonishment touched her face. Her eyes turned from disbelieving blue to disbelieving green.

Grasping her face in both hands, he kissed her. He kissed her until every last angry word between them had been atoned for. He kissed her until every ugly memory they shared had been erased. And when he was convinced that all the past had been put to rest, he kissed her until every dark shadow of the cave radiated with the light of love.

ADAM COULD HARDLY wait for Amy to return home from softball practice. He'd torn himself away from Janette and now it was all he could do to keep from jumping with joy, and giving away his secret. "I have something to show you."

Taking her by the hand, he led her outside, down the narrow path to the cave, refusing to answer her questions.

Once inside the cave, he stepped back to allow Amy a full view. She stood speechless, her gaze traveling up and down the spotless granite walls of the cave. Finally, she bent over to touch the glistening white sand beneath her feet.

Convinced at last that she wasn't dreaming, she straightened and turned, her eyes soft with tears. "Oh, Daddy," she whispered. "The cave is cleaner than ever." She flung her arms around him. "Oh, thank you, Daddy. Thank you, thank you."

"Hold on there, sport." Adam held her at arm's length. "I think you better thank the person who's really responsible."

Janette stepped out from behind a rock and Adam turned Amy around to face her.

Amy let out a gasp. "*You* cleaned my cave?"

Janette nodded.

Not knowing what to think, Amy glanced back at her father. "Does this mean Janette and I can be friends?"

Adam squeezed her shoulder. "It means you can be more than friends. As soon as we can manage it, the three of us are going to be a real family."

Amy didn't need to hear another word. Shouting with joy, she flew into Janette's waiting arms.

Not wanting to be left out, Adam joined them, and the three of them hugged and kissed, refusing to let even the rising tide force them apart.

EPILOGUE

THE LIGHTS DIMMED and a hush settled over the audience. The music started and the curtains began to rise. Cameron Taylor's *Girl with Gull* filled the stage. Amy was so perfect, she could have been painted by the master's golden brush.

The crowd applauded in approval, then suddenly rose to its feet, the applause thundering beneath the star-studded sky, and filling Janette's heart with unspeakable joy.

From the back of the amphitheater, Janette smiled up at Adam, her happiness that much more complete because he was by her side. This was the second time that night that the crowd had reacted with a standing ovation. The first had been for her father's painting called *Nightwatch*. And to think she had almost not chosen that painting. If it wasn't for Amy the painting would still be a thorn in her side instead of a warm glow in her heart.

Amy had picked out the painting, saying the policeman had made her feel safe. Safe. Janette had hugged the word to her heart. That's when she realized the true symbolism of her father's work. *Nightwatch* had been his way of expressing his concern for her welfare, not an indictment of her behavior.

Suddenly it had occurred to her that by avoiding the paintings that spoke to her on an emotional level, she had failed to dramatize her father's best work. He hadn't been able to communicate with her through the usual channels, but he'd tried to communicate with her through his work. He was still communicating through his work, and that was the wonderful part of it. Now that she had Amy and Adam in her life, there was no room for anger or resentment. And without either one of these feelings, the subtle and loving messages implanted in her father's paintings had become perfectly clear to her.

She looked up into the loving face of her new husband. They had been married for only a few weeks, but already she knew that it was a marriage made in heaven. And nothing, not even the pending lawsuit that she and Adam had filed jointly against the hospital could mar the future.

She marveled that *Girl with Gull*, the portrait that had once caused her such grief was directly responsible for bringing Adam and Amy into her life. She only hoped that her father would forgive her for making one change; she'd given the seagull in the portrait only one leg, in memory of Pogo.

Adam bent over and kissed her on the nose. "I love you," he whispered.

She smiled. How wonderful to have someone in her life that could communicate so honestly and openly. How wonderful to be able to respond just as honestly. "I love you, too," she answered him.

The applause died down and the audience sat. Janette noticed that Virginia and Wes were the last to take their seats. Virginia's new makeup and hairdo made her look years younger, and Wes had managed to interest her in sailing. Yet, despite the changes in Virginia, Janette still sensed the woman's resentment toward her.

It was Janette's fervent wish that Virginia would eventually come to accept her, and not feel that she was trying to replace her in Amy's affections. Janette hoped that maybe in time, Virginia would learn that there was room in Amy's life for everyone who loved her.

And when that day came, Janette's already perfect world would be more perfect still. She tucked her arm in Adam's and leaned her head on his shoulder as the curtain began to rise again, and all the warmth and love and humor of Norman Rockwell's *Welcoming the New Baby* filled the stage.

Adam gazed at her wonderingly. "Are you trying to tell me something?" he asked.

She shook her head and laughed. Her father used art to express his feelings, but she had other ways to express hers.

"No," she said softly. "But it is an intriguing idea, don't you agree?"

Adam didn't answer her, but he applauded louder than anyone else in the audience, and the grin on his face was as broad as all get-out.

Harlequin Supperromance®

**Experience the exotic world of
Hong Kong in Sharon Brondos's
latest Supperromance novel
EAST OF THE MOON.**

Sarah Branson knew her trip to Hong Kong
would be fabulous and she was not disappointed.
What she didn't expect, however, was that she'd
become involved in a mystery over smuggled
diamonds with tall, dark and handsome James
Leigh, a man who literally swept her off her feet.

Coming in June.

EAST OF THE MOON (#505)

EM92

Harlequin Superromance®

Coming in June from
Harlequin Superromance
A new novel by the author of
Blessing in Disguise

A MATTER OF PRIVILEGE
By Lorna Michaels

Family secrets...

In the privileged world of Texas philanthropy, all is
not what it seems. Worldwide Press's ace investigative
reporter Stephanie Barrett comes to Houston to look
into a possible fraud at the prestigious Madison
Foundation. What she finds—a story of tragedy,
blackmail and betrayal—could destroy the Madison
family ... and her newfound love for foundation
director Reed Madison. Reed's sister, Toni, is in love
with her brother's consultant, Matt O'Connor. Toni
doesn't care that Matt is confined to a wheelchair, but
Matt is determined that she'll never know the true
circumstances of the accident that disabled him.

A MATTER OF PRIVILEGE
A story of love and courage
Superromance #503

SRMOP

"GET AWAY FROM IT ALL" SWEEPSTAKES

HERE'S HOW THE SWEEPSTAKES WORKS

NO PURCHASE NECESSARY

To enter each drawing, complete the appropriate Official Entry Form or a 3" by 5" index card by hand-printing your name, address and phone number and the trip destination that the entry is being submitted for (i.e., Caneel Bay, Canyon Ranch or London and the English Countryside) and mailing it to: Get Away From It All Sweepstakes, P.O. Box 1397, Buffalo, New York 14269-1397.

No responsibility is assumed for lost, late or misdirected mail. Entries must be sent separately with first class postage affixed, and be received by: 4/15/92 for the Caneel Bay Vacation Drawing, 5/15/92 for the Canyon Ranch Vacation Drawing and 6/15/92 for the London and the English Countryside Vacation Drawing. Sweepstakes is open to residents of the U.S. (except Puerto Rico) and Canada, 21 years of age or older as of 5/31/92.

For complete rules send a self-addressed, stamped (WA residents need not affix return postage) envelope to: Get Away From It All Sweepstakes, P.O. Box 4892, Blair, NE 68009.

© 1992 HARLEQUIN ENTERPRISES LTD.   SWP-RLS

"GET AWAY FROM IT ALL" SWEEPSTAKES

HERE'S HOW THE SWEEPSTAKES WORKS

NO PURCHASE NECESSARY

To enter each drawing, complete the appropriate Official Entry Form or a 3" by 5" index card by hand-printing your name, address and phone number and the trip destination that the entry is being submitted for (i.e., Caneel Bay, Canyon Ranch or London and the English Countryside) and mailing it to: Get Away From It All Sweepstakes, P.O. Box 1397, Buffalo, New York 14269-1397.

No responsibility is assumed for lost, late or misdirected mail. Entries must be sent separately with first class postage affixed, and be received by: 4/15/92 for the Caneel Bay Vacation Drawing, 5/15/92 for the Canyon Ranch Vacation Drawing and 6/15/92 for the London and the English Countryside Vacation Drawing. Sweepstakes is open to residents of the U.S. (except Puerto Rico) and Canada, 21 years of age or older as of 5/31/92.

For complete rules send a self-addressed, stamped (WA residents need not affix return postage) envelope to: Get Away From It All Sweepstakes, P.O. Box 4892, Blair, NE 68009.

© 1992 HARLEQUIN ENTERPRISES LTD.   SWP-RLS

"GET AWAY FROM IT ALL"

Brand-new Subscribers-Only Sweepstakes

OFFICIAL ENTRY FORM

This entry must be received by: June 15, 1992
This month's winner will be notified by: June 30, 1992
Trip must be taken between: July 31, 1992—July 31, 1993

YES, I want to win the vacation for two to England. I understand the prize includes round-trip airfare and the two additional prizes revealed in the BONUS PRIZES insert.

Name _____

Address _____

City _____

State/Prov._____ Zip/Postal Code_____

Daytime phone number _____
(Area Code)

Return entries with invoice in envelope provided. Each book in this shipment has two entry coupons — and the more coupons you enter, the better your chances of winning!

© 1992 HARLEQUIN ENTERPRISES LTD.   3M-CPN

"GET AWAY FROM IT ALL"

Brand-new Subscribers-Only Sweepstakes

OFFICIAL ENTRY FORM

This entry must be received by: June 15, 1992
This month's winner will be notified by: June 30, 1992
Trip must be taken between: July 31, 1992—July 31, 1993

YES, I want to win the vacation for two to England. I understand the prize includes round-trip airfare and the two additional prizes revealed in the BONUS PRIZES insert.

Name _____

Address _____

City _____

State/Prov._____ Zip/Postal Code_____

Daytime phone number _____
(Area Code)

Return entries with invoice in envelope provided. Each book in this shipment has two entry coupons — and the more coupons you enter, the better your chances of winning!

© 1992 HARLEQUIN ENTERPRISES LTD.   3M-CPN